CW00539654

"The human body is not an instrument to be used, but a realm of one's being to be experienced, explored, enriched and thereby— loved deeply."

~ *(Deliberately misquoted) Thomas Hanna*

ROUGH ATTRACTION

THE DOMINION OF BROTHERS SERIES: BOOK 4

TALON P.S.

BESTSELLING BDSM EROTIC ROMANCE

BESTSELLING EROTIC SERIES

THE DOMINION OF BROTHERS SERIES

WRITTEN BY TALON P.S. & TARIAN P.S.

Five Brothers at Arms share a lust for control and bondage; now they are living the BDSM lifestyle openly, and they are the very Masters who can provide satisfaction to the world of Taboo.

Plenty of people love their kink, but when the Dominion of Brothers arrive in New York, the Lifestyle gets an empowering supporter; with not only a boost in stimulation, their fellow Lifestylers also get a guardian. As it just so happens, the Brothers will stop at nothing to protect their friends, loved ones, and those who look to them for the freedom of consensual sexual expression.

BECOMING HIS SLAVE

DOMMING THE HEIRESS

A PLACE FOR CLIFF

ROUGH ATTRACTION

TAKING OVER TROFIM

RIGHT ONE 4 DIESEL

TOUCHING VIDA~VINCE

SEDUCING HIS THIEF

UNSUSPECTING SAVING

MASTERS' GOLDEN DARK SIDE

Submit your desires within the Dominion of Brothers and submerge yourself into a world of Dominance and Bliss, but get ready~

"I'm about to make you wet."

Talon ps.

ROUGH ATTRACTION

THE DOMINION OF BROTHERS SERIES: BOOK 4

MM-Romance / Billionaire Romance / Cocky Bad Boy with a Besotted Heart / Erotic-Romance / When You're the Affair / Raw Passion / Sexy Car Collection / Family Bonds / Sexy Men Row / Smoldering to Scolding Burn Right Out the Gate / Explicit Language

Like brimstone and caramel. When two men come together with a Rough Attraction that burns as fast as Nitro-fuel in their veins, it's hard to find the cruise control and trust that they can make this last for the long run.

༺ཡༀ༻

Life and relationships aren't always neat and clean, or come in perfect little packages. Maxum St. Laurents knows this all too well. After being in a four-year relationship that does everything but bring him pleasure and fulfillment, he finds himself struggling to keep working at it. It doesn't help matters that the man who satisfies every need and want he could have is the man he is having the affair with. And for Maxum, affairs don't translate into long term relationships.

Darko Laszkovi just couldn't help himself when he spotted the handsome man ranting over a flat tire on the side of the road. Moreover, he couldn't be happier when the reward turned into an insatiable lover he hoped to keep for the long run, something he never found himself desire of previous lovers. But, despite the rough attraction that holds them to each other like power-magnets, when Maxum struggles to let go of a toxic relationship that doesn't work, Darko's patience and understanding that we aren't always where we want to be, gets tested to the max.

ROUGH ATTRACTION

THE DOMINION OF BROTHERS SERIES: BOOK 4
WRITTEN BY TALON P.S.

DEDICATION

To Talon

&

To our Bug and Bobcat

Special Thanks goes to: Alison Greene & Nick Hasse for keeping us Dyslexic-Disaster-Zone free.

And to our wonderful Beta Readers: Alyn Love, Ethan LJubankovic, Tina Moran,

Michelle Regan Friedoff & Kristina Kirkpatrick Semiche.

TRADEMARK ACKNOWLEDGEMENT

The author acknowledges the trademarked status and trademark owners of the following wordmarks mentioned in this work of fiction:

Vehicles:

    Bugatti Roadster
    Bugatti Veyron L'or Blanc
    Pagani Zonda F Roadster
    Auburn boat-tail Roadster
    Ford Tungsten F-350 Roadster
    Fisker Luxury Sedan
    McLaren MP4-12C F1
    Devon GTX
    Austin Healy
    Jaguar XKE sportscar {referred to as modified}

Alcohol Brands:

    Bodegas Dios Baco Imperial Amontillado Jerez
    Daniel Bouju Cognac
    Remi Martin Cognac
    Butchertown Black Ale
    Imperial Iba Black Ale
    Föroya Bjor Black Sheep Black Ale
    Point 2012 Black Ale

Misc:

    Le Bernardin Restaurant
    Gramercy Tavern Steak House Restaurant
    Volkswagen's Ehra-Lessien Test Track, Germany
    Dream of you – song by Schiller
    Harold and Maude - film by Hal Ashby with Paramount Pictures
    The Birdcage – film by Mike Nichols with United Artists Pictures
    Beekman Gehry Tower, NY
    Woolworths Tower, NY

TABLE OF CONTENT

ROUGH ATTRACTION

CHAPTER ONE

Darko cruised along the highway, keeping to the right lane. It was morning traffic time, and he was not in such a hurry to put him and his chopper into the Death Race 2000 against New York's finest; At least that's what it typically felt like when trying to dodge the all too many *gotta get there first* zigzag drivers of a typical New York morning commute. *Let them have it.* As for him, he'd get to work when he got there and that's all the morning drive ever was for him.

The morning was just like any other. That is until he spotted the striking mancandy stranded on the side of the road, cursing at a new model Mercedes. Even the feuding expression on the man's face as he passed, had Darko licking his lips and his cock itching to reach out and touch someone. *Dayyum* Both convinced him instantaneously the man was worth a day's good deed and he quickly pulled off into the emergency lane, turned his bike around and rode back down the shoulder to the car and his beau-in-distress.

He kicked the motorcycle into idle in front of the Mercedes, swung a leg over, and strolled up to the side of the car with a gait that spoke more about cocky seduction than mechanical know-how. Pulling the gauntlet glove free from one hand, Darko let his fingers drift lightly over the glossy paint, as if to caress her curves. The car was so new, he could smell it, even on the highway of rushing traffic and its acrid stench of exhaust fumes.

He glanced down to inspect the rear tire— flat as a twink's chest, however, the *man* was anything but. Tall, perhaps just breaching six feet, this would put the man, eye to eye with him— sun-streaked, golden-brown hair and completely out of place with the polished exterior of this man. Maybe he groomed it back nice and smooth this morning, or maybe not. Regardless it was now disheveled in his aggravation.

The hint of tan to the man's face and hands marked him for an outdoors man in favorable weather, and the stark muscles hiding under the expensive looking, light grey suit and crisp, white shirt, said he was in good enough shape for some serious sheet rumbles. Of course, as far as Darko's assessment went, it wasn't hurting matters at all, that the man was packing a sweet looking ass inside the tailored slacks either.

Darko bit back the impulse to lick his lips, but the view of eye candy the man exuded was worth the stop already. "Looks like you got a flat?" Darko stated the obvious with a mischievous smile.

The man spun around, "Obvious, is it?" Not at all amused, nor gathering too quickly he was about to be rescued.

Oh, and he's got some fire to boot, Darko thought to himself and now his cock was more than itching for a scratch or two from this brisling man. Getting to romp around with Paris on more than one or two occasions had certainly cranked up his appetite putting him on the manhunt for a new playmate. But back to the rescue at hand— "You need some help?" Darko turned sincere in the offer.

"I can change my own tire, if I could just find the fucking tool kit to do it with." The disgruntled man pivoted on his heels, throwing his hands up in the air in a shouted gesture towards the car, more frustrated with himself than anything else it would seem. The hands lowered, landing at his hips, and he turned back to the offer of assistance. "I've had the car all of half a day, and already it's got a flat, and I can't find anything." All that fire, in a blink, leveled off to an admission of defeat. *Control at its finest in this one.*

A few of the golden highlights of hair now hung misplaced around his face, touching smooth round cheeks that softened a hard stare. A pair of lips, despite tightening into a grimace, were absolute kiss-candy as far as Darko was concerned. Just then the man's eyes caught the light of the late morning rising sun. Brown would not be the color Darko'd use to describe the eyes, because at just the right angle they lit up like coins tempered with a mix of copper and polished bronze. Reminded him of Tiger's-Eye stone. He liked how they shimmered, glancing at him. Moreover, Darko enjoyed how his eyes dropped to check him out just as his own gaze was drifting down for another appraisal of the frame underneath the handsome face that just caught his breath, mm-hmm— *dayyum.* Darko soaked up the sight and then finally offered a smirk of understanding, "My brother had one of these."

"It's my first. Will certainly be my last as well," Mister-knight-in-shining-armor threw out a few vows of retribution.

Darko stepped up, helping himself, where he opened the door, reached behind the headrest of the driver's seat, and pressed the hidden concealed button. There was a soft click under the rear seat and when he lifted it, it exposed the hidden compartment there. Inside, he fetched a black bag that would make the job of rescuing his rough tempered, knight-in-*shiny*-armor all the easier.

He strolled back around toward the rear of the car but not passing up on the chance to brush against the man's backside as he passed in order to steal a frisk with the same fingertips, he used to feel up the car. It almost seems like a game of *tag your it*, when his beau-in-distress followed right behind him and might have chanced a touch of his own when he stepped in close to watch.

Darko began assembling the extended crank bar. "You see, the snobs that designed the car decided they didn't want to see the tools or the spare tire. They thought the sight of them marred the rich physic of the car's design." He lined the extension bar through an indention just above the bumper and pushed in until it caught and he began to crank it around.

His beau-in-distress bent over and could see the dark object lowering down from the under carriage. His spare tire.

Darko dropped down, reached under, unfastened the caddy and tugged the tire out from under the car.

Another twenty minutes later and he had the car good as new. Nor did he fail to notice that during the rescue mission, the man was eyeing *him* about as hot and heavily as Darko had him.

"You don't know how much I appreciate this." His rescued-man glanced at the watch that might have cost more than the car. "I might actually make my meeting after all." He watched as Darko placed the flattened tired into the trunk along with the bag of tools. Those glinting eyes tracking more so on the cords of Darko's arms as they flexed with the movement than on the tire being placed in his car. "I'm not sure how to repay you—" he pulled a business card from his lapel pocket. "But if there's anything you could—"

Darko twisted, grabbing the knight by his suit coat and yanked their bodies to collide together. His mouth instantly crashing over the other man's, in an avaricious kiss. Darko licked over his lips, soliciting entry and with barely a note of hesitation, his knight gave it to him. The feisty and richly dressed businessman tasted like one of those fancy coffees and a hint of fruit jam on toast, but it was his tongue that had Darko swelling in his pants. Because the man consciously kissed back; the caress of his tongue was powerful, hungry, and completely pliable against his own, as if this man was made to fit him, reminiscent of a pair of rich leather gloves. He could just imagine the man fucking with a pair on and that visual put a finality to his impending hard-on.

Darko released the suit coat, gliding down the man's arm until he clasped around his knight's hand, and moved it to grope the established erection in Darko's jeans. And for a tasty treat, Darko gave him a sample of his plaid hips, rocking forward, to grind the hard bulge of his cock into the man's palm.

Darko let out a groan and an embarrassed smile broke over his face. *Grrrhhh*— that had just been too damn good, striking when the man was least expecting it. He was about to move in for another kiss when Darko realized what he'd done to knight's suit. He leaned back, glancing down, making a slight clicking noise through his lips and then stepped back. The suitcoat and white shirt were now ruined with black smudges of tire soot from Darko's hands.

The man's eyes, burnishing with the same heat Darko'd just felt himself, dropped in response, discovering the same exact condition in which the kiss had precisely left him in.

Quickly, Darko snatched the business card still in his knight's hand and pulled the fancy pen from the man's shirt pocket, leaving more smudges. "Looks like I messed up your pretty clothes." Making no actual apology, Darko scribbled over the backside of the card then tucked it back into the man's shirt pocket, along with the pen. His hand lingering just long enough to let his fingers feel the firm body behind the shirt and tweak over the hard nipple hidden there. Yet again, leaving further evidence of Darko's touch in a hand-print of grime. "That's my address. Be there for dinner. Tonight. Bring the suit— and I'll pay for the dry cleaning. Stand me up, and the suit is your problem." He grinned; a rather self-satisfied smile that held no hint that he might actually feel bad for messing up the man's expensive clothes.

As storm brewed on that face— still shocked and smoldering from the kiss held back any horror or rage that it was at the price of his threads.

Darko turned, heading back for his ride.

He sat on his chopper, closing up his leather jacket and pulling his gloves back on, all while he watched the reflection of the man behind him through his rearview mirror. His knight wore the expression of a well kissed man and Darko was feeling all his bets on it would be enough to bring him calling.

Darko wasn't thinking about who was at his door when the knock came, that was until he opened it. His rescued *knight-in-shiny-armor* stepped inside, brushing passed a rather surprised Darko, even if he did his best not to show it.

Closing the door, Darko couldn't help but feel a little smugness coming back from earlier. Clearly his chips paid off. Though admittedly, he hadn't actually expected the ruined suit and kiss ploy to work. But, if he had any other thoughts, they were instantly gone when he turned, only to have his body thrown back against the door. The man he'd just let in, pressed against him with surprising strength, along with an impressive hard-on. His knight crushed his lips with his and when Darko felt the tempting tongue lick across his lips— he let *him* in. Lips hot and demanding as if they'd waited all day for a second taste of the other.

Just then, his guest's hand dropped down, going right where Darko had placed his hand this morning.

"*Mmmm,* seems like you got yourself a flat." He pressed the heel of his palm in harder, grinding Darko's cock to accept his hand, which was eagerly hardening to prove the claim wrong. "There. That's better." He pulled away, wearing the smug look he'd just stolen from Darko. "Just as I remember."

"I guess there's no need for ceremony for kissing on our first date then?" Darko asked, his eyes half lidded with satisfaction.

"How was I supposed to turn down a proposition like that?" The knight's expression added to the growling tone which stirred desires that perhaps hadn't been set ablaze in a long time for the other man.

Darko waited for a retake of that kiss, but instead, his guest turned, and began a tour of the living room as if Darko's presence in the room was no longer registering with him. Darko watched as the man slid the long, double-breasted wool coat off then folded it over one of the chair backs and turned, standing there glancing at him. He looked radiant in the rich threads of a smoky-grey herringbone suit. And just like the one he wore this morning, it was tailored to every line of his body in smooth perfection. The inky off-colored purple shirt transcribed well in a muted match with the dark grey, and the look was finished off with an obsidian black tie. Darko felt the low *grottled* growl kick off deep in his chest— damned if he could get used to looking at the man-candy.

The knight went back to his strolling about— stopping to glance at things in the room as if he could discern everything about the homeowner just by what was there, and what condition each clue in. The knight's hands absently undid his tie then started on the buttons of his shirt. He stopped along the wall unit, picking up a picture frame— two scull rowers in the early dawn light. The surface of the water casting a hazy reflection of burnished-gold, leaving the rowers in dark silhouette. Darko's guest glanced at the trophy that sat next to it and ran his fingertip across the brass plate, then inspected his fingertips— distinctively noting the lack of dust. He read aloud— more contemplative, "New England Regional Championship Regatta – Master's Solo Division." His left hand tugged at his tie, pulling it free then he shrugged his suit coat off and dropped it over the back of the sofa, his tie followed.

Even now, without the presence of a fancy car, Darko saw the man before him— the knight in *shiny* armor still fit, rather than himself being seen as that gallant knight who'd done the actual rescue. Just something about this man's demeanor made him shine like dark glossy paint in the dim light of his living room. His knight toed the dress shoes off next, pausing for only a moment to read over the framed poster on the wall showing a straight-on view of several muscular men seated, lined-up one behind the other in a fierce tug of oars. The caption at the bottom read— *Real athletes row. Everyone else just plays ball.* His knight turned, looking at him as if deciphering— fan, fanatic, or involved player?

Darko decided to let the man find out for himself, licking his lips as he watched the strip show continue and then the shirt came off, finding its way on yet another form of furniture.

"I really didn't expect you to show. I didn't plan anything for dinner," Darko confessed out-loud to break the silence.

The man stopped and looked at him, "You got a phone and an address, right?"

Darko shot him a perplexed glance.

"Take out will do—" and the man headed down the hall. "After I've fucked you!" he called back.

Darko smiled to himself. *That suited him just fine.* Only when his intended didn't venture back, Darko went looking for him, finding him in his bedroom standing at the dresser. His guest's watch and wallet now placed on top. His finger pressed to his wallet as he glanced around as if he was forgetting something then quite purposely moved toward the nightstand, next to the bed. He pulled the top drawer, found what he was looking for, and tossed a bottle of lube and a few square foils onto the bed.

His pants were next to come off then he dropped down on the bed with a bounce before positioning himself into the perfect *come-hither* pose, leaning back on the headboard. "Do you plan to get naked with me? Or do you always fuck with your clothes on?"

Darko walked to the dresser, snatching up the wallet and flipped it open.

"I didn't know I was paying for this," the man on his bed commented smoothly.

"You're not," Darko assured him and read the name on the driver's license. "I just wanted to know who I am about to fuck—" He returned the wallet to the dresser and looked at the man. "Maxum St. Laurents." If Darko thought the man looked utterly tasty in the dark suit, he looked even more mouth-wateringly desirable in the nude, especially stretched out over his bed as if he owned it.

Full and heavy, Maxum's penis sprang from a shallow nest of dark, silky hair. Bigger might not make the man a better lover, but it was certainly prettier to look at; cut, pinkish, with strong veins. It matched Darko's eight uncut inches of dark, rosy flesh, though he figured he might have the man on girth. Darko watched, transfixed, as the knight stroked himself and the first excited pearlescent drop appeared.

"Enjoying what you see?" Maxum asked from the bed.

Darko folded his arms over his chest, nearly chewing his lower lip off at the delectable view, while he remained leaning back on the dresser to enjoy the show a little longer. "Oh, I was liking it this morning when I pulled over to steal that kiss off you." He took a deep breath and let it out with a groan. "It's just getting better."

Maxum flipped his cock with his thumb, letting it slap back hard against his belly. All for show. "Are you just gonna stand there or are you going to join me anytime soon?"

Darko made a half-hearted shrug, "You know, I've lived here three years now, and I don't think my bed has ever looked as good. I'm liking the new accessory upgrade."

"Wait until you try it on."

Darko pushed off the dresser and pulled his t-shirt up over his head.

A hungry verbal growl of approval came from the awaiting man, "View from this side of the room looks good, too."

"It's about to get even better," Darko offered the languid lure and stepped to the foot of the bed, easing his zipper down, brushing the sides down, slowly enough to torture his guest. His thumbs caught his briefs and tugged them downward, just far enough to let his cock spring free. Letting the edges snap up just under his scrotum.

Maxum's gaze licked over the approaching man's body. It was far better than he had imagined. In fact, from what he could see, as Darko unzipped his jeans and the dark tanned flesh of his uncut, swollen shaft sprang free, the man was perfection to the satisfaction of any desires a man could speak of. "Ah, fuck you're a sight to see." His breath picked up, his veins pumping hard with his need racing through him. Damn, he was dying to get inside him already. *Heady lust.* Maxum stroked his cock with a flattened palm, watching with flaring hunger as the man eased down on the bed, one knee, next a hand, then the other, and slowly came crawling towards him. His host's cock bobbing from his jeans as he crept closer, dropping his head down to Maxum's leg and kissing as he did so. First to his ankle, soon after applying a wet one towards the underside of one knee then the next— *ahh, shit*— then his thigh.

Before Maxum even was aware of his motor control, he offered his own shaft up for a pass of his host's tongue, and the man didn't refute him. "Fuck yes," he hissed at the first glance of the man's moist caress. Not even a faint teasing one. The man licked him with full-on contact with the flat of his tongue from stem-to-stern of his erect rod. Blue eyes, like cobalt glass, looked right up at him. Maxum nearly chuckled as it occurred to him the lights were still on. *Almost* —because, precisely when he started to think this was funny, his man's mouth came right over the head of his cock and was instantly working it over. All thought, funny or not, was gone. The tongue pressed against the soft underside of Maxum's glans and damned if his hips didn't practically come flying off the bed in response. "Oh, fuck yes, that's it," he groaned with considerable encouragement so the pleasure would continue.

Darko took that as his cue— *and oh yeah, this man was in dire need of having his junk worked over.* He hooked both of Maxum's legs in his arms and rolled with a hard push, bringing the knight's entire body with him until Darko was on his back with Maxum's knees straddled to the sides of his head, and he swallowed his knight's cock down without pause.

A trail of curses blasted overhead, fueling his motives, and he worked double-time over the turgid flesh with his tongue; using the muscles of his jaw to tighten around the shaft, adding extra hug to the sides of Maxum's cock. Darko pushed his hands up to stroke the fine-tuned body, feeling out smooth ribs and a soft, rippling muscle that tapered down to a trimmed waist and then that ass. Oh, yeah, the ass— it *felt* as good in his hands as it had *looked* in the expensive slacks earlier this morning.

Taking hold of Maxum's hips, Darko began to lift him, pumping the thick member into his mouth. *Mmmm*— but he couldn't help himself to like how Maxum tasted and smelled. All manly-man and exquisitely groomed.

Albeit, before Darko had much of a chance to enjoy it as thoroughly as he planned, Maxum was moving, his cock popping free from Darko's mouth, and was moving down his body. "Hey, I wasn't done with that," he objected and sat up to lay a wet claim over the retreating body with his mouth.

Maxum's response only managed to come out as a groan as that wet morsel of a mouth laid a trail up his chest as he attempted to position himself down over his host. He forced himself to slow to a crawl, enjoying the trail of pleasure this man, who rode up on a chopper to save the day, gave him. Maxum glanced down his chest to the blue eyes, dark with lust stared up at him, watching, while his danced out, seeking out one of his nipples. Maxum's eyes eyes floated closed just when those lips clamped down on one— the sight turned sensation jolted through Maxum's entire body. He sank lower to have more, pressing into the exquisite mouth sucking his now pert disk. But the surrendering body of encouragement only tested Maxum's already lack of pacing. "Fuck, babe. I gotta have a taste of your ass right now," Maxum growled, hoping this lover would not only understand, but also be complacent about his sudden compulsion.

Maxum couldn't hold back, his hands finding, and gripping the already open fly of his host's jeans; he rolled to his back and yanked the man's body up over him. Every inch of Maxum's body and need, arched up to meld seamlessly against Darko's. Their mouths came crashing into one another, while Maxum's hand sought out their cocks, already grinding into each other as if mating snakes. He grasped them both in his fist, stroking over them together. "Oh, fuck," he cursed, drowning in this energy of raw pleasure. *Like the very first time he slid into the seat of his brand new Bugatti.* How his whole body hummed and tingled with exhilarated anticipation of the first test drive on a German track, knowing he wouldn't have to hold back on the throttle. He could push the car to its ultimate limits and still push further, and the car would take it. The man stretched over his body, hot and grinding with him like the exotic roadster laying tracks, taking everything he could dish out, and welcomed even more of it.

Making the exchange even hotter was having the lights on— seeing every detail— every nuance of the other man's body. Maxum sat up, forcing his host up on his knees, straddled over his own legs. He glanced down at the uncut cock, swollen to its fullest, just waiting. A drop of clear fluid hung from the slit, beckoning him. Maxum needed no further invitation, and he was there, licking down on that gorgeous piece of meat.

ᏒᏯᎧ

Darko let out a loud groan as Maxum practically bowled him backwards to sit back on his heels while his knight tongued over his cock like he was licking the last remnants of a favorite flavor from a dinner plate then swallowed him up in one movement. Maxum didn't just suck; the man was gobbling him up as if he were a man starved of the pleasure. Bent backwards, Darko tried to prop up on an arm and watch Maxum work him over. But fuck, if it wasn't the best cock sucking he could recall, forfeiting technique with unbounded enthusiasm. Thus, Darko surrendered his back to the bed and it was all he could do just to stay sane.

Right when he was delivered to the edge of losing that last nanometer of sanity, Maxum was flipping him without request, hands spreading his cheeks wide and that mouth with its hot, wet tongue, showing no signs of slowing down or backing off, came down over his hole.

In an instant reflex, Darko's hands fisted into bed covers that had already since been pulled from their proper placement and were well tussled before he and Maxum had even gotten to the riding portion of their night. He buried his face and moaned— followed up with a hiss— then moaned again. Damned, if the guy wasn't igniting all his torches. It felt *soooo* good, unlike nothing he'd had. Oh, he'd been rimmed before, but not from a hungry beast, as he was now. Maxum's face was full on buried in his ass. His tongue alternated between broad licks, to firm tongue-fuckings, and then full-on suction. Darko knew he was in for the ride of his life when two moistened fingers slowly found their way into his well-loosened ass going straight for his glory spot.

He slammed his face into the bed covers and relented to the onslaught of intense pleasure, gasping in its wake. *Dammit*, his mind and body simultaneously agreeing to take bottom placement right about then.

It was a good thing he already volunteered in silent agreement to bottom, because once his ass was well sucked and washed over, Maxum was lining up behind him. He heard the rustle of foil, a moment later he felt the cock sliding down his crevice, rocking and sliding—

rocking and sliding— then slowly pushed in. Darko curled up and gasped with the initial stretch. It had been too long, but Darko wasn't about to say no now, because he wanted it. He wanted this man, anyway he could have him, and with any luck, he'd have Maxum both ways.

He forced himself to relax, his back arching, angling his ass to have that cock all the way up inside him, and he rocked on his hands and knees, nudging back, impaling himself inch by exquisite inch to stretch past the preliminaries.

Maxum dropped a heavy hand down on the man's back steadying himself more than anything, as the exotically free-spirited man worked his own body down on his cock. Full-throttle— pedal to the metal— race for the gold— cords of desire chant in his ears. Yet, as the countdown— *on the mark, get-set, go!* invite backed itself onto his cock and the lights lit up a brilliant green, Maxum just sat there, mesmerized in the glory of that signal to go for a moment.

He was swimming in the beauty of this man, who'd somehow lured him to find him with unspoken promises of raw euphoria and was now real and in the flesh. It took a long moment to decipher real from fantasy.

When Maxum felt the other man's balls slap back against his own, the shell shock of freedom shattered, and his body responded. Hips withdrawing back, his brain zeroed in on the exquisite sensation of the man's tight ring hugging his dick. Sliding back once more,

Maxum rammed all the way in, nearly throwing his lover face down on the bed.

"Fuck, baby. I want, no— I need to pound your ass."

"Stop talking and start pounding then." Mister blue-eyes shot the verbiage over his shoulder at him, and that was all the permission Maxum needed. Moving his hands to the man's hips, Maxum braced himself, and pulled out, hammered in, and set the pace for an unrelenting hard fucking. Every stroke from there promised no respite until they had both plastered each other in spunk.

The room filled with the curses and groans of intense pleasure, and it smelled so fucking good. The sweat of their bodies ignited the colognes they both wore; blended notes of basil, rum, and something citrusy mixed with the lure of what Maxum wore, carrying a woody and chocolaty smell. All this coiled about with the scents of human musk and sex. *Fuck, it was really good.*

Despite Maxum's pummeling, Darko managed to hold his ground underneath him, hands fisted into the bed covers to anchor himself in place. His arms locking firmly under him to counter back, matching Maxum's pounding, his ass meeting Maxum's hips in a regular slapping rhythm. Each thrust into Darko's tight channel, Maxum's cock nudged his glory spot and sent ripples of pleasure searing through Darko's body.

Darko's arms and legs began to tingle, his muscles turning to rubber, as his orgasm built inside him until he feared he wouldn't be able to support his own weight.

He forced his body to comply, turning to glance at the man driving into him; his knight was definitely shining now, glowing with a profound hunger, and a sheen of sweat beading over his skin.

Maxum switched a knee for a foot on the bed and began changing his angle with each thrust, grinding in circular assaults. Each slide into his ass driving him insane, and Darko found himself slamming his face into the bed, biting into the covers. His cock, jutting up his belly and aiming straight for his chin, and was threatening to fire off any moment. Every onslaught against his body sent out some strange, strangled expressions that echoed back in a sound. And though he wasn't sure how to define them, he did seem to be making a lot of them.

"Damn, babe, your hole quivers around my cock when you're ready to come. Go ahead—" Maxum hissed, "let loose." He pushed home, angling just right to catch his lover's glory spot, one last time, sliding across it until he bottomed out and stilled there, feeling the body under him clench around his cock with the spasm that was destined to run a course through the man's balls and shoot out the evidence in white jets of cum, all over his torso and the bed. Maxum saw the movement of an arm, knowing full well the lover's hand laid home around his own cock. He watched the display of strained muscles in his lover's shoulder and upper arm, gauging the vice gripe that was being attributed to his cock's handling, even while the man grunted and moaned with each convulsion under Maxum. Damn, it looked good watching and feeling this delectable man— feeling the ability, or perhaps the desire to become completely addicted to him.

No matter for that now, he wasn't done yet. Maxum pulled out only long enough to flip his rendered lover over then came down between Darko's legs and sank back inside the lush walls of his ass. Maxum pumped, picking back up where he left off forcing the man to ride out a flood of aftershocks. Each one a tantalizing squeeze around his cock as he drove inside his ass until Maxum couldn't hold back his own orgasm any longer.

He pulled out, ripping the condom from his cock just in time to fire off his load, adding it to the spillage already painted on the man's torso. So intense, as Maxum's muscles contracted and tore at him, he could barely manage to bark out the groans he wanted to express as jet after hot jet of cum erupted from him until every ounce of bodily strength spilled out with the last milky white drop. When it was over, Maxum came down hard, almost crushing the body under him. Yet, he was pleased to find no harm was done when arms caught him and welcomed the weight. So, he gladly surrendered to the embrace.

He could have easily drifted into a deep bliss then and there, but the calloused hands that stroked over his back felt nice, a lingering contact that called him to stay alert. Don't let it end yet, take the moment for every drop of indulgence he could. Of course, the first try to rev up some physical strength barely got him up on his elbows, but as he did, there were those deep-blue eyes watching him under a lazy gaze that equaled his own. And they chuckled at each other.

Maxum couldn't figure it out, but his lust was so well sated at that moment, he found himself touched with some bizarre form of intimacy. At least that's what he thought it was. Because he heard so many speak of it, but he'd never known it himself. Like some mythological occurrence. The next thing he knew, his hand was caressing the side of his head, brushing aside the wavy, coffee-colored hair, now plastered to his forehead from the sweat. "I don't know your name," Maxum whispered as his gaze drifted over the man's features, rugged, European-cut facial features, and some American-grown bad boy.

"Did you want to know my name?" Darko asked, seemingly fond of basking in the post bliss for a while longer with or without particulars.

Maxum nodded as his attention became transfixed on the man's lips, even as his body was sluggishly starting to wake up again. Their legs were stitched against each other, while their chests seemed to be in a raspy competition for the small space of air between them. Such an oddity to be sharing this afterglow with a stranger, yet he liked it, all the same. Maxum felt the blood trickling back down to his cock, it was crazy, but the twitch against his thigh said it was happening. His attention went back to those lips, realizing he hadn't kissed them nearly as much as he wanted to, and he nodded again, not sure what he was agreeing to any more.

"My name is Darko. Darko Laszkovi."

And right at that moment, Maxum dropped down over Darko's lips and molested them with a hungry kiss, growling out a husky version of the name in between. His hands moved over Darko's body in a rough caress, mapping out turns and corded muscles to match the body with the name in his mind. Enjoying every inch of Darko Laszkovi, caught under his body.

⁀ᴗ⁀

Damn, a second round, or just some good post petting, was on-the-ball as far as Darko was concerned. Akin to a bonus that few lovers could muster so soon after round one. He hitched a foot up on the bed and pushed off, rolling them both over, until he had Maxum underneath him where he ground against his knight's hip, feeling his cock swelling already as they commenced with deep kissing and petting.

Maxum's hand came down hard, delivering a brash stinging across Darko's ass cheek.

Darko flinched, tearing from their tangle of tongues, and gazed down at the man who'd just delivered the blow. "You did not just do that." He cocked his head with mock surprise. "Did you just spank me?"

"I did," Maxum answered, all too smug about it, and to prove a point, he repeated the affliction to Darko's other ass cheek. "Now, what are you going to do about it?"

"Oh," Darko growled, his arms tensing around Maxum, "I'll show you what I am going to do." And just then Darko's arms were moving down Maxum, catching his knight's legs at the knees and yanked them up until his feet were in the air, and his ass an open target. Darko dropped his hips down, rubbing his renewed hard cock into the accessible crevice, sawing back and forth, teasing Maxum's hole.

He folded down over Maxum, using his body to keep the man pinned in position while he reached for one of the foils on the bed and wrapped his shaft. He stroked the pre-lube from the packet over his thick, jutting cock a few times then lined himself up until the broad glans kissed the tight sphincter.

Eyes burning with another round of anticipated lust, the two men locked with each other's gaze, and Darko pressed in. He stopped when the man under him tensed in a painful strain.

Maxum's teeth chattered, "Easy, easy, easy." He nearly begged, his hands slapping to Darko's thighs to hold him off a moment.

Darko quickly backed away to lessen the pressure but only to return, pushing against the first tight ring of muscle again— repeating it over and over with micro pushes until he felt the invitation from Maxum's unused, hungry hole, and ushered in at least two thirds of his length before reversing to withdraw all the way out.

He liked that look he got from Maxum— *need* consuming the man to relent and be taken, so long as the night did not end between them. It was the equivalent of a Nitrous oxide system pumping the booster fuel into an engine that loved high octane in the first place, though all too often the consumer got duped with little more than leaded substitutes— leaving them still needing and wanting.

Darko was as equally unaccustomed to the intensity of sensation as his knight obviously was but unwilling to deny reveling in it.

One more time, he grabbed Maxum's hips, positioned the head of his cock against the relaxed opening, and in one smooth push, he shoved himself all the way in, eliciting a gasp from the man under him as the shock of sudden penetration filled all of his knight's sensories.

❦

Maxum fought to control his breathing while adjusting to the stretch and burn, but after years and years of longing, he found his body surprisingly accepting the man who'd just flipped him to bottom.

He'd taken and now it was being fed back to him. He liked— lusted— hungered for both without ever having realized it. His senses tumbling as if he'd had a few too many drinks, rocking his body in a wave of salacious involvement. The slide of Darko's cock igniting a lost need that now screamed to awaken and be devoured by this man.

❦

"Oh god, it's so tight inside you," Darko growled. There was no way he was going to last long inside his knight. Not if he went on the rhythm he intended and he wasn't about to hold back any more than Maxum had with him.

He pressed Maxum's legs down and leaned back, creating all the access one could get from another's body and pistoned inside him until he was deep inside the other man's nethers.

Nerve endings fired off inside his body, scattering in all directions. The obliterating pleasure was far more intense than Darko had ever shared or received with another man. Despite the overwhelming sensation, he drilled in harder and faster, unwilling to deliver less than half of what he felt himself.

"Oh fuck— oh fuck—" Maxum was gasping under him. Open hands grappled against Darko's thighs trying to ease the assault of pleasure to a more comprehensible level, but Darko didn't comply. And just to be sure it was every bit as explosive, he reached between them, taking Maxum's cock in his hand, and began jacking him with just as much fury as his own cock shafted inside him.

They were both panting and grunting together, cursing that such a mismatched fucking could be so obliterating and intoxicating to both their minds and bodies.

Darko could feel his orgasm coming, igniting a stampede of a thousand angry stallions. It was going to be too good to leave bagged up. He withdrew, instantly ripping the condom off and ground Maxum's hard-on against his own cock. He leaned over to the side and drove several fingers into Maxum's ass and crooked his finger up to catch the man's prostate while his other hand joined Maxum's already wrapping around both their cocks and rocked against him.

Their foreheads met; eyes locked— cobalt against tigers eye. Darko tried to kiss him, deep languishing washes of tongue work but impossible to maintain against the heightened breathing to support the racing machine.

Every muscle in Darko's body clutched tight and went into a violent shudder. So intense, it assailed him with the concentrated explosion of euphoria, even his gasping expression struggled to break past his strained jaw muscles.

Maxum's fist clenched around their cocks and his body bucked against him.

Darko knew the man was coming with him, but damned if he could find the strength to pry his eyes open to watch him.

Maxum's growls were echoed by his own, while pulse after pulse of semen shot out in thick white ropes of frothy liquid that splattered over them both.

As the last of the aftershocks settled and relinquished control of his body, Darko dropped to the mattress. His body completely spent and his mind instantly drifted into a nebulous haze, lulled there by the elixir of their combined panting. He couldn't even muster the energy to rise up and kiss the man. Though, he desperately wanted to. He let out a deep guttural sigh, "Remind me to kiss you endlessly until your lips are raw when we wake and I've regained my strength." His slight chuckle turned groan— slipping into sleepy, sated oblivion.

CHAPTER TWO

Maxum St. Laurents paced his office as he listened to the meeting via satellite over the network phone, however his mind was on the man he slept with last night. So impassioned, his veins burned same as a racecar hopped-up on jet fuel to have more of the man he now knew as Darko and consumed him with this need. Every part of the night had been powerful, rough, and carnal. *Fuck, he loved it like a junky on a new drug.* So much so, that, instead of sneaking out early in the morning, as he had intended, they went at each other again. He couldn't remember the last time he woke up with a man's lips around his cock, but that was exactly what Darko had done to him. Washing his morning wood with his tongue and when Maxum couldn't hang on any longer, Maxum flipped the man over, and shafted his ass hard and relentlessly. Only to repeat the frenzy when they showered. Soaping that beautiful manly body was too much temptation. He recalled the timbre of his own voice deep and gravelly, as he moaned—

"Mr. St Laurents?" the man's voice coming from the speakerphone disrupted his daydreaming.

Maxum stopped and turned to look at the phone sitting on his desk as if seeing it for the first time— and that it talked, was completely alien to him.

"Mr. St Laurents?"

Maxum blinked out of his daze. "Yes." He cleared his mind a moment to gather his thoughts back to the conference meeting where they should have been. "I'm sorry. What was that again?"

"Have you gone over the MLP reports?"

"Yes."

"And are you ready to move some money that way?"

"That would be an altogether *no*, on that. The reports are hopped up. Their backing funds aren't substantial enough to fulfill the promised paybacks." Maxum returned to his desk chair and sat his restless body down.

"Stivvenson and Stephens are growing anxious on your lack of moving funds into the MLPs and on the Nasdaq. They want to know when you're going to move forward and begin high yield investments," the voice on the other end of the speaker took a challenging tone.

Maxum rocked back in his highbacked leather chair, his hands in his lap, relaxed as if he were talking about what was for lunch. "You tell them to settle down. Now is not the time to start dumping all of our investor's money into high yields. The flux is still very unstable."

"They're threatening to withdraw," the challenger reiterated with a note of concern rather than more arguing further this time.

"Then you tell them we're not in the business of throwing people's money away. If that's what they want, our best wishes for them. Nevertheless, I will not squander this company's funds along with theirs. I've made them far richer than they were when they came to us eight years ago. I'll do it again. Stivvenson and Stephens need fast cash in hand to start their new markets. Yet the product is unproven, which is why the backing isn't there for them. Hence, the reason they are pushing for individual investment with promises of high yields. I am not biting down on the bait. We are not in the business of crowdfunding and now's not the time to start cracking our nest eggs." He glanced at his watch. "Gentlemen, anything else? I have another meeting to catch."

"I believe we've covered everything today," a new voice in on the conference spoke up to answer.

"Very well, Brent, will you call the meeting adjourned?"

"Of course, Chairman," the new voice responded to the addressed name.

Maxum jumped up, grabbed his suitcoat and pulled it on. "Gentlemen." He punched a button, disconnecting the line and headed out in a rush, advising his assistant to postpone the rest of his day until further notice, and out the door he went.

Maxum followed the direction on the GPS and found the motorcycle shop just shortly before lunch. He sat outside, watching as a few men walked about on the other side of the large display window. All three wearing dingy, blue coveralls smudged in grease, but neither of them was his man.

What the hell was he doing here? Last night had been incredible, this morning even better. Beyond even that, to be so consumed inside the storm of lust that he let Darko fuck *him* after he'd rutted the man until he was drained of every drop of his seed.

Maxum was about to start the car back up and leave while he still could, when just then the man stuck on his brain, and libido, walked into view. There was no mistaking the half-naked man. *Where the hell had he developed such perfect muscle tone?* Maxum involuntarily licked his lips in anticipation of licking Darko's entire body over. His cock throbbed painfully in his slacks, calling up the memory of their romp from last night. He'd woken up that morning with his cock inside Darko— looking at the desirable body now he knew— *it hadn't been enough.* There was no leaving now.

"Hey, Darko!" One of the guys called towards the back just as Maxum stepped in, but Maxum already had the man pinpointed. "You got company!" the other two, working on a gutted Iron Eagle, jeered amongst themselves.

Maxum ignored them as he strolled past, not waiting for the invitation. He hadn't planned to do anything but invite Darko over for a night, or perhaps it might take the whole weekend to get enough of him, but that was all, just ask and get out. Yet, one look at the man up close and Maxum was doomed to fail in his restricted plan. Muscular arms tanned from hours of being outdoors were soaked to the elbows in black crude, while sweat sheened across his back. All of the above perfectly packaged with the firm ass, gift-wrapped tightly in faded jeans.

Darko turned and faced him, his front frame was doubly enticing— the sight slammed Maxum. Sweat and grease had never been his style or so Maxum thought, because right now, it was the sexiest thing he'd ever seen on a male body. Outside of a healthy glaze of spunk.

His mouth watered instantly for a taste of Darko and he knew he was hooked.

A sheepish grin came over the man as Maxum took a step toward him while he was trying his best to wipe some of the oil off his hands with a shop towel. "Surprise visit— I like those," Darko welcomed him with a voice as dark as a Bohemian black lager. A thumb moved up to lazily glide over some invisible itch, leaving a black smudge across the golden skin of a pectoral muscle, just above a tight pale, mauve colored nipple. Had it been edible, Maxum would have already jumped the man to lick it off. Just the sight had Maxum breathing deeply, and some proverb along the lines of, *if he kisses me, that's it, we're fucking*, danced through his head.

"Hey, Darko, looks like you might need some space, so we're cutting out for lunch early. We'll be a while!" One of the three at the other end of the shop, called out.

Darko gave a slight upward nod of acknowledgment, but his eyes didn't leave Maxum, dark blue eyes brimming with lust.

"Didn't think I was so obvious," Maxum commented, not in the least shamed or concerned at the moment, but rather amused.

❦

"No, but I am." Darko rolled his lips in and licked over the top one seductively as if savoring some fond memory as his gaze drifted over the silk suited man standing before him, "Plus, I might have mentioned something along the lines of getting throttled by a knight-in-*shiny*-armor." Darko then glanced out the window to the collector's model in the parking lot. Silver sides with black trim and fenders. Chrome manifold pipes laced out the side of the engine panels and the added feature of whitewall spoke tires gave it that Great Gatsby roadster look. His baby sisters, who were all about Steampunk fashion, would approve. "Nice armor today." Darko's eyes glided from the car outside and back to the man standing inside, his voice teasing like a dribble of melted chocolate just begging to be licked away. "So, what happened to the Mercedes?"

"Had them take it back." Maxum shrugged.

"And now you have?" Darko let the question ring out, to offer the man a chance to brag about his replacement ride.

"A 1936 Auburn Boat-Tail Roadster." Another mild shrug, "I've had this one for some time."

Darko stepped in, closing the gap between them and leaned in, "I like this one better," Darko spoke as he delivered a tempting kiss that licked over Maxum's lips.

The air left Maxum's lungs. *That's it.* "Can you get out of here?" Maxum was nearly growling with lust. His head falling against Darko's forehead, exchanging deep gasps of hot breath.

Darko kept close, purposely teasing him further with the heat of his body, "What did you have in mind?"

"I only came by to ask if you had plans for tonight, but just looking at you has got me so hard, I doubt I could sit down without my cock busting through my pants."

Darko's grin deepened, his eyes shifting his focus once more to the unique car outside that screamed antique classic steampunk racecar, but what mattered most right now was it didn't have much room for playing around in. "No back seat," he verbally pointed out, turning back to Maxum.

"I'm sure you have a broom closet around here somewhere," Maxum sputtered, not caring about the particulars of where as he leaned in to steal a kiss from Darko, who reciprocated and fed the need instantly.

Darko let the kiss linger until he could no longer stand so close and not touch the man by any other means but their lips. He pulled his head back wrenching the lips apart. "I have an office," he offered in a heated groan.

"There's a desk?" Maxum growled.

"Yes."

ॐ

"Perfect." Maxum's tongue lapped out from his mouth, reaching to have the taste of the man's mouth returned to him. Just then, out of the corner of his peripheral, Maxum saw the blur of black hands coming up, and he instantly caught Darko's wrists, before the greasy brute could mangle yet another suit. He held Darko steadfast, while his tongue found its target and laved over Darko's, sucking at it before chewing on his lips, which got the man he was kissing, and holding back at the same time, growling.

Darko playfully tested Maxum's grip, pressing more of his weight into the hold, and Maxum's hands tightened further around them, holding ground.

"Oh— if you think we're doing this without me touching you, you're wrong." Darko pushed into him and began walking Maxum backwards towards the small office room in the back corner of the shop.

"I have to return to the office after this."

"Don't you keep a spare suit there?" The debate was on.

They reached the door, Darko's eyes peered down at the handle with a wry grin and waited. Maxum let one wrist go, to grasp the doorknob, and that's when Darko moved in for the kill. Darko's hand was instantly fisting into Maxum's suit coat and shirt, just as before, and forcibly pulled them together, and devoured Maxum's mouth with a burning kiss.

Maxum opened the door and shoved Darko inside the room, not bothering with the lights, "You're a pig," Maxum growled, shutting the door and then began stripping his clothes off.

Darko let out a light sinister chuckle, his eyes filled with carnivorous flames of lust as he watched Maxum undress. "I've been called many things before. *Pig*— isn't one of them."

"Shut up and get those jeans off," Maxum barked, the aggression in which Darko matched him had him already panting hard with urgency, not that he had any need for helping him get there. He was hooked on this guy the moment he brutally kissed him on the highway yesterday. It was as if being swept off his feet in some twisted male, cavalier romantic way. And he had liked it right from the start. However, if Darko didn't start undressing soon, he was going to rip his clothes off.

Maxum tossed his crisp white shirt, now painted with greasy handprints to the floor, along with his suit coat. He toe'd his dress shoes off then unfastened his belt and unzipped his pants. One hand slipping in to stroke over his tormented hard-on as he watched Darko peel his tight fitted jeans off his hips. "I've been wanting to fuck you all morning."

"I believe it's my turn," Darko protested mildly, with a cocky quirk to one brow.

"Oh no, I'm fucking you. But I'll give something in return for now." Maxum closed in, dropping to his knees and without asking, sucked Darko's cock into his mouth in one quick movement, taking every dark-complected inch into his hungry mouth.

He pushed in, burrowing his face in Darko's groin until Maxum felt Darko's body stop against the desk edge. He let out a groan, savoring the feel and flavor of the man now engorged in his mouth. It'd been too long since he got to enjoy this and was going to have it until the man came. When he felt the surrendering sigh from Darko's body, Maxum let the cock slip from his mouth, and he moved lower, running a trail of open-mouth kisses along the underside ridge several times then moved even lower to wash Darko's balls with his tongue. First one, then the other.

Fuck, he was dying for this, as his hand dropped down to fist over his own shaft, and slowly delivered a few absentminded pumps before taking Darko's cock in the other hand and began to work him up, licking him over from sack to tip. Maxum felt the sting on his scalp as Darko's fingers raked into his hair and curled in tight, jerking his head in a tilt, to give himself a better view of the action he was receiving. Maxum kicked it up a notch by sucking in the bulbous head and lobbed it around on his tongue. Molesting the eye-slit with his tongue then gave it a power suction to get every drop of pre-cum from him, then topped the whole act off with a tight groan that was sure to reverberate into Darko's shaft.

The curse overhead confirmed it and Maxum was pleased that the man was so receptive to his needs. *His* needs, because he had to have this— craved the taste of a man's body, a man's cock on his tongue. To be a man and loving the act of devouring another man.

"Oh shiiiit!" Darko cut out a long curse through clenched teeth, his hand held tight on Maxum's scalp and his thighs jumped under the tension as his cock pulsated in Maxum's mouth then shot out an immaculate release.

The fist Maxum still had wrapped around his own dick, started pumping. Stopping only long enough to blindly feel for the foil already waiting in his back pocket and then prepping his erection while he swallowed down the prize Darko's body shot down his gullet. Dark, richly briny, an exotic candy all to his own palate, not unlike dark malt scotch. He just couldn't get enough of this. And he still nurtured Darko's cock, playing in the extra skin with his tongue even as it softened until Darko forced him to let go. "Fuck. That was incredible." Darko's way of applauding him, and then folded down, diving into his mouth and kissed him full on. That too, was something Maxum hadn't had in a long time. He let out a growl and pushed up to his feet, into Darko's arms, pressing against the man's body and deepened their kiss, wrangling with the tongue that sought to share the flavors from his own.

"Damn you." Maxum tore away with a growl and pressed his head against the side of Darko's face as he strained to catch his breath.

"Hmmm— a blow job like that and now you're cursing me? Seems rather contrite," Darko joked as he nudged against Maxum's cheek with his nose, trying to roll him back for more accessible kissing, but finally just grabbing Maxum's chin and lifted him up to be taken.

"You're like a dru—" The last word swallowed up by Darko's insistent kiss and for whatever reason Maxum thought to argue this, relented. Their tongues rolled together, clashed. Maxum was operating on instinct, licentiousness and pent up frustration. At no point was their kiss a gentle exploration, but every bit as explosive as a savage war. Hot and consuming, a rendering of self, an unquenchable thirst. He wanted more and he needed it now, and his arms were instantly seeking out Darko's legs, hoisting him up, and placing him flat on his back on the desk.

Maxum wasn't thinking control as he lined the tip of his shaft with Darko's rosette. The grip of Darko's hands as they took hold of Maxum's hips and pulled, said he wasn't either, and Maxum sank in, pausing only to relish the first gasp they both shared.

He eased back as the ripple of pleasure moved over him and seated its epic pulse at the base of his balls, then pushed until he was all the way in. Darko's body tightened around him like a fist, a slight curse husked from his own lips while shifting side to side to get that last micron of depth, and yet another gasp.

Once that first delicious feeling was gone, Maxum began moving pumping in and out of the lover he had stumbled across, and he lost control of himself. The salacious slide of his cock inside Darko's tight walls was as intense as the emotional face that looked up at him, equally consumed with this blazing bonfire they shared.

Their eyes locked in each other's gaze as Maxum found a grinding rhythm that suited them both, their raspy breaths echoed in the small office as they both became nothing more than consumption and frenzy.

Maxum couldn't think, he could only feel, and not all was purely physical. There was something about the rugged looking, hedonist, he was currently molesting. Resembling the exotic car you didn't just take for a test drive, you became addicted to them.

Sweat beaded up on his back, knocking his cologne into high gear, scenting the stale air of the room that was just as quickly becoming coated with the smell of their sex. Maxum liked the smell. No potpourris, just two men and men's cologne battling to overpower the smell of grease and machine shop tools.

Maxum kicked up another notch in his pace, feeling the intensity building at the base of his spine. Darko, too, was groaning in staccato breaths created by Maxum's relentless pounding against his ass. The slap of his balls not only added to the sound of their bodies and expressions but also stimulated both their passions, sending him plummeting towards the desired explosive release.

Only, Maxum wanted to hear more than just groaning from Darko and he bent down at his knees and angled his pistoning drives upward to get the money spot.

Darko tossed his head, his hand coming around his cock and began to pump frantically to normalize the intense pleasure that ripped through him. "Mmmm, *fu*—" The word morphing into panting huffs and then it hit. Darko's head slammed back into the desk, only to curl up with the rest of his body as it contorted with his orgasm.

Maxum was right behind him. He stood straight then slammed against Darko's ass as hard as he could and seated his cock all the way to the bottom where he remained, growling like a menacing animal as he shot out his load. The sound that bounced off the wall and came back at him didn't even sound remotely human, but it was him, and matched every bit of what he was feeling. And when it drained from him, he collapsed over Darko in a heap of panting nothingness.

Dingy oil-stained hands came over him in a lazy caress over his back in a weak attempt to cuddle before falling back to the desk. The gritty feel of the touch reminded Maxum of the grimy handprints they likely left behind— *oh hell he just didn't give a fuck right now.*

Maxum laid there until the moment of panting chorus gave way to awkward silence and he stood, easing out of the man he was so hooked on. He snapped the spent condom from his dick, dropped it like a trophy in the waste bin, and disappeared in the small bathroom. The bathroom light flickered then shone down on him with a yellow glare as he looked at his reflection and the grease marks on his jawline and shoulder. "Fuck," he cursed turning his head for a better look. He slathered his hands up using the degreaser goop from the jar on the sink edge, lathered it up and made a futile attempt to clean the mess off as he silently contemplated how he felt about them.

He snatched several paper towels from the dispenser, wet them down, and tried to wipe off the grime marks from his shoulder. He tried to get pissed standing there staring at them, or rather, he was trying to condone their presence.

The black smudges becoming a symbol of where he should not be, but the anger never came. Not about where he was or that his lover had dirtied him. Sure, he cared. He cared when it was an insult to his senses. This wasn't the same. Darko challenged him, he didn't insult or act as if Maxum wasn't even there as a real person. He closed his eyes and leaned forward until his forehead touched the cool surface of the mirror and just stood there, mentally dismissing the thoughts. *This was just—*

An arm reaching around him, turned the water on, disrupted his thoughts and Maxum stood up, coming back against Darko's chest. The hand in the sink squeezed a clean, white cloth then moved in to wash Maxum's soft dick, while lips equally soft kissed his neck. And dark blues watched him intently over his shoulder through the mirror's reflection of them. "Having second thoughts about me?"

"No," Maxum answered, just a little too hastily, but he didn't want thoughts getting in the way. "Come spend the weekend with me." But instead of answering him,

Darko reached around, taking his still smudged jaw and pulled him to turn around where he landed right into a slow tender kiss, perhaps too tender, inviting an emotional intimacy, but Maxum didn't care about that either, right now.

CHAPTER THREE

Darko had actually persuaded Maxum to alter their plans to stay at Darko's place instead, under the insistence that he wasn't about to sleep in an unfamiliar bed on a night before practice. Maxum thought it was a rather lame excuse, until he went and watched from one of the bridges just down from the boathouse. The eight-man rowing scull glided across the river's surface in the early morning sun. Maxum sat forward on the bench where he was mesmerized by the physique and fluidity of each of the men. There was something about certain sports that got a man's attention, like rugby and soccer. Sculling was now among them.

The late October wind whipped across the water, then leaped up over the bridge where he stood to slap his face with the impending arrival of a New York winter. He pulled his wool coat in tighter, wishing he was on the boat. Although they were wearing much less, their bodies pumping with the exertion of the sport meant they were warmer than he was.

While the view was spectacular, the scull was steadily pulling off up river and out of sight, so he decided to head over to his place, grab an overnight bag, and to do a few extra things, then change out cars. He even timed it right, getting back to the boathouse just as Darko was stepping out to look for him. To which, he was more than happy to steal Maxum away and take him back to the flat.

All day and into the next, Maxum and Darko lounged on the sofa watching gay porn and took free play with each other's bodies. There never was the request or hinting— they simply did when the mood arose, which was quite frequently. If Maxum had been booze, Darko would be several sheets to the wind.

He was not an unblemished man of sex. Darko knew what he wanted and wasn't afraid to be adventurous and had plenty of willing subjects for his menu. Even so, Maxum seized his desires in a way he'd not felt with any of them. The man didn't flirt, he invested. His intensity was a constant brush against Darko's nerve endings, rousing some long forgotten slumbering part of his body, working him into a frenzy.

"So how adventurous are you?" Maxum nudged the man who was sprawled across his lap.

Darko gave him a queried expression. "As long as it doesn't entail me having to call one of my brothers to bail me out, I'm game."

Maxum chuckled, "I was thinking along the lines of food. *Le Bernardin* is having their food and wine tasting social tonight. I have a reserved table there. I just wasn't sure you'd be willing to suffer through overpriced, overly designed fancy food."

Darko twisted so he could look up at him, "Those things appeal to you?"

Maxum's gaze dropped over him and he scratched at his lip with a finger, almost like a nervous twitch. "Mmm, yes, they do."

Darko only smiled. "Then let's go."

"Good. Get dressed and put on a tie."

"Alright, but don't expect me to wash my hands," Darko joked.

Maxum stalled suddenly, just as he'd gotten to his feet. His hand sought out Darko's and slowly brought his fingers up to his mouth and sucked on two of them. A light groan rode on his sigh as his tongue tasted remnants of their earlier hand jobs. "I agree." He smiled playfully, letting Darko's hand go and headed for the bedroom where he'd placed his overnight bag and suit hanger, earlier.

An hour and half later, they were pulling up in front of the Waldorf Astoria on Park Avenue. Much as the lavish hotel didn't surprise Darko, what did was Maxum pulling up into the valet did. Oh sure, rich folk always did that, but not with a car that cost more than an average person's lifetime income. If it had been his Austin roadster, he wouldn't have allowed a minimum wage valet college kid to touch it. Yet they zipped right in and Maxum left the keys in the ignition as they hopped out. The second thing that took Darko by surprise was the sudden feeling of a hand at the small of his back. Darko snapped a glance at Maxum, just before they made it inside. "So, this is a touching date?"

Maxum stopped and something haunting threatened just under his face, but his hand hadn't fallen away. "Do you not want me to?"

"No—" Darko shook his head. "I mean yes, just didn't expect it. High society and all."

Maxum seemed relieved. "At five grand a pop, I'm allowed some PDA. That or I stop coming." With his comment, Maxum's hand pressed a little, urging them inside.

"Somehow, I doubt one toss of five grand is going to have them balking." Darko smirked as they made their way down the large corridor filled with people crowding towards the banquet hall.

"They do, when I go to anywhere from six to eight of these a year." He chuckled just as they stepped into the event hall, and the air of food, wine, and money met them head on. If it had not been for the comforting contact of Maxum's hand still on his back, Darko was sure he'd have turned right back around and left. He'd been to socials, been around wealthy people, but he knew full damn well he didn't fit in. not without some heavy amount of lascivious naughty lifestyle hosting. However, he did like fitting into the arms of the man next to him very much, so a little social unease was tolerable, considering the pay off.

Almost right away, a few social butterflies in the crowd approached to greet Maxum. Each time, Darko noticed, the man stroked his back before withdrawing away to shake hands or grasp their shoulder for a cheeky kiss-n-greet, then right back to his original position, to stroke over Darko's back or side like a signal that said *I know you are still here*. He liked that most of all.

As they continued to steer for the bar, there was no way to make it without a few more stops. But once there, a heavy sigh came from Maxum which brought on a certain chuckle from Darko. Clearly, the faux pressure valve release was brought on by all the ladies' vulgarly innocent attempts to touch him. Whether it was for his looks or his market value didn't matter. What amused Darko was, with each one, Maxum seemed to sweat them more. The man was purely 100% gay-angus-beef.

"So this PDA— is there a limit?" Darko teased, more so to adjust the man's thoughts back to a perspective comfort zone.

Maxum's fingers leafed one of the wine lists on the bar and slid it over to browse the selection for tasting. The arm around Darko drew tighter, pulling him in for full body contact before turning to face him with a part content, part smoldering expression. "Usually, if the term *'get a room'* has to be mentioned, I think they expect us to cordially make our exit." And to prove a point, Maxum leaned in and kissed him. Nothing too arousing, but it wasn't a *zip-in zip-out* peck on the cheek either. Maxum's soft lips lingered on his own, delivering a subliminal message as if to tell every fiber of his body— *finally, I found you.*

Damn but if he could learn to love this guy. 'Hmmm and how much does a room cost here?' he laid on a heavy bad-boy smirk.

The evening event went on. Live music to entertain. Non-stop sampling of foods— some so fancy and exotic, Darko couldn't bring himself to taste. He made several tight-lipped expressions to prevent them from being shoveled into his mouth anyways, which his rich lover was taking some delight in doing, like a new game he'd never been allowed to play before. Food, of course, was followed up with more wine. Working their way from the light and fruity to the more dark and robust.

The banquet hall in itself held a rich flavor; dark umber walls tricked out with burnished gold and navy dinner tables and a few high-bar tables peppered the floor. All of which corralled around a center banquet of all-you-can-eat hors d'oeuvres and amuse bouche. Maxum was in his element, enjoying the event as much as Darko would enjoy being at a rowing race. He had to admit the trade-off was still in good running with him. Nevertheless, he was starting to eyeball the balconies that overlooked the ballroom, noting that none were in use— and it was far easier than getting a room, with a dash of naughty to boot. Maxum had abandoned his post for a restroom break and no doubt, the ladies would be moving in like vultures to pine for a moment of his time with no one at his side. So, Darko retreated to the main bar ordering up a dark ale to remedy his palate. He had the need to balance the fancy fare with a bold malt flavor more to his liking, and familiarity while he waited for the equally likable, bold flavored man to return.

A gingered-haired gentleman, dressed in a nice tan suit came up beside Darko, landing his elbows on the bar heavily, his eyes landing on Darko's body with like measure. Darko only smirked, his gaydar meter pinging hard into the red. One was always bound to approach. He saw the *tells* written all over the man's face; married, straight, sex life unfulfilling, and still at a loss of how to fill it. This type so often moved in on who they hoped was experienced enough to lead them to the fulfillment of their closeted needs.

Darko chuckled to himself, *a perfect prey to be turned into submissive material.* He brought a finger up to his mouth, cloaking the silent laugh as he licked over his lips. *Why, he could even hook him up, if the mood to be so nice struck him.* Which he didn't— not here— and not on his date. Though Darko had offered no invitation, the man had clearly loaded up on his liquid courage and thus began the small talk.

Darko e wasn't on his own turf, had he been at the Tavern, Club Pain or, *hell*, even the occasional visit to the Leather Strap, he would have been clear about what the definition of *piss-off* meant. Instead, he stopped himself, just in case *Mister Ginger* was a client or close friend of Maxum's. Either way, friend or not, Darko gave no encouragement toward further conversation. Eyes straight ahead, nursing his stout. None of that seemed to deter the other male any. That was until Maxum was back at his side, just when *Mister Ginger* popped the question.

"So, any chance I can get your number?" Mister Ginger's eyes dropped to the floor nervously.

"He's not a rent boy," a possessive tone came over Darko's right shoulder and he turned to see a displeased expression from Maxum.

Darko didn't for one second think it might be for him, and he dropped his head back, catching Maxum by his tie, and pulled him over for a kiss. "But *he* is what happens, when you leave your honey within range of the flies." Darko joked to make light of the encounter.

Something changed in Maxum at that moment, making Darko reconsider that maybe some of the fuss really was for him. The mar in Maxum's expression was fixed and wiped away for him. Maxum seemed relieved and with a smile that said as much, he bent down over Darko and kissed him several more times. Each one becoming longer and deeper until they were locked in a kiss that said it was time for that room, or maybe the balcony he'd been eyeing. Even said as much with a growl, when Maxum pulled away to catch his breath.

"Don't make me have to say it twice," Darko teased.

Maxum responded with a low groan and a turn of his head. "Mmmm, let's get out of here then."

Hours later, with the moon beaming through the glass walls of the bedroom, the two men lay spooned into each other. Maxum was wrapped around Darko, keeping him pressed back against his chest as they both quietly listened to their breaths settling after a long run of love-making. Maxum's cock was still seated inside Darko's ass, enjoying a few post-coital pushes, at the same time nibbling on the back of his shoulder.

Darko had an arm tucked under his head, the other held fast to Maxum's thigh, still draped over his hip, lest he decided to stop too soon. It was the first time they hadn't gone after each other like wild animals, racing to mark each other with spunk. Rather it was slow. Copious amounts of touching and kissing—and awesomeness. His eyes flickered to the clock. One hour and fifteen minutes. Talk about a stretch. A hand came around and pulled his face around to smear him with wet kissing and licking.

"Thank you," Maxum sighed with content.

"For?" Darko shifted around to look back at him better.

"For a perfect night."

"And the rent boy?" Darko wasn't really meaning to antagonize him about it, but he was just a bit curious enough to tease him.

The taunt got him a burnishing kiss and a growl to boot. "You're too fucking handsome to be owned, but I didn't want anyone thinking any less of you." His embrace tightened, pulling Darko to settle against the perfectly sculpted chest that pressed against his back.

Spooning was always an ideal comfort, but never before had it seemed like he lay with the perfect fit as they both snuggled in for slumber. He felt Maxum's lips pressed permanently against the back of his neck. "But you know, I could come up with a lease with option to buy plan for you," Darko managed to suggest before he'd drifted off too far. The heavy sigh of silence behind him was more than what Darko had expected, though. He even felt the slight tension in Maxum's body and the pinch to his heart that Maxum didn't even laugh the suggestion away. Rather withdrew from it. Another *tell*— only it was one Darko would have preferred not to have picked up on.

CHAPTER FOUR

Maxum's Monday was like any businessman's Monday— hectic, with every hour of his schedule booked with more than one meeting he could humanly attend to. Tuesday was little better for him, and when a sudden drop in certain stocks meant he had to concur with a telecast meeting with CEOs in Hong Kong, he barely squeezed out time to make the call that would cancel his dinner plans.

"So, how is my knight in shiny armor? I didn't expect to hear from you until later."

Maxum almost forgot why he called, as the dark caramel voice of the man on the other end seeped into his mind and took form there. "Uh, yeah, I'm afraid I have to cancel on you. Meeting with clients in Hong Kong popped up."

"Turning me down for Chinese food, huh?" Darko chuckled at him from the other end. If there was a note of distrust, Maxum didn't pick up on it. *"Well, don't come complaining to me when you're hungry an hour later."*

"I'll try not to." Maxum let out a relaxed laugh, but fell silent, just lingering on the phone, not sure what to say, but oddly he wasn't feeling compelled to hang up either. He even found an unexpected comfort when Darko didn't cut the call short, the wayward conversation that held little importance except to be company. Leaving him in a comfort zone he seldom had these days yet would linger with him through his trip.

Maxum was due in sometime tonight and had told Darko he'd call once he was in, so Darko was surprised when he heard the knock on the door, and glancing out the window, he spotted the familiar exotic car.

"Did you really come straight—" His words cut off when Maxum stepped in, dropping the suitcase down on the floor then reached out grabbing him up, and pulled him in for a lingering kiss. It was by far the best *glad I'm home welcoming,* he'd ever experienced and while one arm floated up to join in on the embrace, the other still held onto the door to steady himself as Maxum's tongue was clearly sweeping him off his feet.

Without breaking the sensual kiss, Maxum reached out and took the door from Darko's hand, swung it closed then wrapped him up in his arms once more, and deepening the kiss.

Okay, so he was definitely feeling swept off his feet.

Darko started walking backwards while Maxum keep in tandem, like a smoldering dance set to the rhythm of their mutual desires for each other. Not allowing the connection to be severed for anything more than a few words spoken against his lips. "I was thinking I would cuddle the hell out of you before we went to your bedroom," Maxum chuckled.

"Not bedroom— kitchen."

"Mmmm, kinky. I can handle doing you on the kitchen table."

"Food—" his attempt to debate the purpose of the kitchen voyage interrupted with more kissing, along with some disrobing of a suit coat from Maxum, that went flying over the back of the sofa as they passed it. Darko broke free of the lip loving. "As in, I am cooking some dinner."

"Mmmm, but you're the only one I am hungry for right now." Maxum came at him with the full gusto of his physical appetite.

Damned, if the guy didn't turn him on nonstop. Darko felt the bulge building in his jeans, and Maxum's hands hadn't even wandered there yet. While *where* Maxum's hands did diverge felt incredible, Darko's body was screaming for him to get to his cock sooner rather than later. And, as if his silent prayers were being answered, Darko found himself shoving against the counter while Maxum worked his way down his body undoing the jeans to get them removed like he was starved for what was inside them.

Darko leaned back on his hands, catching the counter, as Maxum manipulated his legs and tugged his jeans from one leg then the next. His eyes flickered to the steaks on the stovetop grill but were immediately pulled away from thoughts of dinner to the tongue lasciviously trailing up his thigh. He let out a hiss, letting his head fall back as his hips thrust out to greet the mouth making its way up.

Darko's teeth found his bottom lip, his head still kicked back on his shoulders, and hands held onto the countertop edge with a vice grip as he surrendered his body to the lips now mouthing over his cock through his briefs. *Damn, how did he go all week without this?* He had to wonder.

Maxum's hands came up on the backsides of his thighs then up over his hips, fisting into his briefs and down they went. His cock popping out to be greeted by the pressure of the man's face, smashing against it, sucking in a deep breath as if sampling Darko's scent to remember what he liked most.

"I need to turn the grill off," Darko hissed, but the intel didn't seem to register in the man kneeling before him. A hand caught Darko's left thigh, pressing it to widen and Maxum dove in. His lover's free hand scooping his balls aside, and a warm wet tongue found its way over his taint, licking him all the way up then over his sacks, sucking on one, then the other. Giving each of Darko's fleshy orbs a final washing, before licking his way up the underside of his shaft and up along the hard ridge, until finally circling over the mushroom cap.

The steaks sizzled and crackled on the stovetop grill until the smell of charred meat started to fill the kitchen.

"Maxum, I need to—"

"Don't fucking move," Maxum growled.

"Hey! Those are porterhouses on the grill. If they burn—"

"I will take you out for dinner when I have had my replenishment of you. And, by out, I mean an expensive dinner." And without another word or letting Darko reach for the stove top, Maxum took the full length of Darko's cock into his mouth, sucking him down entirely.

Darko growled out as his cock bottomed out in Maxum's throat. "Oh god, that's so fucking good." More growling escaped him and his hand, on its own accord, found the back of his lover's head and held him as his hips rocked in and out a few times before forcing himself to pull out and let the man breathe as he also stretched over to turn the grill top off before burning his apartment down. "Deal," Darko hummed the word out and was immediately being sucked back into Maxum's mouth.

After Maxum had had his *phallacio* fix, the two men changed clothes, loaded up in the car and headed out for *Gramercy Tavern* for the promised steak dinner. Maxum tried not to let his head suffer over his pleasures with this man. Not even when Darko's arm went around him as they waltzed into the tavern area to eat, rather than heading for the restaurant section, did either man seem concerned of any looks they might draw to themselves. Be that as it may, more importantly, Maxum didn't worry himself that someone might make any presumptions of the change in his life or who he was with. Simeon never did steak. In fact, the only time Sim did anything that wasn't vegetarian was when it was costing Maxum a grand a plate at some charity dinner function.

He fought back the groan, knowing he'd just invited his own troubled thoughts to drown his good mood. That was another place— another time— not for here or with this man.

They took a small corner booth that allowed them to sit catty-corner to each other and looked over the menu. But, if there was a moment to be awkward, it never came. Darko struck up a conversation as if they belonged right where they were. No past or residue to shadow their evening.

"So tell me about your very first collector's car."

Maxum blinked toward the man nearly surprised by the question. He shouldn't have been, Darko was a man into manly things. Simeon had never taken interest in his collection, just that Maxum showed up in which ever model Simeon thought was going to impress his friends. Darko looked over the menu, occasionally looking back at him, waiting for him to tell the story. He felt the smile warming his face, burning away everything else from his thoughts and for the first time in a long time, Maxum felt completely at ease, and all too comfortable.

A smile returned to his face that Darko could feel as Maxum pulled up the fond memory.

"My first car was a 1955 Austin Healy. Damned thing didn't ever run, but I liked looking out the window of my apartment and seeing it in my parking spot. Was seventeen at the time and I didn't make enough money to afford the repairs so I got a second job. Before I even got it up and running, I had my eyes on yet another car.

I decided then I needed a career that was going to afford me my addiction."

Darko was about to ask another question but was put on pause when their waiter arrived to take their orders. An answer Darko had yet to determine since they had talked nonstop since their arrival. Whether Maxum noted his hesitation, or he was just accustomed to heading the table, Maxum spoke right up with a plan. "Yeah, I'll have the butternut squash with lobster and Brussels sprouts soup." Maxum glanced at Darko. "Did you decide on an appetizer?"

"I trust you," was all Darko said, enjoying watching Maxum take charge of the moment.

Maxum chuckled with a small shake of his head and added to their order. "Very well then, we'll also have the raw oysters and the duck liver mousse."

Darko's head popped up with quite the expression on it, "Duck liver mousse?"

"You said you trusted me."

"Well— I mean— it's just—"

Maxum merely gave him an amused grin and Darko's brows must have dropped half way down his face with the returned expression. "Yeah, okay, I'll try it once."

Their waiter nodded and conferred, "Very nice selection, and do you need some more time for your entrées?"

"No—" Darko spoke up, "We'll both be having the Kobe steaks cooked rare with just a hint of blackened seasoning, the leeks-n-mushroom side, and potato dumplings with the sour cream butter sauce."

It was Maxum's turn to give a surprised look. "You did notice they don't have Kobe steaks on their menu?"

Darko matched him with a smug smile. "Ah, yes, but then it's a steakhouse and all high end New York Steak restaurants know to carry it." He rubbed his fingers together to signal it was carried for those with lots of money. "You just have to be in *the know* to order it."

Maxum nodded, Darko was right. Kobe was expensive and rarely listed on a menu, but, if one could afford a Kobe steak, they knew it was there for the asking. He glanced up at the waiter waiting for the confirmation, "Is the Kobe available?"

The man smiled happily, "Why, yes, sirs. Arrived fresh yesterday."

Maxum nodded.

"Excellent. Two Kobe dinners." The waiter scribbled the selection down, made a slight bow and hurried off with their orders.

"So did you ever get the Austin running?" Darko quickly set the pace back to cars and hot rods.

Maxum grinned proudly. "I did."

"And what will it be that catches your eye next?"

Maxum chuckled and leaned over to plant a playful peck on Darko's lips. "You mean besides you?" He returned to his rested posture. "Hmmm, not sure. Eventually I want to add the McLaren F1 or perhaps the Devon GTX. Either one is an exceptional car to have as well." He scratched at his lip and made a chuckling sound, "I have a hankering for movie cars, too, but one of my favorites doesn't exist anymore. Crass bastards really did run it off a cliff and they only had the one modified Jaguar XKE sportscar."

"Wait. You mean the Hearst Jaguar from *Herold and Maude*?" Darko laughed.

"Yeah, you know the movie?"

"Who doesn't?" Darko took a long drink from his chilled glass of dark ale before continuing, "So, no Bugatti for you? Or is that out of your price range?"

Maxum laughed a hardy laugh, "I already have two." He nodded with a warm inward smile, "and they're among my favorites. I picked up the Bugatti Roadster with two-tone, matte black-n-matte blue color scheme several years back, but the moment I laid eyes on the Bugatti Veyron L'or Blanc, I knew she had to be mine. I sold off three of my others just to get her. I already have plans for a trip scheduled to Volkswagen's Ehra-Lessien Test Track in Germany in the late spring, to ship both cars over to run them wide open."

The smile Maxum had on now, as he talked about the *once upon a time* top-secret, thirty mile oval track, was worth more than the cars he talked about, and it had Darko falling for him. There was something about him that put Maxum in a class all by himself.

A self-made business man that afforded him whatever he wanted, yet he lacked the ego that was customarily found with such status. Maxum was laid back with nearly everything Darko had seen him in, except maybe his lust for raw, unadulterated sex.

He gave off an air of regalness that only lent further to the pet name he'd tagged him with as his knight. Yet, inside all that, as Darko listened to Maxum talk about his experience racing down the last fifteen mile stretch as fast as he could push the limits, Darko also saw a kid, waving his prized *Mickey Mantle* baseball card, or something that was equally heartfelt, inside. Maxum St. Laurents may be wealthy, but he was human, too, and that was the part about him Darko liked best.

As the next hour and a half passed by, talk over food went from cars to motorcycles. From Maxum's trip to how Darko got involved in sculling. Maxum asked questions like how the *in-your-face* iconic name came about for the Greenwich Queens Rowing Team and he listened as Darko ramble on about his faster than the highest average pace that made it impossible for him to compete any other way than as a single-shell rower.

They could have been best friends just catching up on each other's lives, with an equally invested interest. Only theirs came with some exceptionally steamy extra benefits, which— as the night dwindled down both were feeling rather eager to get on with.

After a hurried drive back to Darko's place, which showed off Maxum's driving skills to match his car; he now sat completely naked in the corner of the sofa, stroking his cock as he waited for Darko's return and was completely taken by surprise when the man came crawling over him from behind the sofa. Stout legs bound with uncanny strength, anchored around Maxum's head with his knees propped on the back, while Darko lowered down until his face came over Maxum's lap, putting them both in the perfect vertical sixty-nine position.

Maxum didn't waste any time taking to the man, burrowing his face into the musky scent of cock and balls being offered up to him. He reached up locking onto Darko's hips and pulled him down until the man's groin was smashing him in the face. His nose buried in the tanned flesh, he sucked the soft flesh into his mouth, moving from one nut to the next, washing each thoroughly with his tongue, and inhaled deeply to enjoy a full banquet of smell and taste. Enjoying every aromatic flavor of the man and hummed his appreciation.

His thoughts skipped several beats when he felt his cock sink inside the warm, moist cavern of Darko's mouth that sent out a warm ripple of pleasure. *Damn it, if this man didn't know how to feed him.* Maxum's arms tightened around his lover's hips, crushing him even harder against his face as he swallowed every inch of Darko's still partially flaccid cock down his throat. Moaning at the joyous sensation of having it thicken inside his mouth. Swelling hard flesh pressed against his tongue until he was nearly gagging with the now spectacularly swollen shaft.

Simeon never let him have this with him. In fact, Simeon didn't like his own cock messed with beyond a hand job. It was a wonder why the man didn't have it cut off, but then if Simeon had done that, Maxum would have dumped him in a heartbeat. If he was going to have a man in his bed, he's going to be a complete man, cock and all. Here, Darko didn't thwart him, and so far allowed him to revel in his oral obsession. As Maxum figured, the man would likely even make him partake if he even thought to skip over such luxuries. Nevertheless, it wasn't the case. Maxum loved a man's body, loved tasting, smelling, and feeling every inch of it. He was addicted to it. The male body was his fetish and Darko suited his fetish perfectly.

Yet, Simeon had his good points, having been the perfect partner on his arm; making himself the near perfect trophy husband. Simeon's feminine wiles made him a social butterfly hit at all the parties and public socials. Befriending the wives of all Maxum's partners in record time, he went to a calendar full of luncheons and teas with them, essentially making himself the perfect *pet-gay* friend. Simeon kept the women entertained and feeling important, that alone made Maxum's clients happy. However, Simeon was sometimes too flaming for his own taste. Not the androgynous male beauty Dane Masters' brother Vince was, but most definitely a *queen*.

Not so was the man presently flipped over him, sucking on his cock, proffering his own to him. Darko was pure dark lust and all alpha male that surprisingly seemed to enjoy flip-fucking, definitely a new thing for himself. But he was addictively hooked at the moment on the open invitation to vent out his deeply suppressed needs with him. He almost laughed just imaging Simeon's reaction if he had ever asked him to top just one night.

Maxum brought up his fingers, soaked them down with saliva and reached up circling Darko's tight rosette and pushed in. He was rewarded with a ripple that trickled down Darko's body at his doing. The sensation was exquisite, kicking his rapaciousness up another notch.

Maxum moved his fingers in and out slowly, enjoying the silky sensation of Darko's inner walls. He twisted and crooked a finger catching the sweet spot and the effect reflected in Darko's mouth tightening around his shaft.

"Oh god, fuck me, your body is amazing." He groaned aloud, licking Darko's thigh while he watched his finger slide in and out the puckered entrance, as his lower regions were being drowned in utter bliss. Maxum hadn't expected his appraisal to be taken as invitation, but that was exactly how Darko took it.

Coming up off his body, Darko's cock slipped from Maxum's lips with a loud pop and was quickly tossing Maxum over to his hands and knees on the back of the sofa. "I'll be more than happy to oblige you."

"Wait." Maxum resisted a moment, he was still in *eating* mode, and wasn't through with Darko's cock yet. He'd had every intension of tasting his spunk tonight.

☙❦☙

"Ah, no way, honey. You said *fuck you* and that's exactly what I'm going to do. Besides, it's my turn after all." Darko's hand magically procured the foil package and tore it open in his teeth, then rolled on the condom while his fingers smeared a small amount of lube around and in Maxum's hole.

Just a couple of teasing kisses of his cock against the tight pucker and Darko was sinking inside. His lungs hissing out a loud expulsion of air as he slowly sank all the way to his hilt. Heat and the tight clench of muscled walls wrapped around his shaft, engulfing him in the promise of terminal bliss. What was it about this man that it felt so much better when fucking him than any other man he'd been inside?

Darko let his head fall back on his shoulders; eyes closed just letting every nerve-ending dive right into the heat his cock was soaking up. He growled what he hoped would sound like pure approval because damn, it felt incredibly good. His fingers clenched into Maxum's hips, knees shifting as he prepared to drill into the man.

(•ᴗ•)

Maxum curled, fisting into the cushion back, curses groaning from his throat. That first sweet stretch of pain was easily coated with Darko's touch of honey, as his cock started sliding in and out of his channel. The exquisite elixir of somatic lust started to work on him like a primed Formula-1 car, warming up on the tracks. His own cock lobbed up and down, his pre-cum drizzling out the eye-slit. "Oh fuck, that's incredible. Yes-s, fuck me." And he pushed back letting this forbidden lover know he was ready for him to let loose and burn up the tracks.

But, as eager as Maxum was to get to the pounding, his driver was seemingly reluctant to get to it. He shot a pleading look over his shoulder and was met with deep blue eyes that weren't just looking at him but looking into him with a euphoric glaze. His hips sliding slowly in and just as slowly came out. A hand let go of Maxum's hip and was suddenly swiping over his own chest, his lover licked his lips with a hum and those blue eyes rolled to the back, taking his head right along with it when the nearly-nine inches of thick uncut cock slowly bottomed out inside Maxum's hole. "Fuck, you are so fucking beautiful, but dammit, Darko, I don't know how much longer I can hold on with this slow motion stuff. I need you pounding me—" Maxum growled, "Fuck me, goddamn it." He pushed back only to feel both hands back on his ass, keeping him in place, and damned if Darko didn't make him endure it longer.

Maxum had every intention of getting dressed and leaving as soon as they were finished with their fuck fest. But just as much as his first time with Darko, he was so fully sated, he fell asleep coiled up with the man's arms and legs around him. He'd just get some sleep and slip out at first light. But when morning came, he lingered, idly helping himself to a shower, telling himself he'd skip out after that. Now, he was standing there looking at the man lounging in the bed with a *to die for* body, Maxum still couldn't bring himself to leave.

He needed to get out of here. It was all wrong. He shouldn't feel so transfixed with anyone as much as he wanted this one. However, already his cock was tenting under the towel wrapped around his hips. Even his ass, that until this last week and a half had been cock-free since he finished college, was aching to be stuffed again.

Darko stirred in the bed, a hand floating over chest muscles, scratching then fell idle across his stomach. Maxum took a deep breath and groaned. *Maybe just one more toss and then I'll go.* He told himself.

Maxum crawled up on the bed positioning himself over the tantalizing body he'd just been admiring and planted a hand to either side of his head just hovering over him as he stirred awake.

"There you are," the sleepy tenor whispered up at him. Darko rolled squarely on his back between Maxum's arms. His hips coming up off the bed to seek him out with a lurid invitation and he moaned a silent need for him.

"You sleep like the dead. Lucky for me everything was easy to find," Maxum suggested, trying his best to not sound nearly as ensnared as he truly was.

Darko pulled the towel from Maxum's waist and tossed it to the floor, just looking up at him with some sinister amusement as if daring him to do something about it. His hips came up again pressing his morning, turgid cock against his own, knowing damn well what he was doing to him.

He wasn't leaving. Not until he had this man fucking him again and then he planned to drill him back. Darko had secured that with just the simple brush of his cock on his. There wasn't a passive bone in the man's body and that was a problem.

"You look frustrated," Darko teased him, his hand pulling on their shafts together still grinding his hips up to add to the friction.

Maxum groaned, "This can't work out between us."

"Then why are you still here?" Darko's hands never stopping, not even a hiccup in what they were doing.

"Because you're addicting."

"Well, in that case," Darko's arm came around Maxum's shoulders. pulling him down for a kiss. "Want some candy, little boy?"

No sooner had their mouths met, Darko was rolling them both over until he had Maxum on his back and right away was moving down his chest, licking and kissing his way farther down. His hands grabbed hold of Maxum's thighs just as his mouth found his cock. In choreographed movements, he lifted Maxum's legs up while Darko dropped his mouth down over his lover's shaft, taking him all the way down.

"Ah, fuck," Maxum gasped but the shock and awe didn't stop there. Darko released his cock and then the purpose of his legs in the air became evident when Darko's mouth closed around his freshly showered ass. "Ah fuck! Ahh fuck!" His hands sprang over the hands that held his legs.

Darko sealed his lips around his tight opening and ran his tongue in circles, gently, but feverishly urging the ring of muscles to relax. An indiscernible chain of growling and moaning escaped Maxum's mouth as he fought to anchor himself against the crashing sensation attacking his sensitive hole.

With each circling, Darko's tongue probed deeper into him until he fucked Maxum's ass with his tongue.

Maxum was still sensitive from last night, giving him little to no defenses to the new attention. He felt Darko's growling tremor against his hole. The low sound vibrated through his cock and his toes curled— *dammit it, he was so done in.*

CHAPTER FIVE

After their morning romp, Darko fell back to sleep in his arms. It took everything Maxum had to rip himself from around the exotic body, but he had to go. His love affair with a beautiful man was over, time to go back to the reality of his life—

—and the man he was still involved with.

Glancing back over his shoulder at the empty spot in the bed, the spot that seemed to have been reserved for him, and even now seemed to call him back. Like some subliminal message that he was doing this all backwards.

Maxum slipped out, leaving Darko's place before his lover could entrap him any more with his favorite mancandy. The guilt stricken introspection had bombarded him in the middle of the night, forcing him awake. He lay there in Darko's arms, silently berating himself. The storm of thoughts and emotions plagued him until his head pounded with the migraine of them. The handsome body— sound asleep, next to him, the perfect and all too wrong match for his love life. Yet, Maxum had played the coward and couldn't bring himself to walk away from it; rather he consumed every mouthful he could. Now it all would have to come to an end and already he was feeling the withdrawal pains.

He drove out to the Atlantic Beach, watched the tide come up, letting the winter wind whip at him with a cold blast until he could no longer stand it, then got back in his car, and with a heavy heart headed for Kennedy Airport where he picked up Simeon Correl— his boyfriend for the last four years.

Maxum made the extra effort to meet his partner at the terminal rather than wait for him curbside. An effort that was greeted with little more than a kiss to his cheek, as Simeon passed off the carry-on to his waiting partner's hand. Maxum froze in a stupor, feeling completely disregarded, a chauffeur or bellhop rather than a partner. The kiss noting more than a penny for his tip.

He closed his eyes, beating back the judgments that threatened to surface from deep inside. Thoughts argued and excused that Simeon was not Darko, and it was unfair he should compare them. However, that didn't undo the hollowness Maxum was left with when Simeon made no attempt to make his own stamp on his heart.

Right away Simeon was rambling on endlessly about his trip, his dreadful sister's wedding, and not once stopped to give him a kiss to say he was happy to be back. "It was a good thing you didn't go. You would have been miserable. The food was absolutely boorish and I know how you are about your food. And my mother. Oh, don't even let me get started there. I don't think the woman stopped talking the whole time I was there—"

Well, that explained it. Maxum now had it on insight whose side of the family Simeon favored but he didn't bother to mention it, he wouldn't get a word in edge wise if he tried.

"—but at least I can say one good thing is that the weather out in California is absolutely scrumptious." He let out a musical sigh, "I could just live there all year you know. Maybe I could get you to come out—"

Maxum's mind wandered, as it always did when Simeon was on a roll of prattling. Sim could go on forever and never say anything that required him to participate or respond to—

"Maxum?"

"Hmm?" Maxum blinked, glancing over at his partner who was giving him *that* look, reminding him there were *some* parts of the one sided conversation he needed to respond to. "I'm sorry, did you ask something?"

"I asked if you missed me?"

"Of course, I missed you." He reached over and took Simeon's hand then squeezed it gently. But Simeon was gone from his touch before it could have any effect for either of them.

"No, you didn't. I can see it in your eyes. I swear, I don't even know why I bother."

Oh god, here is where it starts. Maxum shook his head. He could manage a business and their funds, make a rich man out of a pauper, but he didn't know how to steer his partner's pendulous mood swings.

The high-pitched, whining rant ensued like a blur in Maxum's mind, having heard it on more than one occasion. If asked if he could recite it, he had a good notion he might pass a pop quiz. He knew them all word for word and how long they lasted. This was a four minute deal— all until one thing stuck out, when something utterly new was said and it caught Maxum's attention.

"— I even talked to Gonzalo about it when he suggested I come out and stay with them. But I really don't know how I could give up NoHo. I mean—"

"Who is Gonzalo?"

"Someone I met while at a Rainbow social."

"Excuse me, Simeon? You mean to tell me that while on your vacation you were having a conversation with someone you just met, that led to the consideration of breaking up with me?"

"Wha-I—" Simeon started ringing his hands in his lap. "No. Of course not. I just meant— well, I thought about moving out there, yes. But we wouldn't have to stop being together. It would just mean you'd have to fly out to visit so we could have some personal time together— is all." Simeon turned his eyes out the window as if it was the shut-off valve to this newest revelation of news.

It was a good thing they were already pulling up to a red light, as Maxum was certain he might have stomped the brakes, and sent Simeon through the front windshield, seeing he wasn't wearing a seat belt. Always saying it wrinkled his clothes. He was dressed like he just got back from Key West, Florida and here he was in New York, in the start of November. Wrinkles were the last thing Simeon needed to be concerning himself with.

The light turned green, and an impatient driver behind them saw to it Maxum didn't sit too long brooding. "Uh-huh and what other life changing decisions did you contemplate while out there?"

"None at all," Simeon refuted with an arrogant retort. "Oh, but I wish you could have been with me when we went to this wonderful bistro—" and *the four-minute-turned-five* fuss was over and done with. Turn the page and off to the next set of headlines of the *Simeon Huffington Posts* and Maxum knew there was no going back to the old subject. Once something was dismissed by Simeon, there was never bringing it back up. "You would have loved this place—"

"New York is full of bistros." Finding the suggestion peculiar, since Simeon didn't like them with him.

"Yes, but this one was California style."

"New York has California style bistros."

"Well, yes, but it's cold here." Clearly, Simeon's argument was taking on a rather muted defense.

"And your point?"

"My point?" Hands doing double time on the wringing now. "Well, maybe you could move out to California with me."

"My business is here."

"Well, you could open an office there. They have big buildings and clients there, too."

"Except they don't have the stock market there." And that seemed to end the discussion. That was until Maxum had to open his mouth and say something else he knew he shouldn't. "So, will this Gonzalo rent boy be keeping you entertained between visits?"

Simeon's head snapped around, but it wasn't hurt that glared at him, but defiant guilt. "Why— how— why must you say such things to me?" Yet the only thing Maxum could think of in an honest response was: *because I knew you would before you ever left. And that's why I refuse to feel guilty for my own indiscretion.*

"You know, you are becoming more and more butch every day."

Maxum almost chuckled at the concept. "Butch? Don't they use that for the more masculine gay women? Tell you what, why don't I pull out my cock, and you suck me. Let's see if you still think I'm a butch by the time we get to your place." It was likely the rudest thing he'd ever said to Simeon, but far less than what he was feeling inside. So when Simeon turned back to the window, watching as the city slipped by in silence, Maxum let it stay that way and he let his emotional grief chastise him. Knowing, if he was going to try one last time to make this work between them, he was going to have to put his hurts behind him.

When they arrived at the artsy condominiums where Simeon lived in the heart of NoHo, New York, right away, he was back at it again, running around, rambling and, as always, Maxum didn't try to keep up with what was wrong this time.

"I've told Donta so many times, you have to mist the plants, not soak them. Now look, they're all near death." Simeon waved his hand around at the wilting plants around his apartment.

"Come here." Maxum caught him in passing and drew him in.

"But, my plants," his frustrated partner pouted. It was almost cute if taken out of context, to which Maxum tried.

Maxum stepped up to pull his partner into the embrace of his arms. "We can water them together really quick. They'll snap back."

Simeon thwarted the cuddling attempts and tossed his hands to highlight the condition of the plants. "They're already over watered, Maxum."

"I'll buy you new ones then. Just stop running around for a minute, and let me hold you."

"Oh—" the sound idled down as Simeon quizzically watched Maxum wrap around him then lowered to kiss him. Offering first a slow soft brush of his lips, just how Simeon liked it. Letting the billowy softness of his kiss brush and press— brush and press— until he was teased into wanting more, but when Simeon opened up for him, Maxum dove in with a force that had Simeon squirming in his arms very quickly. Simeon finally wrenched free, taking a stumbling step back, "Maxum, you're hurting me."

"How did I hurt you?"

"You know I don't like the aggressive stuff when you force me."

"Force you? Simeon how is it I'm forcing you. I haven't seen you in two weeks. I'd like to feel you against my body for a few minutes, catch up on some kissing. What is wrong with that?"

Simeon cringed then shook it off. "I suppose I over reacted." He tried on a sullen face for him. "I guess I just forgot how overwhelming you can be."

"Was there someone else in California who touched you otherwise?"

"No. Of course not." Simeon made that fidgety twitch thing again, but Maxum couldn't say for sure if it was guilt or something else that made him do it. Not that he was innocent to press for an answer this time. So he let it slide.

"It's just— been awhile."

"Not that long Simeon. You didn't forget. You're just not into kissing anymore— or holding hands— or much anything else for that matter."

"Don't say that," Simeon's tone went up in a pathetic plea, "That's just not true."

"Then come back into my arms and let me finish kissing you."

Simeon rolled his lips a moment to stall.

Maxum could see he wanted to refuse, but Maxum knew how to guilt him into surrendering at least some affection. Because, if it all vanished, there was no sense in staying together. "You fuss about it when you think I don't miss you. Yet, you won't let me have you in my arms, either. Which is it going to be, Simeon?"

Simeon, let out a defeated sigh and reluctantly surrendered back into Maxum's arms, pushing up on his toes to initiate the kiss between them. Maxum reciprocated, but it wasn't the same the second time around. He had to hold back what he wanted to put into

it, because what he wanted to give wasn't acceptable—
or welcomed.

"Shall we go get something to eat?" Simeon suggested,
thinking that the one solitary kissing moment would
suffice him, and now they could go on to other things.
Like spend money.

"Not just yet." Maxum smiled gently for his partner,
"What do you say we just curl up on the sofa a bit first."
He'd *guilted* him into a kiss, now he planned to ride that
gain as far as he could while he had it. Then he'd sell
out.

Maxum moved to the sofa, stretching out and coaxed
Simeon to join him, but rather the quiet moment of
snuggling, he was looking for, Simeon chattered on
about his stay in California, about emails he'd
exchanged with his friend here in town, and something
about needing to go to the hair dresser. Maxum ran his
fingers through Simeon's short strands of platinum
blonde hair while Simeon's hand followed his,
smoothing it back down, shooting him an annoyed look.
Maxum was just trying to figure out what exactly
Simeon needed to have done to it.

An hour of this and Simeon had reached his limit of
sitting quietly. For Maxum's partner, it was about as
enthusiastic as sitting in a waiting room in a doctor's
office.

"Can we go now?" A little saucier than perhaps even
Simeon had meant to sound, because the question was
quickly followed with a peck on Maxum's cheek and a
bat of his lashes.

Maxum forced on a warm smile, "What do you say we
just stay in. We could order delivery and lay about for

the remainder of the evening in nothing but our skins and make love all night."

Simeon looked at him like he'd just lost his marbles but played along anyways. "Like what?"

"Chinese works for me."

"*Eww*— are you serious? Do you know how much MSG is in that stuff?" Simeon twisted from his arms. "But you know Thai does sound good. Pat tells me that new place over on Avenue A has superb Tom Yum soup. Perhaps we could go there?"

"Sounds good, we can walk." Maxum latched onto the option with a cheerful relief that he'd accomplished some arbitration with his partner so soon.

"Walk? Are you crazy?" Once more Simeon's voice went up and gave him a super-sized scoffing glance. "It's freezing out there."

"Well, if you weren't dressing like you dragged the west coast sunshine with you and put some clothes on, it wouldn't be so bad."

Simeon seemed to think he had a better idea and said as much. "Or— you could pull the Rolls out and we could go in it."

"Sim, in case you didn't notice, I picked you up in the Fisker. I am not driving all the way to the garage, changing out cars, then coming back to pick you up so we can go eat at a restaurant that is only three blocks down the sidewalk." Maxum wasn't really ready to give up on the moment he was hoping to have. He'd had a taste of the other side. Of what it was like to have intimacy in the most casual of arrangements and atmospheres. If his life with Simeon were to work out, they'd have to vamp it up a bit, but he would settle for bartering for just a fragment of it. "If you can actually spend the next ten minutes snuggling with me then we'll go."

Once again, Simeon's reluctance was too obvious, but Maxum got what he wanted— *in show* at least. Along with a mumbled side dish of *don't nobody even know what a Fisker is*, to boot. Maxum relaxed back down on the sofa, forcing the tension out of him then rolled to his side, making room for Simeon to lie next to him. Which also took some coaxing, but no amount of bribing or cuddling was going to put in the warmth that just wasn't there. Maxum, for all he felt from his partner, might as well have been lying down with a mannequin.

Ten minutes— on the dot, and Simeon was up and heading wordlessly for his room to change. The silent retreat was his strategy to not invite any further detours.

Minutes later, a scream echoed down the hall, and Maxum was to his feet running for the bedroom. He skidded to a halt, finding Simeon standing just inside the room with his hands around his face. Maxum glanced around but didn't see a reason for the scream. "What's wrong?"

"What's wrong? Have you lost your mind?"

"Why as a matter of fact I have, did you not see it roll across the floor?" Maxum came back with the incredulous response to point out just how insane Simeon's rant was. However, all that did was get his partner going further.

The frazzled man straightened, slamming his fists to his hips. "Oh, so, my bed is ruined, and you want to make fun of me? That's just perfect."

"It's not ruined, Simeon. What the fuck are you going on about?" Not bothering to comment on the *making fun* part. Maxum knew better than take the bait on that argument.

Simeon's shoulders slunk and his eyes bugged out at him in utter shocked annoyance. "Look!" he cried out, stabbing a thin finger in the direction of the bed.

Maxum, once again, glanced around the bedroom, but save for the disorder of the bed linens, which was almost unheard of for Simeon, he saw nothing to warrant the three-bell alarm. "What am I looking at?"

"My bed!" Simeon jabbed a finger at the guilty-as-charged furniture. "Someone has been using my bed! I told Dante he could not use my condo for any reason and look!" Simeon threw his hands toward the tussled bed covers. "I just know if I look, I'll find soiled linens."

Maxum slapped a hand to his forehead then scrubbed over his face while he held back a groan, relenting to his exhaustion of the mini-dramas. "They can be washed."

"Washed?"

The look Maxum got now didn't just convict him of losing his mind, but apparently it really did fall out of his skull. Which he knew it hadn't, but arguing with Simeon had all the logic of placing one's hand on a red lit burner to see if it was hot. There just wasn't any winning.

"Yes, Sim, washed. Now, will you get dressed so we can go eat?" Maxum now saw the urgent need to actually get Simeon out of the house, before the night was lost in mayhem for good.

Simeon staggered over to the dresser and leaned on it. "Oh, I don't know if I can now. I feel a headache coming on."

Maxum was suddenly on the road of tested patience. "Sim, you do not have a headache. Now stop this. We'll change the sheets when we get back."

"You expect me to sleep here?"

"I'll buy you new sheets. There! Will that settle this?"

"New sheets? That's not the point!"

"Then pray tell, what is!" Maxum had finally lost his cool, and let his own voice belt out a notch louder than he cared to do.

Simeon spun, waving his hands to further the drama, "I'll just have to go get a hotel room."

"What? Simeon, what the hell are you thinking? A hotel? They're just sheets, for crying out loud!" Maxum had already sacrificed his composure, but he was not willing to disengage logic. The ensuing changes bringing the heat boiling up in his face.

"My bed is ruined. I can't sleep in it now that it is infested with Dante's spunk."

That was it; all logic for this argument was gone. "Simeon, you used to sleep with him before we started dating. Your *insides* are infested with his spunk!"

Simeon's hand swung out, delivering the swift sting to Maxum's cheek. Maxum froze there a half second, trying to decide if he actually deserved that or not. While perhaps his choice words had, some darker emotion won out, deciding that he had not, and he turned to storm out.

"Where are you going?" Simeon actually followed him as he reached the front door.

"For a drive." Bitter tones escaped gritted teeth, biting back the storm of emotions that were far worse than he was willing to spill.

"At this hour? Traffic will be dreadful."

"That's why we have turnpikes, Simeon." He headed out, not even pulling the door closed as he stalked down the hall.

"Well, call me." A light tone as if it was Sunday and no disorder had just taken place, called out to him.

Maxum slammed to a stop and spun ready to snap, but the door was already clicking shut and Simeon had retreated into his world. The rage inside that wanted to fight, drifted off like steam from a hot street after the rain, deflating the emotions, neither feuding nor relieved. There should have been more to this— but Simeon had dismissed it, or perhaps he didn't even see it at all that there was something wrong— something missing between them, and it left Maxum feeling further emptied than he ever had before.

CHAPTER SIX

Maxum sat at his desk, staring out the tall windows that overlooked the new Beekman/Gehry Tower, where he lived, with occasional glances far down to the park below that sat between the two buildings. He'd been sitting there for almost an hour doing none of the things he was supposed to be doing and all of the things he *didn't* need to be entertaining at all. Like Darko Laszkovi.

Darko was just a onetime fling; a bit of raw play that was like spice and hot sauce to his presently lethargic love life. Bot from the first taste of that man, it was like pumping NOS into his system, and it had Maxum's insides smoldering. When they were together, it was as though he couldn't get enough of the man until they both collapsed in utter exhaustion from the best, revved up sex he'd ever had in his entire life.

It'd been two weeks since he left Darko's sleeping body in the late morning to go pick up Simeon. And it had been just as long since he bothered to see Sim as well, with little more than a few phone conversations. He even pointedly forgot, last night, to arrive at the sushi bar they frequented once a week and where Sim always surprises him with a couple of friends to join them. Never a romantic night alone.

Instead, Maxum had buried himself in work— *sort of*—and at night, as he kept to himself, alone at his flat, his mind filled with intoxicating thoughts of Darko.

He couldn't close his eyes without seeing Darko. Those ripped abs and firm pecs. Deep-blue eyes that glinted in contrast to his nearly black-coffee hair, and shallow ten-day growth of five o'clock shadow. The dark, musky taste of his cock. *Fuck.*

Maxum dropped his head, letting it fall back over the leather backrest of his chair, and let out a groan towards the ceiling. Just thinking about it had him breathing hard. A physical sensation twitched below the belt and he rolled his head to the side, glancing down at his lap— *among other things*. He took a deep breath and let it out with a sighing growl.

Nine days he'd had with the man during Simeon's two week trip. No telling what Simeon had been up to during his visit to California. Maxum wasn't in the dark about his partner's indiscretions, who was habitually easily lured into backrooms or bathrooms for offerings of party favors for party favors. But no argument in the world would convince Simeon the blowjob-for-blow was still considered cheating. So, Maxum wasn't about to feel contrite for his own venture. What tormented Maxum was not guilt for any wrongdoing to Simeon, but rather, he felt as if he was cheating on Darko.

He'd had something so rich and overpriced that now he found it even harder to stay in the muted arrangement he was in with Simeon. Darko added fire to his hearth, but he couldn't go back. Because life with a man that good, couldn't possibly be long lasting.

Still, Maxum could think of nothing else. He was a viral man with a hunger he had never been able to sate, never finding the right man for his needs. It wasn't until he met Trenton Leos and his brother Diesel Gentry, that he thought he might find what he needed to at the very least fill in the voids with his own version of party favors. An island that allowed endless sex— *where ever you pleased to have it.* It was a rich and tantalizing offer. A personal investment he didn't pass up on; yet, even there, he found there was still the one missing element. *A desirable and willing partner.*

The intercom on his desk phone buzzed. He swiped both hands over his face then reached over, punching one of the buttons, "Yeah, Alysse."

"Simeon is on line one."

Shit. Just what he needed. A call from Simeon when his thoughts were anywhere but. He stared at the flashing light on his phone, wondering how long he could just sit there before it stopped flashing. Simeon, his prosaic lover, would probably sit there and wait. The flashing light would burn out before Simeon would hang up.

He punched the speakerphone then the line.

"Simeon."

"Well, there you are, honey. I missed you last night. Are we still on for the dinner party tonight?"

"Did we have plans?"

"The charity is tonight, silly boo-bear."

Fuck. Maxum had already forgotten about the charity tonight. He scrubbed over his eyes with a rough hand to clear out his other thoughts, "Yep, still on."

"I guess you had to work really late last night huh, hon? Sometimes I think you'd never stop working if I didn't come around to brighten your day every so often."

Maxum let out a sigh. "I gotta go. Got a meeting."

"Well, okay, go get him, tiger. You'll come get me say around seven?"

"Sounds good."

"Well, alright, then. Kiss-kiss. I lo—"

Maxum disconnected the line before the remaining words could come across. Then just sat there staring at the phone some more. He landed an elbow on the armrest of his seat, leaning on a tilt to scrub across his forehead. He pulled the center desk drawer out and picked up the business card he kept there and flipped it over. X marks the spot. He reread the scribbled address over and over. Even if it didn't mark the spot it was where his thoughts were.

At precisely 7:00pm sharp, Maxum pulled up along the curb in front of Simeon's condominium building. He watched as his partner came out of the lobby wearing a contrite expression undoubtedly over the selected vehicle in which Maxum had just dared pick him up in. The expression alone warned Maxum tonight would be like any other, Simeon was going to have an opinion about showing up in class rather than flash. Even if Maxum saw the inevitable coming, he still got out and opened the door to be the perfect gentleman to his partner.

"Where's the new Mercedes?" Simeon stopped and gaped at the bucket leather interior and console that came between them.

"I took it back," Maxum answered with a shrug.

"You wha-? Took it back?" Simeon asked in a shrilled pitch, "What on earth for?"

"I didn't like it. It didn't stand up to my standards."

"Standards? Oh, hon, what on earth are you talking about? You're like the only rich man in the state of New York that doesn't have a Mercedes. I mean for goodness sake look out there." He waved to the hood of the car. "Who paints their car like this and still has class?"

Maxum lost his smug amusement; patience for being compared to *other* rich persons was not a strength he possessed for conversation, especially when he was still standing on the passenger's side, holding the door open for the partner who'd just judged him. His gaze floated down the rolling streamline of the sports car, the sides were a royal blue and the top half a refrigerator-white, the two colors came together in streaks that swirled into each like marbled taffy. It was one of the things he loved the most about the car; the rare custom ceramic paint job made it standout even in its own class, and fastly made it one of his favorite cars in his entire collection. "Sim, get into the Bugatti. At two-and-a-half-*million* dollars, I am pretty damn sure it will succeed to impress your friends at the party. That is, *if* they are rich enough to know what the fuck this is."

Simeon's mouth gaped open in silent retort to Maxum's language. Though, at Maxum's scowling glance, he snapped his mouth closed, biting back his snooty remark, and slid into the bucket seat of the high-end German sports car. Maxum took a deep breath closing him in. Already it was starting. He had more money than anyone his partner knew. Yet, because Maxum chose to indulge himself with a love for exotic hotrods for his own pleasure, rather than fancy parties and common luxuries to show off with, he was constantly finding himself at odds with Simeon. *Rather than being seen as a knight in shiny armor.*

He let the slight grin break his mood, as he recalled his afternoon with his cock deep inside the stallion male. His sigh turned to a groan. *It was just a fling, nothing more. Best to shake it before he got hurt.*

A tap on the window, kicked him back into the present; he darted around the car and jumped in. Before Maxum even had the car back on the road, Simeon was rolling out further nagging about the car selection. "I still can't believe you took the Mercedes back. You know how much I wanted us to have that car. Why on earth did you take it back?"

"Because *us* didn't want it. You did and I got it to make you happy, yet four hours after I picked it up, it got a flat. After that, I couldn't find the god damn jack. *And* their road-side service sucked. It was a good thing someone else stopped to help or I would never have made my morning meeting." The memory of the tall, dark, tanned-body of his rescuer flashed in his mind again, and he almost wished Simeon would ask who. He didn't, but the nagging did continue.

"I still don't see why you had to take it back just because of that."

"What's done is done, Simeon. Let it rest." With that, his foot got heavy on the accelerator.

"Well, couldn't you have at least, for tonight, brought the Rolls Royce instead?"

Maxum's foot pressed down even more. The more Simeon barked at him, the faster he wanted to go, some part of him trying to run away and leave his partner behind.

"You know, there's still some time. We could go by the garage and switch them out."

"We're not swapping the cars, Simeon," Maxum stewed. He even felt his eyes roll over once or twice. He was going to blow his top or get a speeding ticket if he didn't calm himself. Forcing himself to once again be the initiator to change the direction of their night, he reached over taking Simeon's hand in his.

"Now what are you doing?" Simeon pulled his hand from Maxum's, with an alarmed look.

"I'm trying to hold my lover's hand. I figured it's the least you could do while you're scolding me just moments before I shell out several thousand dollars for the benefit you're dragging me to," Maxum scoffed, now pissed at himself.

He was trying— *trying*— and now he'd just yelled at Simeon. Which undoubtedly put them right back where they were heading to in the first place. When they came up to a red light, he took the moment to rub at his forehead with the back of his hand. *He just couldn't win.*

Simeon shifted in his place and along with some mental shifting going about in his partner's head. Maxum waited, hoping the guilt trip would work. It usually did. It was a small relief, but Maxum would take it when Simeon settled down, finally stopping the argument, and returned his hand in an offer for Maxum's. But nothing else was given over as Simeon remained silent the remainder of the commute. Nor did it miss Maxum's attention that he might as well have been holding hands with a corpse, for all the affection and warmth he felt from the physical connection. No more present than Simeon was the other night when he asked Sim to cuddle with him. The cold detachment crept inside Maxum, hardening in his bones. Surely this was not what a long-term relationship was supposed to be. Though it would explain why so many people sought company and affection elsewhere outside of their committed relationship. Why was it so much to ask for, to want to feel life and a moment of passion with the same one who was supposed to be in his life forever?

When they arrived at the hotel, the only ones standing outside to even act impressed by what they drove up in was the valet. Maxum came around to join Simeon and offered his arm. He was mentally working up a compliment for him on how nice he looked, but that's when Maxum started taking actual notice of his partner's attire. His eyes trailing down the heather grey and pastel ensemble meant for spring under the white leather trench coat until he noted Simeon's shoes.

"Sim. You're wearing gardening shoes." And he was none too pleased about it.

"They're clogs," Simeon defended.

"Like I said— *gardening shoes*," Maxum gruffed back.

Simeon's tone turned snippety as they walked into the hotel and headed for the banquet hall. "They're in fashion."

Maxum's face went stark mad. "Sim, it's November in New York City. I'm certain your slip-ons are not in fashion right now. Especially for a dinner that cost a grand a plate."

"Well, we had to come in that—" Simeon's hand waved back toward the glass front entrance of the hotel and the car that was parked to the side, still under the valet belvedere. He made a disgruntled face, "Whatever you called it."

"Perhaps you'd like to brush up on your wealthy etiquette 101 before we continue with this argument." Maxum gave him a flicker of his warning eyes. It wasn't beyond him to just turn right around get back in the car and go home at this point.

They paused just outside the doors of the banquet hall of the hotel, "Are you saying I'm stupid." Simeon was bordering on anger and hurt.

Maxum took a deep breath and let it flare out his nostrils, willing himself to calm down. *Just one more time.* Though Simeon was out of line, as far as he was concerned, he knew he wouldn't win this argument. Going home would trump the challenge, but it would not be a productive outcome. He took another deep breath and let it out. "No. I'm sorry, Sim. I didn't mean to get harsh with you." He pulled his lover in and planted a kiss on his lips. Simeon's hand came up, patted his chest then pulled away without ever having opened up to him, and Maxum felt the ever present wall between them. They were more strangers now than ever.

Just playing the part of husband and husband for his clients and Simeon's savvy socialites. "Let's just go in and enjoy ourselves." Maxum forced a smile on for Simeon and his arm tightened around his waist to find some semblance of closeness, but it just wasn't there. And already his partner's eyes were shifting away, looking to acknowledge others as they made their way inside the banquet hall.

As the evening burned on, without ever requiring Maxum's full thought of participation, Simeon was his social butterfly, and as always, never slowing down on the never-ending refills on his drink. When they kissed, Maxum could taste the staleness of the gin and tonic, and he despised it even more than ever. Darko had never tasted as such. He was the flavor of his last meal. The fancy lager in the evening, a mix of toothpaste and fresh brewed coffee in the morning— in a word, Darko was life and he tasted like a well lived man. And it was there with every blistering kiss he gave.

Maxum sat with an elbow parked on the dinner table, his fingers stroked over his lips with a slow, dreamy caress as his mind drifted off following that reminiscent kiss to a faraway bedroom where a man equal to his size and strength had fucked him into oblivion.

"Two pence for your thoughts," Simeon's offer broke through his drifting mind. Leave it to Simeon to say something so cliché and make it completely pretentious. That was Simeon, gay as a two-dollar bill, light in the loafers, and as flighty as a song bird. Maxum used to like it in him, thought it was cute, but now it was as dull as everything else they shared.

Maxum blinked a moment then his eyes drifted to his non-loving partner. "Ready to go home?" the question showed all his lack of interest.

"But we've only been here a few hours." Simeon was prepared to put up a fuss, "I thought for sure we'd stay for a few drinks and then perhaps join the others at the Limelight."

Maxum ran two fingers down his temple, the pressure slicing through the headache he felt coming on. Always the same, Simeon dragged him out to these functions because he liked showing off that his beau could afford healthy contributions. Then it was club hopping all night. Usually, by the time they made it home, Simeon was too *tankered* to be a decent fuck. Maxum was tired of it. "I'm tired, Sim. What do you say we call it an early night? I can pop open a nice bottle of sherry. We'll stretch out in front of the fire—"

Simeon shrugged the suggestion off. "Well, we can do that any time."

Maxum's hand dropped like a gavel. "Funny, cause I don't recall us doing that *anytime,*" he fired off. Only, he could see by the way Simeon sniffled then rubbed at his nose, someone had already given him a bump of *something,* and there'd be no convincing him to come home now. He felt the irate tweak in the back of his skull, wondering if Simeon had given anything in exchange for it. Just considering it might have happened killed any desire to kiss him now. Unintentionally, he glanced through the crowd and then he spotted the likely suspect across the room, who just happened to be glancing their way with a rather smug and satisfied look on his face. So many times Maxum had chosen to ignore it, but he couldn't bring himself to do so tonight. He stood from his chair, his hands absently checking his pockets for his keys and wallet then grabbed his jacket off the back of his seat. "Good night, Simeon." The departing farewell was cold.

"What? You're leaving me?"

"I'm sure Emilio will give you a ride in exchange for a ride." Maxum could see right away— Simeon was going to go into a tantrum of denials. "Don't bother, Simeon, I already know you give him head in exchange for lines of coke off the toilet porcelain. Just once, I wish I'd get blown for all the money I donate for your bragging rights at these fundraisers."

CHAPTER SEVEN

Darko heard the pounding on his door, stirring him from a deep sleep. He was dreaming of someone. His hand dropped to the hard-on he'd developed in his lucid state and stroked over it through the fabric of his briefs. *Yeah, that feels good.* Perhaps the sound had only been part of his dream. Already, he was drifting back toward his fantasy with intentions of making it a wet one.

The return of an insistent rap repeating on his front door told him otherwise.

With a loud rebellious groan to sound off his reluctance, Darko crawled out of bed, and headed for the door. Not attempting to make himself decent. Whomever it was, daring to knock on his door at this hour, deserved the shock of see him in his boxer-briefs that did little to hide the thick cock straining to get out.

He glanced out the window blinds, spotting the Bugatti down on the curb with the unique custom blue-n-white swirling paint job. *Only one person he knew who might ride around in something like that.* He cracked the door, not releasing the chain just in case, but as suspected, it was his new man, Maxum, minus the heat in his silent, emotionless face. Darko edged the door closed, released the chain, and then opened it back up, leaning an arm up on the doorjamb above his head. "You look like someone who doesn't need any demands put on him." Not that Darko wouldn't mind if the guy made a few demands of his own on him— *namely the present condition of his fully awakened cock.* After all, it'd been two weeks since he'd seen or heard from Maxum. He could use a good refill. However, Darko could see right away, it wasn't why the man was here. His cock would have to wait.

"Am I that transparent?" Maxum looked up at him from a bowed expression that nearly pleaded to not be turned away.

"No, but I've worn that face a few times myself." Darko opened the door wider, inviting him in. "Come in and sleep with me. I'll keep you warm." He closed the door as the troubled man stepped inside, then locked it back, and headed for the room with a slightly sleepy saunter. "But don't get any ideas of copping a feel. I'm not that kind of guy."

Darko held the covers open as he waited for his fly-by knight of the night to join him. Maxum didn't look at him, or speak, his hands seemingly on autopilot as he undressed. Yet, there was some definite gear-movement up in that head of his. Firing off with as much sputtering as shitty fuel burning. *Yep,* Darko thought, he'd been there once or twice and he knew first hand it was pointless to ask. The mind and emotions were going, but there wasn't an answer to be given just yet. Even the kinder expression of *are you alright,* would come across more as an irritation than anything else. It was best to let Maxum talk when he was ready. Darko's job for tonight was to do nothing but be a warm body so Maxum wouldn't feel so alone in the darkness of whatever was tormenting him. In essence, to be the guardian of his body while the mind was emotionally vulnerable. Darko knew this and wasn't offended by it. Because sometimes being the warm body at the right time was the best thing to be. Strangely, that's what he wanted— *to be the best thing for this man.*

Maxum finally lay down next to him and Darko pulled him against his chest, curling up with him. Letting the warmth of his slow deep breathing kiss the man's ear and neck, and nothing more. He grinned to himself when Maxum took a deep breath and let himself go in his arms. It was exactly what the man needed and Darko had given it to him. *Sometimes it pays to have a psychologist for a brother who specializes in sex and relationships.*

"I think I just broke up with my boyfriend." The man in Darko's arms confessed aloud in the darkness of the room.

Darko fought the flinch the confession caused him. He'd suspected there was another in the scheme of things. Why else had Maxum just up and cut everything off? "Good," Darko muttered as he snuggled in closer, taking in a deep inhale of the man next to him. Still capturing the cologne, he had on, a deep dark manly scent of lemon, champagne, basil, and rum. A man's cologne made to attract other men.

"Good?"

"Yes, good. I don't like having to share."

Maxum let out a slight huff, his head sinking even deeper into the pillow. "I shelled out ten grand tonight and didn't even get a blow job."

"Is that the going rate these days? Damn, and to think I fucked you for nothing more than cheap Chinese take-out." Darko followed his quip with a chaste kiss to the broken man's jaw. He knew Maxum was bordering on a need to vent and that was counterproductive in his bed when it happened to be about another man. He pressed against Maxum's body, grinding his already hard cock against his hip, just long enough to distract the man's thoughts well enough away from what had chased him here. He wanted Maxum to feel the *present* along with his presence. *This* Him— not the other's. To know that what was here was right, rather than the guilt Maxum was starting to feel for the other man he'd just escaped. Another warm kiss against the back of Maxum's neck and Darko settled against his back relaxing towards sleepiness.

Maxum took a deep breath and let it out in a long slow breath that seemed to take an age to be completed. The tension refused to let go of the man's body even as the room filled with silence, all but the still-ticking of thoughts running through his head.

Darko kept silent. It worked the first wave; it would most likely work on the second wave as well.

"I don't know why I'm here." As predicted the wave of stunted emotions declared themselves in the dark room.

Well, that was certainly not something Darko wanted to hear Maxum say and there wasn't anything he could come up with that could shift it, so he kept silent, and tried not to tense up with the rejection. He snuggled in again, making sure his breath caressed over Maxum's neck and shoulder. Keeping the rhythm deep and slow, a lulling warmth between them like their first night together.

"I don't even know how to be with you."

Darko kissed his neck once more. "Well, I like walks on the beach. Staying home and fucking, which apparently, I am willing to flip-fuck for you. That alone says something about our compatibility. I like red meat and dark ale. I also like being outdoors, and on the water. Particularly rowing. Concerts in the park and long drives to nowhere for no reason."

"What is this? Gay harmony? I'm being serious here." Maxum stared over his shoulder at him.

Darko shifted up on an elbow and looked at him right back. Hard place for a man to be when his body had led him to the very spot it wanted to be, only to have the brain argue with it once there. *Only one way to silence it.* Darko caught Maxum by the chin and pulled him around, and before his tarnished knight could contest it, Darko dropped over his mouth, slanting just enough to open the invitation. His lips swiping over Maxum's lower lip and sucked it in for a tender nibble. The rebounding man gave to him instantly, his lips opening and his tongue darted out to take Darko in.

Darko could feel the intensive need in Maxum, a yearning that hadn't been quenched in a very long time. Something neither of them had been able to find in a lover— *until now.* And Darko wanted their kiss to remind them full-force before Maxum's brain could get in the way again. He rocked up against his body, his mouth surging up like waves crashing against Maxum's lips, searching for more.

Darko's arms tangled under Maxum, pressing him up as he gave the deeper kiss he wanted so desperately. Tasting more than just the fancy dinner that got washed down with a potent malt scotch. He tasted the man, the one he couldn't get enough of. Breaking only enough to catch his breath. Yet was endless as Darko ate Maxum's lips and sucked on his tongue, his mind swarming in the warm tranquility of their kiss until he was completely breathless. He followed it with a few last chaste kisses then dropped to his side, pulling Maxum to spoon against him once again, and with a satisfied hum, was ready for blissful sleep.

Maxum hadn't come here to fuck. He came to escape the empty demands of another, but he couldn't deny he really did want to get inside Darko after being kissed like that. His cock stiffening with each throbbing thought against his thigh. Like an addict, he was already becoming hooked to the fire that burned inside this man. *As a consequence, addictions were always bad.* But hell, he was already here. He twisted— or so he tried. Darko's strong arms tightened around his waist and hips preventing him. It was all he could do to look over his shoulder to find the alluring dark profile of this rugged man falling asleep behind him. A faint dreamy smile on his face as if perfectly at ease with their pairing.

Maxum pressed against him, the cheeks of his ass grinding against the erection that matched his own, but

Darko didn't reciprocate. "You're serious? You're going to go to sleep after a kiss like that?"

"Mmmm-hmmm," Darko hummed, doing his best to suppress a grin. "I told you, I'm not that kind of guy."

"What the hell is that supposed to mean? Because, as I recall, we pretty much hit on everything on our first date," Maxum chuffed, and none-to-happy about the firm restraint Darko's arms kept him in.

"Exactly, but I'm not the kind who messes around with a date that up and vanishes. For that, there will be no fornication on our second date. It helps build frustration." Darko kissed the back of Maxum's neck, his arms tightening around him like a python keeping him in place and stifling any fight in him.

"And what of the third?"

☾☽

It was Darko's turn to draw quiet a moment. He hadn't planned to go this route, but then Maxum's confession of a boyfriend somewhere out there made *him* the affair and that meant *this* was temporary. He didn't like it, now a light had been shed only to find a dead end. So there was no sense investing further, right? Just enjoy the sex and keep the heart uninvolved. Except, Darko had a feeling he was already too late for that part and he needed to know, before he allowed himself any more room to fall for the man. "Maybe before we invest in our third, you'll answer a question." Darko's arm loosened around Maxum as his eyes rolled open to look at him.

Maxum dropped to his back meeting his gaze. The tension that built in Maxum's body was all too noticeable and Darko did what he could to make it less. "No demands, just asking for a truth. It's not hard to give it. If you want to show your respects for that person and perhaps the time you spend with them, then it's not hard to give a truth." He leaned down and kissed Maxum. First to his lips then delivered one to his temple where all those migraine-causing thoughts dwelled. The gears that clearly had a wrench tossed in them and he whispered to him. "Even if it's only going to be for a short time."

Maxum didn't relax, he fell. His mind and emotions tumbling inside, into a wrecking ball of shit, because he did like Darko. No, it was more than a *liking* and he meant to *respect* him, as a man should be. As someone who he enjoyed being with should be, but he had not been truthful. He could change that now. "Ask." He swallowed hard, because he knew it still wasn't going to be easy.

"When you went back home to him, did you sleep with him as if nothing else had happened?"

Maxum let out a puff of air, unsure of how the question made him feel. His hand came up, landing on his head, and raked through his hair until it was parked between head and pillow, where it stayed as he stared up at the ceiling, looking for some teletype answer when there was none. Only, he did feel some bizarre relief, because the answer wasn't going to be as painful as he feared. Because at that very moment he knew, he didn't want to hurt Darko. "I never slept with him at all."

Darko reached for Maxum, taking his jaw in his hand, and pulled him around to look at him, their eyes meeting in the darkness. Lonely, pained eyes, "Not at all?"

Maxum shook his head slowly, the words came out drained, almost lethargic and definitely defeated. "I tried to cuddle with him. I wanted to hold his hand. I wanted my relationship with my partner to feel like this. *Connected.* Only, no matter how hard I tried or looked to have it there with him, I couldn't find it. I want someone to be forever in my life. I'm an investor. I want my home and sex life to be the same as my money. I don't want a stranger in my bed. I don't want to start all over with a new face and new pet peeves every couple of weeks or months. I don't do short term investments. I want the same man day in and day out to build and grow old with. And I failed."

"Maybe it never existed? A shady investment. Or its life has perished? Company went belly-up. Or you found something that feeds your life better than anything else ever has before. A new up and coming company or innovated idea that has the future in mind like green energy," Darko's suggestions paused in thought, maybe more metaphors that would speak to him, "Life changes around every bend. Investments have to have a flex fund, don't they?" Darko dropped on the pillow, though still looking deeply into him.

(·ω·)

Maxum should have laughed at him, for the analogy he'd just given, since Darko had already confessed one night about not knowing squat about investments. But Maxum was beginning to counter that the hedonist was more than just bronze, drawing from whatever knowledge he did have and changing out a few words to turn it into *Maxum St. Laurents laymen terms.*

Maxum turned his eyes back up at the ceiling, his thoughts ironing out until the ticker tape in his head came out blank. While everything Darko said made sense, he still didn't have a clue what to do with himself or the partnership that had given him no satisfaction in almost as many years as they had been together. Or what to do with the man who lay at his side right now. The man who had given him all he would have liked in those years in just a matter of two short weeks. To top it all off, Darko made more sense in his prattling attempt to put things into perspective, than any attempt Simeon might have ever made. Then again, he couldn't think of a time when Simeon ever gave much concern for his thoughts. At least not lately. *Okay, not in a long time.*

He tossed the disgruntled shit from his mind; repositioned and glanced at Darko and the face watching sideways from his pillow. "So what can I expect on our third date?"

A smile sprouted from the pillow, "Funny thing you should bring it up. Wanna take off with me this coming weekend?"

"It's Thanksgiving weekend." Maxum blinked at him at the unexpected holiday invite.

"Precisely, perfect time to get away from it all. Good food, lay around all day— I'll let you take full advantage of me— or whatever we want."

"We?"

"Yes, *we*. It's an interesting concept, the word *we*." The offer slowed as Darko's eyes started to drift closed and actually began to drift back to sleep. "Sleep. No demands tonight," he whispered lastly.

Maxum rolled to his opposite side, inching back into arms that took a natural position around his waist and hugged him before turning heavy with sleep.

He hadn't expected this. It was what he needed— to just be with someone who understood, who would lay with him and not demand anything. Yet, he could not refute that Darko was like pure grain alcohol to an alcoholic. Outside of being unexpected, Maxum wasn't sure how to decipher his emotions. The man burning in his lust was now stepping outside the bounds of his definition of an affair. As much as he fought the idea, it was hard not to feel anything but an apex of bliss as he nestled against Darko. As if the man had been machined to precision perfection for just him. Like his German cars.

Getting away, doing whatever *we* want to do— maybe in some gay-friendly bed-n-breakfast up the coast of Connecticut or a quick plane hop to Martha's Vineyard. It sounded like the best offer he'd been given. Then maybe he'd be able to just fuck the man out of his system once and for all, then get on with his life without him.

He closed his eyes feeling his mind drift, maybe that would happen, but admittedly, he still needed a little more of Darko Laszkovi, have his fill of him before calling it to an end.

CHAPTER EIGHT

THANKSGIVING DAY WITH THE LASZKOVI FAMILY

Maxum drove up to the address he was given. He glanced out the window to the dwelling, which even for Astoria, wasn't the typical townhome, but *home* it mostly definitely was. As in *private* residence. He glanced at his GPS as if perhaps it was trying to fool him or something. "Was this not supposed to be a bed and breakfast?" he asked it as if *Gladys,* as he'd named the GPS unit, would actually answer.

While *here* was far from anything Maxum was expecting, the place was certainly a gem to have. Standard in the way of being the common Astoria brick upright townhome, yet that's where the standards left off. For starters, four stories high and four windows wide meant two rooms across. A set of stairs led up to the front door on the second level plus a utility entrance down on the ground. The real bonus though, was the gated driveway with parking spaces both in front and, since the driveway went down along the side of the townhouse, meant there was more around back, too. Along the sides of the building, he spotted two more sets of windows centered in the middle, but only on the upper two floors. *Two bedrooms across and three down.*

Maxum growled, scrubbing his hand across his face as he began to seriously contemplate turning around and leaving. He distinctly remembered Darko saying he had ten brothers and sisters. A townhouse with twelve rooms— *yeah*— he didn't need Gladys to explain any further for him. He was just about to pull off when his phone rang. It was Simeon. He stared at it while it both rang and vibrated in its holder on the console. Simeon had called yesterday. Not last week, not over the weekend, not Monday— *yesterday*— to make sure he was going to be there for *his* Thanksgiving social at the condo. It would be just like last year. Him and about six or eight flaming queers, Maxum didn't know. His fingers swiped roughly over his lips and gripped at his chin recalling his discomfort. Sure, they were all gay and they all had a commonality, but he had to ponder if perhaps they were still very different. After all, you don't compare a jaguar with a fluffy Persian cat, do you?

The phone went silent and Maxum felt some relief as the anxiety of the ringing went with it. There had to be some dark ominous reason for why he tensed up every time Simeon called. *Was it just his own failure as a man trying to be in a relationship or was it really over and done with between them?* He glanced back out at the large home of brothers and it struck him how walking in *there* wasn't nearly as agitating to his system as the thought of going over to Simeon's to eat some strange, mutated vegan concoction that he would call duck. Afterwards, he would sit quietly and listen to Sim brag about this or that in front of the gaggle of friends. At some point, Sim would even lean over his lap and pat his thigh, perhaps make one of those— *isn't that right, dear—* type remarks as if he were actually included in the conversation.

Darko was wrestling with his older brother, Pyotr, over a prized cluster of red grapes when Darko's phone started ringing from his pocket. He pulled it out seeing Maxum's I.D. on the screen. He held a hand out to ward off his brother while he took the call, "Hey, are you on your way?"

"I'm already here and you better have a damn good explanation as to why we're not loading up on a puddle-jumper heading for Martha's Vineyard."

"Pull through the gate. I'm coming down." Darko hung up, instantly going to the wall and hit the codes that would signal the courtyard gates to open to let Maxum in, then headed for the stairs.

"Hey!" Pyotr called after him. Darko ground to a halt at the top of the flight, turning to glance at his brother just in time to catch the string of grapes Pyotr tossed at him.

"First kiss has the most bearing." Pyotr winked at him.

Darko tugged at his ear, giving his brother a sheepish look. "Sorry to say, but we're well past the kissing. We're up to fucking now." He added a little wriggle to his brows playfully.

"You're one move away from losing him just for dragging him to a *family* reunion. You're going to need that sweet kiss to stay his ass."

A deep grin melted over Darko's face. "Thanks, Pyotr." He popped several of them in his mouth, smiling when the sweet red flavor burst on his tongue. Then dashed down the stairs to catch his lover before he could escape.

"Did you teach all your brothers the tricks of sex?" Cliff asked from the table where he had been watching the wrestling match.

Maggie brushed past Cliff, her hand patting him on the back. "Yes, he did," she spoke with a note of gleeful experience.

Pyotr conferred with a wicked gleam, none too shameful either.

Downstairs, Darko rushed out just as Maxum was getting out of his car. Darko couldn't help but put on the brakes to take in the sharp image of the man and his shiny machine. He kept back a moment just enjoying the view with a wry smile all his own— *damn if he didn't love looking at that man*— like his machines, Maxum was built of precision lines. Muscles proportioned his body perfectly like a Greek athlete— exotic and unclassified. And always smoldering hot. "Another?" Darko finally stepped out toward him.

"I collect them, remember?" Maxum's answer was short, though it still held a note of sportive sarcasm. They both knew damn well he did.

"So what are ya, rich or something?" Dark smirked playfully.

(ᴖᴗᴖ)

"Or something." Maxum eyed Darko tightly. He was two seconds from turning around and leaving, but the sight of Darko was too tempting to leave behind. His dark hair was tossed as if it'd never been brushed this morning. The muscles in his arms looked pumped like they did when the two of them would get rough and he had to wonder if his strange lover had been inside working out or tussling with another man. The notion alone agitated Maxum.

(ᴖᴗᴖ)

Darko could see the dark displeasure in the man's eyes, he approached cautiously, directing his own attention to the car Maxum stood alongside.

"Ford Tungsten GT." He'd seen one in a magazine before, but it looked even more striking up close. He walked along its length, letting his fingertips glide along the curves. *He liked this one.* Sleek. Sexy. The smoky colored tungsten steel made it look mean like the man who drove it. Maxum, for all his sleek and sexy exterior, looked like a man who could rule the world with his little finger— and Darko had it on first hand, the man could screw you to a wall with his dick.

It was likely that the only thing Maxum *was* afraid of, was *him*— but Darko had no intentions of letting his knight-in-shiny-tungsten-armor run away. He stopped with little more than one arm's length between them. "So, how many cars do you have anyways?"

Maxum shrugged, "Well, not nearly as many as say, some of the more famous collectors."

"And how many is that?"

"One for every week of the year, if I skip holidays."

Darko's smirk screwed up.

"Okay maybe not that many, just yet, but enough to need my own garage."

"Garage?" Darko stepped in front of him, now closing the space between them with a mischievous grin. "Garage space is always at a premium in New York. I wonder—" he tilted his head down then glanced at Maxum from under predominant brows. "How much would you charge for a space?"

Maxum was still trying to hang on to his irritation, but he couldn't stop himself from playing the game of banter with Darko, since they were both just so damn good at it. "A couple of blow jobs and several hard-fuckings a week at least."

"Hmmm— that's kinda expensive." Darko brushed Maxum's hip with his hand, "But, I think I can swing it. I'd have to probably put in extra hours, though." He glanced around, but didn't see an overnight bag with

Maxum, which side-tracked his implications. "Where's your bag?"

Maxum huffed then. "I'm not staying." He retreated from Darko's touch, but only enough to lean back against the mustang. "You see, when you mentioned you wanted me to spend the weekend with you, I figured you were luring me to some Astoria hidden treasure. Like maybe a bed-n-breakfast that just happened to be gay friendly." He cocked his head with a suspicious expression. His eyes darted over the four-story house that loomed behind them. "This doesn't look like a bed-n-breakfast."

Darko closed in again, pressing the man into the car, and brushed his lips over Maxum's. His voice dropping an octave and turning husky with bewitching suggestions, "Well, the bed is inside and if we lie with my cock deep in your ass we just might both fit in it—" he licked out with his tongue to tease Maxum. "and it is definitely— gay— friendly. And then in the morning there'll be pancakes and Serbian sweet breads." And then Darko kissed him, a deep lingering embrace of his lips to deliver the taste of his tongue to the other man that was both sweet as the red grapes and intensely hungry.

Darko shoved full body into him harder as he pushed past his lips, into the hot cavern of Maxum's mouth, and inhaled him all at once. His kiss searching steadily for his tongue so that it was everywhere, possessing, tasting— branding.

In an instant, Maxum's body lit up, blood tingling and his arms coiled around Darko's body, locking on. Darko's fists clutched at his starched white shirt, grabbing the collar to pull him closer. Darko was everything he remembered— full of unrefined finesse. Power and steel, covered in hot, butter-soft leather. Insistent— and more. Never had a man's kiss alone made Maxum want to throw down right where he stood and make love as he did with this man. Darko made him long to be closer to him in every way.

He ran his hands down Darko's body, feeling every bulge of his shoulders, every ripple of his chest. Maxum's palm flitted down the rippling six-pack— and kept descending. *Oh— so —slowly*, he dragged his hand over the other man's erection. Darko hissed in a shocked breath, breaking the kiss, and hardened against Maxum's touch.

Smiling, Maxum reached for his fly.

Darko groaned. "If you're not planning on staying, we—"

Maxum palmed him again, silencing him with a squeeze around his trapped cock, and then flicked the button of his pants open. He pushed the zipper down, a bare rasp in the otherwise quiet. Maxum found Darko's cock straining up passed the waistband of his briefs and he ran his thumb over the sensitive crest that eagerly released a droplet of pre-cum.

Darko's head pressed against his with a deep surrendering huff, "Damn it, I love it when you touch me," he groaned some more. He grabbed Maxum's jacket up in his fists and started walking backwards towards the door, towing the man with him. He released

Maxum only long enough to fumble with the door handle behind him, got it open, and resumed the deep probing of their kiss, dragging Maxum into the house. They were no sooner through the doors into the downstairs rec room that Darko was pushing his jeans open, then dropped a hand on Maxum's shoulder forcing him to his knees. "*Dammit,* I want you to suck me," he demanded, with a low and throaty growl.

Maxum didn't hesitate, giving him what he wanted. His tongue eagerly darted out and licked over the broad tip of his cock, whipping around the partially skinned mushroom cap of the swollen red glans. Maxum took him all the way in his mouth, surrounding the man's cock with a tight suction of his cheeks while his tongue made vicious work over the sensitive nerves.

He drew out, letting it pop free of his lips, and replaced it with his fist. He stroked Darko from base to tip, sliding the foreskin down the shaft away from the glans, then moved in, running his mouth down the side of the throbbing shaft, up and down, over and over. His fingers groping over the engorged mushroom cap, smearing the leaking pre-cum and saliva as he did so. He leaned back just taking in the sight of Darko's erection. Fuck, if the man didn't have a gorgeous cock. A good eight or nine inches, thick and riveted with veins that pulsed with red blood. He pulled Darko's stiff shaft down from his belly, sucking the flanged head into his lips. He gnawed at it tenderly before releasing it, letting it slap back to his belly.

Darko groaned, his hands slapping to the wall to steady himself. And Maxum could hear the strangled curse to keep back any commands.

Maxum wanted so much more of the meal. Simeon was small in every way and actually didn't like Maxum lavishing any attention on his cock other than a simple hand job and only then while he was shafting him from behind. Simeon for all his gloriously gay cliché, wished he'd never had a dick at all, but unwanted to undergo a sex change.

Maxum had no problems being a man that liked to fuck other men. Moreover, Darko was pure raw man that fed that desire. He closed in, burying his nose in the shallow nest of black hairs that nestled around Darko's cock, inhaling the musky scent of his body. Definitely all man. He tucked down lower, licking over Darko's balls, sucking one in his mouth to roll over his tongue then the other, using his lips in a tight hold to pull at the tightening skin.

☙

"*Ahh*, god," Darko let out a husky growl, letting his head drop back into the wall. Damn, the man had a mouth and knew what to do with it. He sucked on him hard with an all-encompassing demand. When Maxum was done, Darko knew he'd be little else but a melted pup, willingly surrendered to anything the man would demand from him after this.

As much as he wanted to continue and divulge the man his meal, his own needs couldn't withstand any longer, roaring for him to take over. He threaded his fingers into Maxum's hair loving the soft silkiness against the calluses of his hand. He let the contrast distract him a moment longer, up to the point when Maxum took him all the way in and his slit kissed the back of huis lover's throat. Every ounce of air spilled from Darko's longs at that moment, and a wave of unexplained pleasure and urge crashed over his body, and then exploded at the same time. "Oh fuck." His hips curled forward and Maxum's hands were suddenly locked onto his hips, pinning him in place.

"No, damn it," Darko gasped, his every breath rasped through his larynx as his body pulsed with more need. If he didn't start fucking the man's mouth, his knees were likely to go weak under him. He needed some control in this.

Darko bucked, trying desperately to pick up a rhythm that sank him into Maxum's throat, but the more he pushed, the tighter Maxum's grip became, until he backed off all together. Darko's near bursting cock slapped against his belly and he hissed wildly. Needing Maxum's mouth back.

"If you want me to stay, you'll have to endure my craving fetish. And right now, I need to eat your cock," Maxum growled.

Darko's hands were instantly clamped around Maxum's head, curling into tight fists in his hair, forcing him to look up at him. Their eyes locked onto one another like fiery demons fixated in a battle of carnal lust. Darko's hips rocked slowly, purposely so his dick slid across Maxum's face, back and forth, caressing him with more of the leaking pre-cum, and mixture of saliva. The scent of sweet salt filled his senses, stoking the hunger inside him. Back and forth, the hard organ sawed over the man's cheek then pressed against his lips and Darko let go of his hair. Splayed fingers reached down the back of Maxum's neck and over his shoulders, quaking with his teetering control.

Everything about Darko appealed to Maxum's senses on a primitive, base level, and his own body hummed with the awareness of it. He turned his freed head and sucked in the mushroom head of Darko's cock. His eyes still on the man watching him. He sucked and gnawed on him until Darko's eyes fluttered closed and his chin jutted up with tension, hiding no expression that he was completely entrenched in Maxum's salacious sucking. How could Maxum not give favoritism to such a man who had surrendered to himself to his own oral fixation?

He sucked him all the way in, wrapping Darko in a stormy sensation with his tongue, rolling and sucking hard over the full length of the shaft. Bringing him all the way in and withdrawing, only to suck him all the way in again.

Maxum felt the tightening pulse in the heavy vein against his tongue. His own body responding with an equal pulsing in his ass, just imagining the engorged cock shafting into him, violently out of control, until he screamed with raw release.

Fists clenched into the shirt at his shoulder and locked on, Darko cried out, releasing a deep guttural moan as he held Maxum tight, hips quaking, and bucking forward, involuntarily as Maxum's mouth filled with the hot froth of semen. He swallowed the first shots down then pulled away, letting the next splatter over his lips. He rolled and smeared them over the purple glans licking and sipping the last drops that spit from the slit.

Maxum wasn't given much time to play with the messy pool of cum, when he felt Darko's immensely strong arms yanking him up, and immediately came over him with his mouth, licking over his lips and the icing of spunk. Just another somatic urge he liked from the man. Kissing after head. Sharing the taste of each other's bodies And nothing timid, Darko kissed with full on force before, during, and after. His passions never falling weak, except perhaps when Maxum was sucking him off.

"Dammit, I want you fucking me right now." Darko growled in his mouth, not even a fight for who was going to top the other. Darko's dick, well sated now, wanted his ass ravaged, and easily offered himself up for more of Maxum's commands. But a rap at the door drew the brakes on faster than a bucket of cold water.

Maxum froze, coming to reality that he was in another person's home, and was about to fuck this man before even meeting the host.

Another knock on the door, "*Hey. Stanislav just pulled in. Pyotr asked if you could put the brakes on long enough so that he can at least get them inside the house before Frannie pulls any of her shit,*" Darko's brother Trofim called from the other side.

Darko let out a long rumble and kissed Maxum, drawing him up in his arms before answering. "Yeah. Though I don't know how much good it'll do," Darko called back to the door. His eyes never leaving Maxum who was watching him, calculating. He could see Maxum's eyes all business now, watching the numbers crunch, and he was analyzing, weighing the gains.

"I'd like to see him. Even if it's just for five minutes. I haven't seen him since I left, Darko," the voice a dark plea.

"It's good, Trofim. It's all good."

Darko's face warmed just then, a look that took Maxum by surprise, but he still didn't like the concern over this *Frannie* arrival.

"So what's the deal with Frannie?"

Darko's expression bucked some. "You, me and several more of my brothers are going to burn in hell according to her."

Maxum yanked back, breaking free from Darko's warm arms. The November chilled air seemed to breach the walls and sought out his spine. "I thought this was supposed to be a gay friendly weekend."

"It is." Darko reached out, catching his hand and laced their fingers together, tightening to keep him. "But my baby brother Stanislav is as forgiving as his bride is evil. We haven't seen him in two years. We didn't even get to see his wedding. So, Pyotr hopes to get him here for all of us and he's willing to deal with her some to do so." He pulled a reluctant Maxum into him with just the sheer strength of the one hand tangled with his. "Don't worry. Pyotr makes a good barrier when it comes to people's misplaced hatred." Darko gave him a playful peck on the nose. "Come on, let me take you upstairs to meet everyone before she comes in and dampens the mood."

Upstairs, Darko ran through the introductions, "This here's Trofim, who just moved back last spring after living in the UK for five years. Trofim this is Maxum."

Maxum and Trofim shook hands. "You look familiar."

"If you've picked up a magazine then you've seen him. He models for cologne and men's fashion. His body is all over the women's magazines." Darko shot him a wink.

"And the men's." Trofim quibbled for his defense.

Darko chuckled back at him, "Yeah, he's quite the supermodel." He reached out to snag his brother into a rough hug.

Trofim dodged him, slapping the muscular arm away. "Well, I wouldn't go that far." And before he could execute a counter attack, Maggie was stepping between them to be introduced.

"Hi. I'm Maggie." She ignored the offered handshake opting instead to closed in for a hug and a warm smile.

"This here is Maggie. Pavle's ex-wife."

"Ex?"

Maggie rolled her eyes at Darko. "Well yes, but we were best friends before, and still are."

Next up for introductions was Sasha and his twin lovers, Isaac and Isaiah. Maxum recognized them as well, but he kept silent over that bit of knowledge, not wanting to invite any discussion about his involvement with the owners of Club Pain. It wasn't a family friendly atmosphere type conversation for sure.

Next, Maxum was led to a frail looking young girl just barely out of her teens from what he could tell. The decorative scarf that wrapped her head absent of hair, along with the dark circles under her eyes, giving too many clues to a present illness.

"This here is Kimmi. Pyotr's newly adopted daughter." Darko pulled her in for a deep hug, tucking her head under his chin, and the young girl wrapped herself around him to complete the hug. "Kimmi here should be world famous for giving the best hugs." Darko bent down, kissing the top of her head.

"You said adopted?" Maxum looked at the girl too old to be adopted.

"Yeah. Kimmi is Cliff's sister. Cliff being Pyotr's lover." He twisted his arm around to point to the *bratting* boyfriend that belonged to his oldest brother. "But my brother became so taken by little Kimmi, he asked if she would be his daughter, and she and Cliff accepted."

Maxum offered a smile and saw a happy face peek through the veil of her illness when she glanced up at Darko. Who, in that moment, seemed just as taken with her as he claimed his brother was. Maxum sensed more to the story, but being this was supposed to be the quick round of intros, he decided to leave it alone.

After the extended Kimmi hug, Maxum was quickly being led toward the living room where he was brought face to face with a man who was clearly Darko's genetic match.

"This here is Pyotr. Headman in the family. Pyotr meet Maxum St. Laurents," Darko said spoken with notable idle worshiping pride that might have gone both ways. The patriarch of the family or the prized lover.

Maxum's eyes darted from Darko to his brother and back again while they exchanged a shake of hands. Same hair, same deep cobalt-blue eyes. Even the shape of their chins and the tanned color of their skin. A few years difference was all that separated them. Maxum glanced around the room, now seeing the astounding familiarity from brother to brother. As if they were a snap shot collection of all the prior years until it came to this one man. But none resembled Pyotr as closely as Darko. As for Pyotr, he was absolutely stunning. GQ's finest. Maxum looked at the man wrapped around his waist, if Darko looked this good now, he was going to be impossible to turn away from in the years to come.

A chuckle from Pyotr had Maxum glancing back at him. Pyotr was studying him with an all-knowing expression that told Maxum he knew what he'd just been thinking and found it equally arousing.

"So this is the man you tricked into joining us for the weekend," Pyotr teased his brother with a wink, letting him know he'd made a good catch.

Darko didn't need to be told by his brother. He knew what he had standing next to him and leaned in offering up a healthy unabashed kiss to Maxum to display it.

"Oh my god! I don't believe this!" a shrill voice blasted in their direction.

Darko and Maxum jerked around to see a young, conservatively dressed young woman standing at the top of the stairs on the landing before the great room. Who then hastily turned heel and stomped back down the stairs she'd come. Stanislav, the brother they'd all been waiting to arrive, turning as well and going aft. "Frannie, wait."

Darko's face went white. "Pyotr, I'm sorry," he whispered.

Pyotr tried to force a smile on, but the pat in the arm he gave did more, "Don't be. Nobody in this house is going to be made to feel ashamed."

"But, I didn't need to be kissing—"

"Stop. You're in your right to do so. A good-looking man like Maxum and I'd be more worried if you weren't kissing him. However, I do believe an apology is owed to you, Maxum." Serious eyes shifted to his brother's date, "As our guest, I hope you don't let my sister-in-law's lack of understanding dampen your desires to be here with my brother." Pyotr glanced towards the stairs, then over to Sasha, "Take your boys upstairs. Play some music for a bit, will you?"

Sasha nodded and soon had the twins heading upstairs.

"What's that all about?" Maxum whispered in Darko's ear as he watched the three head up as told.

"Their parents messed them up pretty bad as they grew up and pretty much flipped when they learned their precious indigo boys were gay. They don't need to hear any of this," Darko explained in a hushed tone.

Pyotr nodded to Darko then to Maxum. "Now, if you'll excuse me." Pyotr turned and headed out after Stanislav and Frannie.

Maxum followed Darko to the window, watching the heated talks unfold down in the courtyard below. He glanced around at the number of family and extended members. It changed everything for him. Darko was supposed to be the hot fuck you take advantage of over a holiday vacation and walk away. Now he was standing here, watching the man and his deep roots with family. With the exception of the one outside, everyone seemed to be connected, close to one another. He looked when he saw Darko's hand go up to the glass, pressing his palm out flat, as if trying to reach out to the younger man down below, looking up at him, and as Maxum took notice, so did all the others. In deep solidarity, they were all gathered at the window watching, trying to reach out, and connect with the brother who yearned to be touched by them. It was all too clear, even to Maxum, the pain of the younger brother's wife's hate ripping at him, becoming a bridge he could not maintain anymore.

And in a matter of minutes, it was over with, Pyotr heading back inside, while Stanislav lead his wife back to their car, placed her in the driver's seat, and saw her off— *without him.*

Darko was instantly at the top of the stairs to meet the patriarch of the family, "Pyotr—" but Pyotr wouldn't have it.

"We have our baby brother with us for a while; let's enjoy his company, shall we?" His arm came over Darko's head and razzed his hair a bit. "The bright side is, I don't have to worry about where you two will be roomed at, in proximity of Frannie's ears now."

"Us?" Darko let his brother's mockery affect him. "What about Cliff? Pavle tells me he's quite a noise maker."

"That's why I bought him a gag for the weekend. Don't suppose you did the same?" Pyotr winked at him and Maxum.

"Oh, you did not!" Maggie made an exaggerated gasp from across the room.

Just then, Cliff was rushing into Pyotr's arms to console his lover and ward off any teasing. Pyotr brought Cliff against him, lifting one of Cliff's arms to drape over his neck and tangled their fingers together on the other side, pressing Cliff back against his chest and kissed the side of his young lover's head. "Mmmm, but I did," Pyotr hummed to tease them all. He whispered something else in Cliff's ear and the two turned off down the hall towards their bedroom, obviously taking some personal time to ease Pyotr's mood before rejoining the family.

When Stanislav came up, his brothers instantly swarmed him.

Maxum watched, feeling like he was a tourist in this family affair, yet a part of it at the same time. Being a part of something, he hadn't counted on being. This weekend was supposed to be the last installment of his affair with the man. Some great sex, some indulgent food, maybe even a nice drive to nowhere for half a day. Then say goodbye, thanks for the steamy weekend, then go back home to try to decide what to do with himself, and if it included letting Simeon back in or not. *Not this.*

This was too real. It affected his fantasy and completely obliterated his definition of an affair.

"Hard, isn't it?"

Maxum's head jerked around to see the glowing pixie-faced Maggie, standing next to him, but he said nothing.

"You thought Darko was just this beautifully rugged man as just a thrill ride and soon he'll ride off into the sunset, then you'll go back to what you were doing before. Like coming home from vacation and going back to work. Now, here you are finding a warm cozy cottage with the white picket fence, parked right in the middle of the most exotic island setting. And don't forget the ultimate garage to park your hotrod."

Maxum's eyes swept over to the man who'd possessed his head and desires beyond recognition over the last several weeks. Then back at the woman who spoke like she had just seen right into his head and knew what he was thinking. *Had to be a family thing.* "I already have a twenty-eight car garage," he answered rather sullenly. Not sure how that was even relevant, but had said it, nonetheless.

"Yeah?" Her eyes lit up, but looked at him like she almost pitied him. "But does it have a white picket fence or smell like a hot salted-caramel sundae?" And then she smiled. The warmest, friendliest smile he had ever seen on another human's face. "What's a heart to do?" she spoke playfully, her eyes twinkling up at him, and then stepped off to claim a hug of her own from the young brother taking center stage.

From there on through the afternoon, everyone gathered, somewhere between the great room and the kitchen, either pitching in to help or stealing tidbits of food to hold themselves off as the whole house filled with the aromatic smells of home cooked food that ignited stomach growling and more thievery. Jovan, who was the second oldest of the Laszkovi family, took charge of the turkeys being cooked in a roast pit outside, while the women took some pleasure skylarking that he was doing it wrong. It wasn't until the dinner birds were brought in and taste samples divvied out to be finger fed to the women, that apologies and *mm-mm-good* praises were offered over for his forgiveness.

Maxum tucked himself behind Darko as they sat together on the brick step to the fireplace hearth, after Darko had released his baby brother, Sasha, from a wrestling hold on the floor. He curled into the man and teased his neck with his warm breath. "You never said you came from such good stock. Look at them all— they're as ruggedly handsome as you are."

Darko grabbed his lover's arm that was draped across his chest and held him in place. "Yeah, well, you only get to have one and that's me."

And only for the one weekend, Maxum thought silently. Just this weekend to get his fill and then get over this infatuation with the man and go back to familiar pastures he had begun to sow years back, no matter how stale they may seem from this angle.

The twin girls made the cattle call from the kitchen and the family and friends herded into the dining area just like that.

Conversations jumped from one subject to the next with as much frequency as the news squawk box, that included local news, cars— Maxum's cars especially, friends and family, and the latest hobbies. Most of that was about rowing.

At the table, it was a closer version of just catching up with each other. Rury talked about what it was like since he and his partner had moved out to Los Angeles just a year ago. Who, then passed the floor, to talk some about Trofim, and his five years in London.

Darko reached over and tussled Trofim's hair and pulled his head in for a hug, "It's good to have you back." The act hinted to some further back-story unlike Rury's move away. While missed with equal expression, it lacked the shadows several of the brothers harbored when talking of Trofim's absence. Notes on the faces, Maxum was well versed to pick up on as a business man who had to read the faces of other businessmen. Always on the lookout for *the tells* of a shady deal and deception. Only Maxum wasn't factoring in deception here, just perhaps Trofim's absence was due to something other than his career choice.

"You say that all the time." Trofim brushed him off, not worrying over his hair anymore.

"Because it's true."

"After five years over there, I'm surprised you don't talk more like them," Jovan commented on the lack of Trofim's strobing accent.

"I'm trying to lose it, but it picks back up whenever I'm around someone who is British."

"I hear it and I think it's sexy." Maggie smiled at him.

"So are the babes in London really freaky hot?" One of the teenage boys cackled up. Of course, it came from the one with more jewelry in his face than the average woman wore as a whole.

"Ever since you left for London, he's become obsessed with the British punk scene." Artyom reached over his son's head and tossed the green hair of his oldest boy, "As you can see." Artyom flicked a gauged earring before letting the teen off the hook for any further razzing.

"Is that what that's called?" Stanislav joked at his brother and nephew.

"I call it: *let's see how batty can I make my mother*," Mira, the boy's mother tried to sound serious. But the blushing smile gave her away, and of course, the younger kids giggled up a storm over their parent's teasing of their older brother.

When there was an opportune pause, Maxum stepped in, "So what took you to London?" Maxum questioned.

A stillness, while brief, still came in like a shadow in the room at the question, but Trofim quickly gathered himself, and redirected the mood. "I needed a break and got a shot at modeling through a friend of Darko's and I decided to move overseas to be closer to the majority of the work. I don't speak a lick of Italian or French, so London was my best choice. Plus, I was able to share a flat with another guy who was also a regular model. It was easier and less travel for me since most of the work is in Europe."

It was a well-rehearsed answer, one Trofim probably told himself often, but Maxum was only confirmed there was something else to it. Especially the way Darko's arm moved around his brother and held him in a quiet hug, not meant to be noticed yet it screamed with buried emotions. The glances from Pyotr and Pavle reiterated his observation.

The conversation shifted again, only this time a word, a singular simple word that was meaningless to Maxum, since it wasn't English seemed to spark a hidden feud that had apparently sat and stoked for nearly a lifetime in one brother. Like a brush fire, nine brothers went from a well stitched family to turmoil. Looking more like the typical American revised family from Maxum's point of view now. At least this scenario made sense.

The rest of them at the table watched in silence. Willing themselves to be invisible. The only thing keeping Maxum in his place was knowing any sudden departure would only fuel it further so he stayed put just as the others did. A hand reached under the table taking his hand. He glanced over, to once more, find the passionate face of Maggie, her smile a little more overwhelmed with the pain she felt for her extended family. Maxum wasn't sure about any of it, nor did he know what to do with her hand. While he may not have returned the reassuring grip she sought from him, he didn't release the embrace, either.

In less time than it would take Maxum to argue a stocks purchase, the dispute turned to resolution, and the outcome was a stronger bond than what it originally started as. Now Maxum felt completely at a loss. His eyes moved to the man he'd known and slept with for only a month's time, feelings he was trying to refute still lurked deep inside, threatening to fill the barren waste land of his heart that another had given little attention to.

For the first time, he questioned if he had this whole thing backwards. Was Darko the very man he should be with? Could a man who fucked so intensely also be a love that lived in the heart as well? He was at a loss to say who Darko was or what he himself would have to do about it. He only knew he had no intentions of leaving tonight. Not yet. So when Darko led him back to the great room to vegetate like stuffed whales on a few pillows thrown on the floor in front of the hearth, Maxum went with his lover without argument.

That night they lay in bed, sated and having even managed to do so without keeping the whole house up. They lay in each other's arms, more awake than they had been earlier during the post turkey lethargic evening.

"You could have warned me, you know," Maxum mumbled against Darko's neck.

"Oh sure. Dear lover, whom I don't even know where you live nor until a few days ago even had your number, won't you please come spend Thanksgiving weekend with me at the Laszkovi family reunion of fifty?"

"I would have said no."

"Precisely why I didn't warn you."

"Just for that I get to go out of turn."

"I might even let you tap it twice." Darko waggled his brows at him.

"That's my line."

"What's yours is mine."

"And what about yours."

"Of course, I didn't figure you the type to share."

"I'm not," Maxum growled.

"Then it's settled between us. If you want to keep me all to yourself, you have to stay."

CHAPTER NINE

While most Americans were either running around taking advantage of the Black Friday sales, or out playing golf if they happened to live in a warm weather climate, or at home watching football, Maxum found himself standing out on the dock of a large boathouse on the East River overlooking the greater city. *Freezing his ass off.* While the sculls were already waiting at the end of the dock, ready to launch. Ten men were doing jumping jacks on the dock to get their blood pumping enough to shed one layer of clothing before loading up.

The winter season so far had been rather mild and aside from a few snow flurries the past few weeks the river was still flowing and no snow on the ground. Though Maxum was told that wouldn't have mattered much if this were a practice, they'd been known to row across the frozen ice to keep in shape over the winter season. To Maxum that was a testament they were dedicated to a sport so few actually knew existed, let alone, participated in.

"So ever row before?" One of the older brothers stepped+6 up beside him.

Maxum was usually good about names but this time, there were just too many of them. They all shared so many features, he hadn't gotten them all down yet, but this one he knew was the doctor. The man who had once been married to Maggie. The adorable woman, who was now off with the rest of the women and shop-a-holics.

"Can't say I have."

Pyotr called out the arrangement over everyone's head to them. "Put him in the coxswain seat then and Darko can take the stroke position in front of him. That way Maxum gets an up-close and personal look at his man in action."

"Darko in the stroke seat means the rest of us getting slaughtered trying to keep up the pace he sets," one of the brother's fussed though Maxum didn't see which one it was.

"Point made. Darko!"

"Yeah?"

"This is for fun not racing so go easy on us." Pyotr set limits on him.

Of course, Maxum didn't miss the rather gloating, wicked grin that dashed across Darko's face, who was apparently more than content to take advantage of something Maxum was sure would be revealed to him soon enough.

Pyotr, Darko, and the doctor loaded up in the eight-man scull first. Darko taking the first slider-seat on the stern end, while Pyotr took the first position at the bow with the doctor taking one of the middle spots. The rest all squatted at the edge of the dock and when Pyotr gave out a call akin to a football huddle, the other five mirroring balancing cranes, carefully stepped in and took their positions in unison. A calculated and well-practiced choreography of balance and counter-balance. No doubt from at least a few spills into the water. Which, maybe, on a summer day wouldn't be so bad? However, today wasn't one of those days to carelessly allow happen.

Bodies lined up and oars sticking out like out riggers, they held onto the dock to keep it in place while Darko reached out to help Maxum take front-row-center for the show. Or in this case *rudder-row-center*.

Maxum chuckled nervously as he contemplated the boat shell that was no more than maybe eighteen inches wide or all of fifteen or so inches above the frigid waters it was floating on. "You want me to fit in there?"

"Well, usually the cox'n is smaller than you, but since you don't row—"

"Fuck," Maxum cursed as he carefully tucked his legs and lowered down in the cramped spot, "My legs are going to be hurting after this."

"Yeah, just be sure you don't damage that middle one or Darko will dump your ass." One of the brothers took advantage of the open door to haggle a brother's lover.

Maxum laughed as he finally settled into place. "Is he trying to warn me you'd leave me if my dick didn't work too well?"

Darko shrugged, shaking his head. "Not at all. We both know I love you for your money."

"HA! Now I know you're fibbing."

While the remaining two brothers were already shoving off in a two-man shell, with a call from Pyotr, the family packed slender shell was pushed off the dock, and away they went. The chant that set the pace was called out by Darko and two other voices which Maxum couldn't make out joined in with responses. A few rough ordered sweeps and then as a team, the seven sets of oars found their step falling in behind the rowing movements of Darko's who set the rowing cadence for everyone else. Maxum could already feel his legs start to cramp and as the boat sped up, the sting of the cold air found his face. Darko's blue eyes seemed to shine like sapphires held out into of the sun. Stunning, and not just in looks within the frame of hair the shade of dark coffee, but the effect they had on Maxum as he watched Darko intently. The strange tribal calls even gave him the feeling that he had a rather barbaric connection to them and the sport. All reinforced with the fluid movement of arms pushing the rows about in a sweeping motion over the water's surface. They dipped, breaking the water's surface, then is a surging strength of both combines effort of arms and legs together, pushed and pulled with a muscle tone that was sure to have Maxum a devoted fan by the end of their journey. Now if he could only figure out what to do with the hard-on fighting for room where there was so little of in his cramped spot. *No wonder they called it the cox seat.*

He was actually rather glad when the chant ended and soon changed over into conversation that broke the hypnotic scene as they headed up stream.

Maxum tried to do more than just half listen as the conversation started up about the youngest baby brother and his twin lovers. While a rather unconventional arrangement that many would dismiss as nothing more than just sex. Maxum had gathered over the past day that the trio went far deeper than shallow definitions. It was still hard for him to fathom or even keep up with the conversation but judging by the problem one of the boys had, a conventional relationship would not be nearly as fulfilling or as healthy as the one the twins were in now. The important thing was the three men were happy with each other and had support from a family of brothers.

"So, what's it feel like to be champions now?" The newly restored family member, Stanislav asked. Not with a tone that he wanted to change the subject but rather he had a few years of family gossip to catch up on. Though Maxum had to lean over a bit to see who'd actually asked and that got him an exaggerated head shake from Darko. *Leaning apparently was really bad.*

"Feels mighty good," Trofim, one of the names Maxum did remember, responded to his little brother sitting in front of him.

"I wish I could have come down to see it," his voice trailed off, and from Maxum's limited view, could have vanished from the group all together until he spoke again. "I've missed too many things. Sasha's wedding— the races— Pavle's divorce." They all laughed.

A pause lent an opportunity and Maxum took it. "So how is it you came up with the name?" he asked. Sure, he'd already asked before but now he got a family team perspective on it. There was always more to a story when more than one person was telling it.

"That part is pretty obvious, we're all gay," Darko answered with a wry grin as they pulled at the oars in unison.

"Hey, hey, speak for yourself," one of the older brothers answered and that had to have been Jovan. Since he was the only one on the boat save the youngest that wasn't gay.

Darko laughed over his shoulder, "I meant everyone on the team. A few even live in Greenwich Village. So that made it legit, but it started off as a goading to get one of the top competing teams to accept our challenge. Rowing competition is structured so that top competitors never go head-to-head with each other until later in the qualifying races. It's actually designed that way so that top teams, aka the popular guys, don't get knocked out of the line-up too early in the season. However, in our case, being the newbies, it was our way to get in *if* we could win."

"And?"

"We beat them twice."

"Twice?" Maxum asked.

"Yes," Pyotr took over the conversation, "The rule is the losing team gets to have what's called a *Repêchage*. A second chance to advance to the finals or a double elimination. So, what can we say, except, we got in the competition rounds. After that, we decided to keep the name because once word was out about an all-gay male sculling team, we had guys and girls from all over coming out to cheer us on. The whole Pride parade if you will. It has been good publicity, both for us as a team, but for the gay community as well." The storytelling paused long enough to give a heads solute to another foolish crew out the water as they rowed by with a less than casual pace.

"Should we race them?" a brother asked.

"Ley them have their moment." Darko butted in.

"So you were saying, Pyotr," Maxum called up, enthralled by their accomplishments.

"We have one of the largest fan bases outside of a collegiate team in the entire New England district," Pyotr added proudly of his team and their fans. "So, the name Greenwich Queens stuck, it's legit yet rhetorical at the same time," he added in mid stroke.

"Damn, I'm sweatin' my ass off— I'm ready to lose another layer," Darko called ahead for the oars to still so he could strip his jacket off.

"Well, you got the cox'n in front of you, put him to work," One of his brothers called back to him.

Darko let out a slight chuckle. "That'd be you."

"What am I supposed to do?" Maxum glanced around as much, or little as the case may be, in the small space he was squashed into, without disturbing the rudder handle.

"Call them to, *let it run.*"

"Let it run?"

"Yeah, only louder," Darko laughed, "So we can all hear it."

Maxum straightened. "Let it run!" he called out with a perplexed expression, not knowing what it meant or what to expect, and right then all eight rowers stopped rowing, lifting their oars from the water and grips locked into their laps.

Darko peeled his sweater off his freshly pumped arms, bulging under the thinner thermal protection of the body armor shirt. Several of the others followed suit, divesting themselves of their outerwear. The unhindered view of his lover's body earned him a lip licking expression from Maxum.

Watching Darko pull his sweatshirt over his head to reveal his muscular form clad in the silk underarmor sport shirt was just a little too much visual candy for Maxum right then. That and the fact there was a whole row of men just like him.

Another coached call from him and the oars went back into motion, as did his lover's body. Fuck, but whoever designed the athletic apparel wasn't thinking about sports or function at all but fucking-eye-candy; those things were made with the fan in mind. Maxum just couldn't stand it much longer, especially with Darko sporting the wicked grin with every pull of the oars. Darko knew full good and well what he was doing to him. Well, two could play this game. He chuckled to himself with the internal dare then reached under his parka to fish out his cock.

Darko was just crunching in on his sweep when his attention fell on Maxum's hand and what his hand was doing. That's when all the blood left his body to pool inside his own cock. A clatter resounded behind him that didn't fully register in his brain until he heard his brother, Rury, laughing at him, exclaiming to everyone what mischief Darko's lover was up to. A set of hands reached up past him taking his hands, and the touch jarred him. Darko glanced around finding he had over reached with his oars and overcame Trofim's and somehow Rury had pulled into them as well.

A few minutes to carefully untangle, plus a few razzing comments from Darko's brothers at his expense, and they were back in motion— heading back for the boathouse.

Darko was already naked and wet when he saw Maxum leaning against the threshold just watching him, and that wasn't where Darko wanted him. He turned the water off and walked over reaching up to cup his jaw and kissed him without having said a word. Maxum's arms fell from the guarded position over his chest and floated down to Darko's hips, but they didn't pull him in like they normally would, and that told Darko his lover wasn't accustomed to open viewed sex.

"You still have clothes on. While I don't mind fucking you with your boots on, wet clothes kinda suck."

"You want me to fuck you in front of all these people?" Maxum asked while Darko still worked to keep his lips busy, nibbling them. Coaxing him to relax and be comfortable.

"What people?"

Darko took Maxum's hands and brought one around, setting it to his ass and pressed it to palm it at will. Of course, he brought Maxum's other hand to his cock, knowing full well Maxum wouldn't turn *that* down. Once he had Maxum in play, he grabbed the man's head in his own hands, and pulled him in for a more intense chain of kissing and nibbling. He slid his hands down over Maxum's shoulders, grabbing clothes as he went. *Only trick now was to get Maxum undressed.*

"You know you want to suck me." Darko started to go for the hard core, below-the-belt kind of baiting, to see if he could get Maxum to rip loose. "Have my meat shoved—" *Kissing and licking interrupted his words, but not his train of thought.* "—down your throat—" *Oh, damn what was he going to say? Oh yeah,* "—while I cum inside you." And that seemed to do it. Suddenly Maxum's hands let go, but only to fight to get his clothes off as fast as he could manage and still have clothes in a wearable condition to put back on later.

☙❧

Shirt— pants— shoes— all went flying over his shoulder towards the locker room, and right away, his hands found their way back to the body that tempted him beyond reason. He walked Darko back towards the shower stall, not stopping until the wall got in the way. From there, Maxum began to work his way down, squatting with his knees spread wide. One hand quickly feeding Darko's cock into his mouth, while his other wrapped around his own, and started an eager pace over his shaft to match his sucking. He felt Darko's hands, one gently steadying his balance yet keeping him right where they both wanted his mouth to be. The other, holding his cock at the base feeding it back towards Maxum's throat with uninhibited lust.

Did it ever stop getting hotter with this man? Always another thing that rushed up to face his own hidden hungers tapped the shoulder of his perversions and invited them out to play without any regrets. No insult taken, to be had or given. Like the resort at Salientis, where fucking without borders existed. But it didn't necessarily take place publicly nor did Maxum have much practice taking advantage of the freedom he'd invested in. While fucking or sucking in front of a crowd was not anything Maxum ever really thought about or had held any headiness for him before. The idea that he could be so into *this* man that it didn't matter if anyone was watching, was what had him worked over into an overload of arousal just now.

His fist tugged along his length, giving an added twist over his glans, and a sharp white flash of pleasure shot with each stroke straight to his balls while he licked his tongue out over the dark flavor of Darko's meat.

Maxum knew he wasn't going to last very long this time. But damned if he was going to shoot off all by himself. He reached around under Darko's nuts, cupping them roughly, then stretched a finger back to tease at the tight rosette. A tight hiss blasted out over his head and the slight shift of Darko's hips moving back was invitation enough. A quick trade of cock for finger, Maxum slathered it up with saliva then once again reached under Darko's sack, found the hungry little hole and gently pushed in.

Jovan's faced turned beet red and he snapped around to face the shower walls; his hands busying themselves washing his body and scrubbing the sparse pelt of chest hairs. However, the sound of his brother and his lover reached his ears despite his trying not to pay attention and *that*, he didn't know how to block.

He tried to look at this whole thing logically. Which, he had to admit was all new territory. He didn't care that any of his brothers were gay, but he had carried some anger with him for far too long in blaming Pyotr. That his older brother's homosexuality had been the cause of their losing their parents and having to flee their homeland. Now, he knew that had never been right and somehow learning it was a huge burden lifted from him, because he didn't want to be angry with his brother any longer. *Still though, he was straight.* This shouldn't affect him.

Jovan swallowed hard at the heavy panting and the curses Darko growled out. The sounds reaching his ears, creating images in the back of his mind— *damn he needed to get out and get laid.*

A laugh to his right had Jovan jerking around to see Pyotr leaning back on the shower wall next to him. Laughing at *him,* but Pyotr's blue eyes were watching *them.*

"I'm not gay," Jovan stammered quite suddenly as if he needed to clarify himself and his sexual orientation.

"I know, but it is only the sounds of sex and love making when you are only listening to it."

Jovan didn't know quite how to respond to that and he couldn't seem to break himself away from watching Pyotr's face. It was as if he could see the porn being played out across his brother's face or something. He saw how it was turning Pyotr on, the arousal burning in his eyes like wild fires and —*fuck*— he wished they wouldn't make it sound like it was *that good. Had they any idea how long it'd been for him?*

Jovan risked a glance over his shoulder when he heard his younger brother cry out. Seeing him just as his hands slapped down on his lover's shoulders, to keep from falling flat on his face as his body convulsed with his release. All this happening while Maxum's cock shot out white ropes across his brother's legs. Jovan felt a sudden heat flash over his face and he quickly snapped his eyes back around to the tile wall and swallowed hard. "Does it turn you on to watch them?" Jovan licked his lips trying to find some semblance of moisture that for some reason had left his mouth dry.

"To see him enjoy and being enjoyed so freely? Yes. Just as much so as listening to them is turning you on."

"But that can't possibly be called love making." Jovan was still trying to come to terms. Ones he could understand.

"No, right now that is fucking. Just pure sex. They're bonding in all of it, in their own way, but right now they are taking pleasure with mutual desire and feeding each other's need.

Jovan eyes snapped to the ceiling. "Well, okay, but I'm not gay," he said dryly.

"Yes, Jovan we both are very aware you are not," Pyotr offered the acknowledgement his brother was obviously needing with a slight chuckle that couldn't be helped. "But just for the record, I think perhaps your left hand *is* enjoying it."

Jovan turned white as a sheet, registering his brother's choice of words, and his head went from the ceiling, dropping to see his hand mindlessly fisting over his erect cock, pulling at with a thick white film of soap suds. "It's been a while. I might as well rub one out here. Seeing how they— well— not that they should be ashamed but— doing it out like this— in front of everyone— kinda says they don't respect each other, doesn't it?"

(ꞏꞷꞏ)

Pyotr could see where his brother had picked out the suppressed common way of thinking, and while the questions were interrupting his own perverse pleasure, he could see Jovan needed some help to open up and understand.

"We are all grown men. Very capable and aware of the things we enjoy and what turns us on. Must we hide it, or lose the moment we are aroused because someone is watching? It's not a disrespect, it's a freedom. A release to enjoy and not worry one's self with judgment. This isn't the public park of New York. It's a footlocker and a safe place for grown men. A woman is raised to always feel ashamed of her body, her pleasures of sex. For her, sexual freedom is unobtainable. To even try to reach for such an open-minded bliss will bring on words like whore, tramp, or slut. Yet, it shouldn't have to be so, and for them," Pyotr jutted his chin out towards Darko and Maxum. "—it isn't."

Cliff finally walked in, naked, and immediately surrendered his body over to Pyotr's hands. Pyotr wrapped his arms around his lover, his hands finding the more aroused parts already in tune to his needs. He leaned in and kissed the side of Cliff's head, whispering, "Are you satisfied your sister is fine?"

A scowling face turned up preferring to just be kissed than have to answer the question, and Pyotr had no problems accommodating the submission. He cheated his eyes away, a sided look, glancing past his young lover to watch as Darko and Maxum now enjoyed some post coital shower-touching in the form of washing each other. Pyotr hoped for the best for them. They certainly seemed well suited for each other. And watching them be so free with their lust for life, turned *him* on considerably. Then again, all sexual freedoms did and Pyotr was soon rubbing his hard cock into the perky ass butted up against him.

Rapid movement out of the corner of his eye had Pyotr purposely burrowing his face in the back of Cliff's neck while he pulled Cliff's hips back to grind against his eager erection. However, Pyotr's adverse hiding wasn't all for the pleasure of kissing the back of Cliff's neck, he was also trying to be considerate of Jovan's feelings by hiding his laughing smile. As he was not unaware of Jovan, frozen in place, staring at them. If Jovan's hand moved any faster, he was likely to fire his cock into outer space.

Darko had been true to his word, they spent the weekend doing whatever the two of them felt like doing, which consisted mostly of sex and laying about. However, they also managed to throw in a daring venture into the shopping world frenzy that was mostly just window-shopping and getting acquainted with one another's likes and dislikes. Plus, some good old fashioned *public-display-of-affection*. They even squeezed in a short drive to nowhere Saturday afternoon after seeing a few of the other family members off.

Focus in the house turned from the holiday affair to the newly adopted daughter, who's illness made every day with her a blessing, and towards the younger brother who had been kept from them far too long. Both in need of healing and the renewal of family bonding.

Seeing he wasn't family, Maxum was thinking he should be one of the ones to go, having overstayed his welcome, and was decidedly packing his things to leave. Darko wasn't too keen on the idea. Only Maxum knew he needed to go before their evening turned into another night of sexual comforts, he had no self-discipline to turn away.

"This just isn't me. I'm not family. It's too weird."

"What? Hanging out with a lover and a healthy family environment? Yeah, weird, I know. I mean, whoever heard of such a fucking thing? The nerve of some people. To actually have what most people in this country wished they had. Hell, most would have settled for half. But, by all means, fucking leave, and throw away a good man all because he has good brothers and sisters that managed to survive, and support each other through their growing spurts in life."

"That's not what I meant," Maxum growled at him.

Darko made a sarcastic gesture with his head and shoulders, his eyes dripping with the expression. "Dude, I am all ears then."

"Wise-ass."

"Yeah, well, you've been fucking this wise-ass, so don't be expecting too much sympathy right now."

Maxum scrubbed over his face with his hand. This wasn't what he had in mind. He didn't want to hurt

Darko at all or argue over what was and what couldn't be. "What the fuck do you want me to say?"

"Let's start with, *a wise ass man once said*. That part should be good—"

Darko's contrite sarcasms had Maxum ready to throw something, seeing how any comment he made was quickly deflected back at him in a retort he didn't know how to argue against. His hands went up around his head, seeing nothing he could throw that wasn't likely going to come back as— *you just broke our grandmothers favorite vase or Jimmy's first trophy*— He glanced about the room, even surprised himself when he folded and simply asked. "Don't you have something I can throw around here?" And just as he turned to look at the man he was mad at, a fat pillow slammed into his head. *Well that wasn't anything he was expecting.* Maxum shook it off, grabbed the pillow off the floor and threw it back at Darko with no real sense of aim, but damned if Darko didn't turn right around and send it flying back at him. Once more hitting him square in the head. Maxum grabbed up the pillow once more— *now he was mad*— and threw it point on towards Darko's head. In a flash, Darko's arm came up in a *wax on wax off* circle sending the pillow off in another direction and off the dresser went the vase Maxum had not wanted to break in the first place. He snapped a look at Darko who was looking at him, cold sober, "That was our mother's. We carried that all the way from Čačak when we fled the civil war."

Maxum was about to beg for forgiveness, but then stopped. If the vase had been that precious, it would not have been in the *spare* bedroom. "You're lying."

"Yes, but then, you've been lying to yourself for some time now. So why should I be the one to have to be honest around here."

Maxum sucked in a hard breath with every intention to start yelling at Darko with a whole bunch of *—how dare you's* and *you don't know what it's like—* Then somehow his calculating mind brought him to a dead stop, as what Darko actually said sank in and he realized not one of his defensives actually fit.

That, right there, deflated his anger and perhaps even him. His shoulders slunk and his head dropped forward. He'd been lying to himself— *but for how long?*

He didn't know—

Maxum sank down toward the floor, twisting so his back fell against the side of the bed and he dropped his head over it, staring up at the ceiling. He let out a long drawn out sigh. "I just don't know what to do."

Darko dropped down on his side, at an angle across the bed, propping his head up on an elbow and looked at the defeated man. "About which part?"

"My four year relationship with Simeon." He let out another sigh, his head rocking back and forth across the edge of the bed as he did. "When you've been together with someone that long, they're the one you're supposed to keep working at to get it to work. People give up all the time. I didn't want to do that."

"But if the two of you weren't meant for each other, all the time and effort in the world isn't going to change that. Sometimes people don't work together in a relationship. It's not because you're being mean or insensitive, it just doesn't work. Or it does, but it comes with an expiration date. Not all relationships are meant forever and you don't know which is which until you are actually there."

Maxum heard, but he couldn't bring himself to say something along the lines of, *okey dokey, I guess that's a wrap on Simeon then.* He did, however, know his heart wasn't in it to stay with him any longer either.

"What made it last this long?"

Maxum was silent for a moment. It wasn't like he didn't know the answer, he did. It just was a shitty one. "There were no lows in it. I thought that meant we worked."

"Come on. Let's go for a ride." Darko patted his shoulder and jumped off the bed to get dressed.

Maxum glanced at his watch, not realizing it had already gotten so late in the night and he wasn't even sure how the hell it slipped past them both. "Where're we going at this hour?"

"You'll see." Darko only said, waving him to come along.

"Fine, but you mind driving?"

Darko stopped, his leg mid-way inside his jeans and a grin melted over his face. His eyes flashed with some wicked, saucy expression then went back to getting his pants on before he fell over.

In less than an hour, they'd dressed and arrived at the motorcycle shop where Darko worked. Maxum bounced in place; his hands buried in his heavy wool coat to stave off the cold night air and tried his best not to look guilty. Even though he knew Darko worked here and had a set of keys, something about showing up afterhours just felt like breaking and entering. In addition, certainly the local patrol officer would see it that way, too.

Once inside, Darko locked it back up and lead the way to the machine shop in back before turning any lights on. Maxum hung back at the door to the room, watching as Darko went over to the workbench and picked up a few things then turned to face him. In his right hand, Darko held up a piston casing with a holding cell made to take a piston rod approximately two inches in diameter.

"*This*— is your Simeon." Darko waved the casing in his hand. Then held up the item in his left hand. A steel drive shaft, only it was square with rounded corners, not spherical like a typical shaft would be and it was about an inch wider than the hole in the piston casing. "*This*— is you." Darko held both objects out and attempted to push the two pieces together. Just as anyone would expect, the square peg did not fit in the round hole. "No amount of time or effort will ever make these two fit together in a manner that will work." Darko carried the display over to a lathe machine, popped the cover, then set and locked the drive shaft into place.

Maxum watched acutely as it only took Darko a fraction of a minute to line up the shaver, close the shield and then turned it on.

Darko didn't even look at the shaft as it was being cut away, instead he looked dead on at him. While Maxum watched as curls of shaved steel fell away, pooling up under the shaft as it was cut and reshaped into something else. When the lathe stopped, Darko popped the hood, pulled out a perfectly round two-inch diameter rod and then slid it into the hole of the casing. "Now, you can be with Simeon." He tossed it carelessly to the floor.

The casing and rod bouncing across the concrete floor in a loud clatter before coming to a stop, which oddly looked like a deformed penis. But, Maxum's attention went back to Darko when he pulled on a leather work glove and scooped up the pile of shavings left behind on the lathe table. Like a giant brillo pad having a bad hair day.

"*This*—" Darko held the wad of curled steel up, "this *was* you. This is everything about you, and what you had to give up just so you could force yourself to fit in *that*." He nodded to the steal dick on the floor then tossed the shavings in the garbage.

Maxum was waiting for Darko to brush past him and just leave him there, gutted and wounded. Stripped of his morale of having a man he could spend the rest of his life with, only to be abandoned in the greasy machine shop with his lonely, withered heart on the floor at his feet. What he got was something quite different when Darko came face to face, grabbed the back of his neck, and pulled him in for an emotionally heated kiss.

Maxum was naked inside it and fuck if he didn't feel the sting of tears in his eyes. He was defenseless against those, too. He was broken down, so lost between what he thought was the right thing to do, and what he felt inside. And in that kiss, he surrendered himself to the man who was hell bent to set him free, but not let go.

Darko released their kiss, but never pulled back, keeping their foreheads together as Maxum held onto him for dear life.

"*This*— this works," Darko's voice was deep and warm like a nighttime brandy meant to soothe all those harbored chills. "We fit. But don't fool yourself, because if in your relationship there are no lows— there are no highs either. A roller coaster can't give you a thrill if you don't climb and jump off a few hills."

As if the man had been machined to precision perfection for just him. The very words Maxum had concluded to himself silently, the night he had run to Darko for consoling for his wrong doings, came back to him now in the very analogy Darko just showed him.

Further to his surprise and weakened condition, Darko asked—

"Stay with me, please. Stay, so you don't go home feeling totally hollow inside. Let me fill that spot, if just for one more night. Please." Darko actually *asked him* to stay and then kissed him again as if he were a long lost lover who'd just come home.

Maxum knew he didn't want to be alone just now. He felt emptied, stripped, his world yanked out from under his feet and all those things made him feel vulnerable. That was something completely new to him. He decided it was best to be in the strong arms of a man who would protect him while he was at his weakest.

They went back to the Laszkovi home. Pavle and Maggie's teen boys were still up, playing video games in the great room, and not in the least surprised or disrupted by their passing as Maxum and Darko slipped quietly upstairs to their room.

They crawled into bed, Darko wrapping around him like a security blanket and planted feathery kisses on the back of his neck and shoulder that in turn sent chills down his body but rather than pool around his cock, they gathered in his aching heart. "I'm going to need a few days alone— to set things right. I need to close the door, but I don't want to slam it in his face either. Simeon doesn't deserve that. Please, I hope you—"

"I know." Darko's arms tightened around him and he kissed him again. "I'll leave the light on for you."

Leave the light on— it meant Darko would be here waiting when he got back— when he was ready. His mind ached as much as his heart did and he was still every bit as lost as he was five minutes ago or even three days go. He lay awake while wrapped in Darko's arms, trying to decide what to do until the grey light of dawn and exhaustion finally took him.

CHAPTER TEN

Maxum had gone home Sunday and spent most of the time glowering at his walls— right along with the empty spot in his bed. He even went as far as dragging one of the leather bound chairs in from the living room into his bedroom. Allowing himself at least the one comfort as he sat and just stared at his bed for several hours, getting up only to hit the bathroom and refill his glass of scotch and ice.

Slumped down in the padding, his gaze fixed, his thoughts were not, shifting just as steadily as the winter sun that moved across the sky, and then dipped below the horizon just outside the glass walls of his room. His mind coming to the same dark ending as he stared at his bed, realizing no one had ever laid there save himself. Eight months he had lived here in the new towering elite skyscraper and he had never filled the position next to him. Simeon had never spent the night here. Maxum had always gone to his place. Endured the discomforts or lack of personal things for a night.

Why had he never brought Simeon to his own bed?

He sat there— perhaps another hour had passed in the stillness of the night, and then the answer came. It came in the visualized image of a well-built tanned body, sleeping soundly in the tossed sheets.

Just as Simeon didn't fill his life with Maxum, Simeon was never to be the person to fill his own life.

CHAPTER ELEVEN

Monday, at the office, was like any other Monday that just happened to follow the largest sales event day of every retailer's year. And for reasons Maxum had never been able to wrap his head around, businesses that had no financial survival relations to whether Black Friday was a good sales day or not, were calling in because so and so is still in the red even after the mega sales day. Demanding to know how this was going to affect their stocks in wind power energy.

By the time Maxum had put out a dozen senseless fires, got through his regular Monday meetings, and global conference calls then made it home, the last thing he was prepared to do was try to talk to Simeon to bring things to a close.

And before he knew it, it was Thursday.

He left the office early and met up with Simeon at one of their usual sushi bars. Maxum was thinking if they were in a public place Simeon wouldn't put on such a show. He was wrong. At first, Simeon seemed to make no reaction, but the tapping of his chopsticks on the plate meant he was letting it stew inside for the upcoming Hollywood style dramatic scene. When it did come, it was clearly an epic achievement. Many Maxum had long since grown immune to and he sat back watching, and waiting as Simeon went through the routine of performances. This was Simeon's neighborhood, not his. He didn't care what on lookers were thinking of them right now.

"Oh, I don't know what to say," Simeon's voice went up in a clear rendition of Albert from *The Birdcage*. Yes, Simeon knew the movie, both the remake and the original, word for word and recited them well when they favored him. "I'm feeling faint. I just don't understand what has brought this on. We were happy." His hand floated up beside his cheek as Simeon shook his head in an act of astonished bewilderment. But there was a sudden shift in Sim's expression, his eyes narrowing at Maxum. "Are you going straight?" the question was more accusation than request for information.

"No, Simeon. I just think it's time we go our separate ways. I am tired of feeling alone when I am with you."

"Yes, but you don't come by. Why I had a small coffee social yesterday and you didn't come. And what about Thanksgiving? It was embarrassing having to make up a story to my friends as to why you weren't there." His hand dropped around his chest as if to grasp at an aching heart, while he turned about scanning the group of people who seemed to be as oblivious to them as Maxum felt oblivious to Sim. It was all about *him* and how Simeon presented himself to his friends. God forbid the trophy husband failed to make a viewing from his cave of misery. *No wonder when you go to zoos the animals are always hiding.* Maxum thought.

When Sim brought his hand to his forehead and claimed a headache was coming, Maxum knew it was their cue to take it back to the condo. The academy award winning stage performance was on the way.

Once they arrived at Simeon's place, he was shuffling straight for the bathroom, the retreat followed with the ruckus of pill bottles. Mostly vitamins and lots, and lots of headache medicines. When he came out, Simeon held what looked like a prescription bottle in his fist and shook it at Maxum with a haggard look about him. "Do you see what you bring me to? I actually went in there and for a second considered killing myself over you!" Simeon shook the bottle again for emphasis then made an overhand swing and tossed it at him. The bottle glanced off Maxum's shoulder, falling to the floor and broke open. Little blue pills went everywhere. "I would have died if I had gone through with it!"

Of course, Maxum had known better than that. Simeon had never been *that* emotionally involved in anything to go that route. Not to mention that while Sim liked his party favors, he didn't have anything so potent or toxic in his home. Hell, Simeon didn't even have poisonous bug spray. Everything was all natural and environmentally safe in his organic abode.

Next came the forced hugging. Sim threw himself at Maxum, wrapping his arms around him. Maxum felt nearly mortified by it. Not that Simeon was heartbroken, but because the whole thing was completely void of any true felt emotions. Like wax and not even a single tear. As much as Maxum had dreaded this moment, fearing he would be sending the final nail into his heart and the pain that would follow, he arrived at the realization that he felt none of that, just— emptiness.

"Enough of the stratagem, Sim." He peeled Simeon's arm from around his middle and that's when the slap came. Setting off a trigger in Maxum as it stung across his cheek.

"I can't believe you'd break up with me! What will everyone think?"

There had been many-a-times when Maxum questioned the validity of being slapped, but this time he was certain from the second it came across his face, he did not deserve it, and without further discussion of his reasons, he left Simeon to deal with the reality of being single on his own.

He was considering a drive, even though his angry heavy foot suggested it would not be the wisest of ideas, but he wasn't ready to just sit in his empty home. Logic was going to lose out when its only card was to go home and be confined— alone. He would not purge there. And he knew he needed to do so before inviting Darko into his life. *Don't be a fall back.* He told himself.

His phone rang, his heart skipped a beat wishing to see Darko's name but it was Diesel Gentry's name that came up on ID. *Maybe there was hope for him after all.*

A few hours later, Maxum sat on the lounger inside Trenton Leos' VIP booth at Club Pain. Diesel's phone call had been an invitation to join them for dinner and drinks at the club to officially celebrate a successful first B/D season at the *Salientis du Deliciarum* Island Resort. A well-deserved applause that had been postponed in the shadow of the attempted kidnapping of Trenton's newly claimed D/s lifestyle slave, Katianna Dumas. After that dark event, Trenton had gone recluse for a while, only now resurfacing, and the respected man's brothers were intent to make sure he stayed out and active. Resuming his position as the Dominus within the BDSM Lifestyle community.

Club Pain had never been a favored haunt for Maxum, but he needed to be anywhere but home right now, if for very different reasons than his friend Trenton. The food, and of course the company with the five brothers, Trenton, Diesel, Dane who made frequent ins and outs to check on things with the club, plus Harper and Marcus, had been good. It was the distraction Maxum needed. Enough mutual commonalities were shared among them all. There was no rap-sheet to compare or compete. Not even an indifference that made one feel less than the man sitting next to him. They talked about food and pleasures just as easily as they talked about business, money, and ideas for future successes. Plans led to a mutual giving of strategies and plausible investments. Eventually it all came to celebrating the Island Resort's two years since the grand reopening under their ownership and its successful first annual fetish season.

Maxum was glad to hear the Event Manager, Paris Dalqeaute had worked out well. Including the news that his request to remain as a full time resident was approved. It was a no brainer really, when the inventive businessman presented them with numerous designs for smaller weekend themes throughout the year to keep both clients of the BDSM lifestyle as well as non-players coming back to the resort again and again.

It also didn't go unnoticed that Diesel seemed to grow uneasy the more they talked about Paris. Something that stuck out, because Diesel was never uneasy about anything— *ever*. Always as rigid as a stone block.

Maxum felt the connection to it— *the emotional rumbling from an ungiving fortress of ideals*. Even as his eyes drifted back to the sea of bodies dancing and grinding on the dance floor; the mocking chuckle he kept to himself as another man stirred the exact same uneasiness in himself.

He felt the buzz in his pocket going off for what seemed like the hundredth time. He reached in not bothering to pull it out to look. The last eighty had all been Simeon. This one would be too and he finally silenced the whole thing.

Someone asked a question in the murmuring conversation. "I may have to set a week aside and go down for a visit again. See my house now that it's finished." Maxum gave his response from the autopilot records in his head, to extricate his thoughts away from Simeon, but not once did his eyes shift away from the dance floor outside the room. He took another sip from his glass wincing at the burning tequila they were all drinking after the first toast of salutation with a shot of Absinthe. *A Dominion of Brothers' tradition.* Maxum wasn't big on either, preferring a bolder darker flavor of scotch or cognac, but right now, it was the effect of the drink Maxum was intentionally torturing himself with. Though, none more than what he was seeing—

The man that haunted his every carnal desire, Darko Laszkovi, was dancing out on the floor with another man wrapped in his arms.

"You should. We're planning to go down at the start of our next B/D season in the summer right after the auction." Maxum heard the response come from Trenton and made some comment back, but he wasn't sure really what he said. His mind becoming infused outside the VIP booth.

He'd been watching Darko dancing with the other man off and on for the last hour now. Not once did he notice the two men kiss, lots of laughing— and rubbing— and prodding. A few spoken exchanges sent directly to the ear to override the volume of the music, but nothing to indicate any deep connection. It didn't make the sight any easier on Maxum. Darko might as well be out there fucking the other man in a deliberate act to rile him up for all the emotion it was stirring up in him right now.

The rage he felt, so hot, it burned his eyes and he finally forced himself to look away just so he could close them. Instantly, the back of his lids played out like tiny movie screens. A stampede of horses strumming through his heart that sounded like thunder in his ears as he watched himself drive into Darko's perfectly riveted body. Only Darko *kissed* him. And did so like no man ever had, the kiss alone was as satisfying as the full act of fucking. During their not so private Thanksgiving run away, they'd spent over an hour just kissing and rubbing against each other. Proving to him it was more than just sex.

The drink was finally loading up in his bladder and he excused himself. Maxum kept his head tucked as he made his way around the dance floor for the bathrooms located on the other side.

While he had been very aware of Darko, he didn't want Darko aware of him. He just wasn't in his right mind and the more he watched Darko with the other man, he wasn't so sure he had ever been.

Breaking up with Simeon was a decision long in the making. Darko was just the light Maxum needed, to see what he wanted in a relationship was not what he had with Simeon. However, he was also getting a wakeup call that what he got from Darko wasn't what he had hoped to fill his life with either. He was finding himself delivered at the very place he was dreading to be in— alone— and a failure.

Standing at the urinal, Maxum closed his eyes as he stood, letting the night of toxic tequila drain from his system, wishing his emotions would drain with it. It came as no surprise when he felt the warm strong arms wrap around him from behind and take hold of his cock before he had even finished pissing.

Maxum didn't even fight it, he gave over his dick and his head fell back on the shoulders behind him, drowning in the hot wet mouth that kissed his neck.

"Even on a free night out on the town, you're still in a suit,." a familiar voice growled in his ear.

"A habit that seemed to keep the peace with my boyfriend," Maxum mumbled, keeping his eyes closed, not removing himself from Darko's embrace just yet. His business in the bathroom done, but still in the hands of the other, he made no move to pull away.

"As in, the boyfriend you supposedly broke up with?" Darko leaned into him, pushing him towards the wall. Maxum's hands shot up to hold them steady, though nothing else inside him was and no chance of getting there, not while Darko's firm hand began stroking his length. "So what does that make me then?" There was a low tenor growl in his ear.

Damn, Maxum didn't want to answer questions, didn't want to have to explain himself. He had done enough of that with Simeon. That part of his life was over. He'd dressed for Simeon for the last time, excused his actions for the last time. While his affair with Darko was not a thing to be proud of, at least with *this* man he'd had some very good prizes at the end of the playing field. "An unstable environment," he muttered aloud. *Affairs never translate into long term relationships.*

"The only thing unstable is that you keep running away to go back to putting cheap gas in your tank. When you know damn well what I have for you is far more satisfying." Darko's hand was steadily twisting as he slid it up and down, creating exhilarating friction that had Maxum panting too quickly.

Maxum couldn't argue that. The heavy buzz had robbed him of any warnings that anyone could walk in on them any moment. All he knew right now was his cock was in the right hands and he wanted it to stay that way. He sucked in a deep breath, wanting every bit of what he felt to be true and safe. He wanted to be lost in this. To come home to this always. He let his head rock back anticipating the feel of a warm kiss taking over his mouth.

There was a shuffle and a few masculine chuckles at the door. *"Niiice,"* one of them crooned, drawing out the vowel to sound out a tantalizing approval with the word.

Maxum's balance stuttered and his eyes flashed open. He snapped around to see the three men coming into the bathroom, their eyes trailing down his front side and Maxum became acutely aware that he was stroking his own dick.

The man who had been holding him wasn't even there. Just haunting him.

Maxum's emotions quickly began to sink even further as he reminded himself what he had always known. *Affairs never translate into long term relationships.*

He tucked himself away and rushed out, not even stopping to make his excuses to Trenton and the others. He would talk to them later. He just needed to get out of there.

❦

Darko could have sworn the blur of dark grey suit had been Maxum. But what the hell was he doing here—in Club Pain no less?

Abandoning his friend and teammate, Mitch, Darko squeezed through the crowd of dancing bodies, but by the time he made it to the end of the bar, glancing down the corridor to the club's exit, whoever he saw was long gone. He turned into the bar dropping his elbows on the countertop, his eyes still going back to the door, unable to shake the certainty that it had been him. He pulled out his phone and called Maxum. Only to get an automated message he wasn't available at the time.

"Did you see something you liked?" Mitch was suddenly beside Darko and called up for a water from Zane who was working behind the bar.

"More than like," Darko answered and waved to Zane for one for himself as well. Mitch looked around Darko's body and down the empty corridor. "Looks like he got away."

Darko turned to face him as he still leaned over the bar. He drank down the glass of water until the ice hit his lips. His thoughts going to Maxum and the several days of silence since their weekend together. Maxum had said he needed time to close one part of his life before opening a new one, but dammit, Darko hated not knowing if Maxum was okay. Or just sitting in an empty house bouncing off the walls because it was now vacant one person.

"After this, will you come back out and dance with me some more?" the offer from Mitch drew Darko from his mind and back to the present.

"You know, any more bumping and grinding with me, and Quentin is likely to catch you, and crack his whip on your hide," Darko joked.

Mitch made a teasing wriggle. A rather comical move given his musculature and size. He even added a playful *waggle* to his brows. "I know. That's what I am hoping for. Sir hasn't spanked me in weeks. Besides, it's my birthday. Figured it was time for me to *not* be such a good boy. What do you Serbian men call it?"

"A brat." Darko shook his head and let out a light chuckle, "As long as Quentin doesn't try to include me on the punishment, fine. I'll help you be bad, *boi deriste.*"

Mitch slapped on a super big grin, "No worries, mate. My Sir likes otters; you don't have enough hair for his pecker's high standards." He grinned more as if it were actually possible, then scrubbed his hands over his chest and the thick black carpet of hair proudly. "Besides, I row faster when my ass hurts."

"It's gonna hurt even more when the chlorine in the pool at the Tank hits it. Practice moves indoors this weekend." The warning only fueled Mitch's naughty smile more, making Darko laugh, drawing his thoughts away from the phantom that had fled out the door.

CHAPTER TWELVE

Maxum's business of financial investments and growth management was located in the Woolworth Tower on the corner of Broadway and Beekman. His own office looking down over the glass atrium roof of the historical Beekman Palace and Steve Flanders square now slowly being blanketed with a layer of white as the season's first snow came drifting down. Right across from him, the Beekman Tower Gehry, where he lived. Albeit his flat was so high up in the tower it was hard to actually enjoy the park at its base below, but knowing it was there appeased Maxum enough to balance out his far more, fast paced life.

He was in no hurry to wrap up his week's business. His Friday was going to be like any other day of the week. Even with the first drifts of snow falling past his window to the ground below. He didn't even wonder if there would be enough that stuck that it would crunch under his feet when he walked across the park to go home. To be there alone, as always. Only this time there wasn't someone out there calling him. Not since he'd tossed his phone across the bedroom and hearing it shatter against the wall. After fleeing Club Pain, and the emotional grief that followed him home, he had pulled his phone out to set the alarm and saw Darko's name in the missed calls. The pain struck so hard, Maxum didn't know what to do with it all. Thus went his phone. At least now, he didn't have to look at the list of calls from Simeon either.

He turned his back to the snowy scenery and back to his computer; checking up on some investments that might work in Dane Master's favor for the restaurant ideas they had discussed last night. Nothing that man did strayed away from his love for sex and the belief that Americans should be open for public fornication. It was a risky motivation for businesses. Yet, Dane Masters had an impeccable track record and not one of the man's ventures had failed so far. Lending truth to the old saying— *sex sells*— but so does having just the right investors involved.

That's where Maxum came in and he knew just the guy who might actually be interested in a restaurant whose servers resembled Greek and Roman servants of the ancient bathhouse brothels. The new venture revived Maxum's mood and he quickly grabbed up the phone and gave his friend a call.

A light knock and his assistant, Alysse, stepped in, dropping some papers on his desk, including a red folder that would contain the week's analysis reports from the US stock exchange. She leaned over his desk whispering, which meant the call was a priority client. "Call on line three."

Maxum scribbled on a notepad— *Toussaint Larou is green*— then cupped the mouth of the phone and glanced her way, both listening to the man still talking on the phone and to the interruption from his assistant. "Who is it?"

"Mr. Almere Glaisphmen," Alysse whispered then left him to his client's call.

"Shit," he mumbled to himself then directed his attention back to the person he was talking to on the phone. "Toussaint, I'll have to call you back later. Yeah, you bet. Thanks." Maxum reached over and switched the lines, his mind as well, going from friendly to business conservative. "Mr. Glaisphmen, pleasure to hear from you. How can I be of service?"

His client didn't waste a word on formalities, cutting straight to business. *"My wife, Coralline, and I are in town for the week and she decided to drag me to one of those wine tasting events. I was rather surprised to not see your name among the attending guests. I would like for you and Simeon to join us."*

"Simeon?" Maxum asked in surprise, "I was not aware you knew my— him." Maxum quickly corrected himself before making any announcements of the said ex-partner in his life.

"Apparently, he and Coralline ran into each other earlier today. She hasn't stopped talking about him since. So she has insisted you bring him."

Maxum cringed at the thought, while Simeon had a way of winning the wives, which always made the husbands happy, Maxum hated bringing him to tasting events because Simeon would inevitably complain— *incisively*— and that always ruined Maxum's own palate. Not to mention Maxum had finally called it off with Simeon. But it Looked like his ex-partner was finding a way around the phone calls he had refused to answer to get back into his life.

Maxum let the phone drop away from his face a moment as he sucked in a deep breath and scrubbed over his face. He knew how Coralline was and if she wanted something, she was prudent enough to see to it she got it or take a man down. Almere Glaisphmen was no small client of his and where he went, a number of others would follow. Suggesting Simeon had a seed of vindictiveness in him that Maxum had never known about.

He suffered himself to swallow the growl along with his own pride and brought the phone back to his ear. Clearing his throat before speaking, "Of course, we'll be there."

"Good. I will be sure to let Coralline know to expect you. See you tomorrow night then." And just like that the puppet master hung up.

Maxum slowly placed the phone on the cradle, his mind elsewhere, and racing with thoughts that could put a formula one car to shame. When the displeasure of having his hand forced came to a boiling point, his hand still hovering around the phone sent it flying off his desk. It careened into the bookcase, shattering into a dozen or more pieces of plastic that fell to the floor.

Maxum - zero— phones - negative two.

"Darko. Dane Masters. You got plans for tonight?" Dane Masters' stern and domineering voice came over the phone line when Darko picked up. It exuded a presence that told the listener right away that turning them down was never an option. Even if he did ask politely.

"None of any consequence. What's up?" Darko's answer, more relaxed and informal than his caller. While he knew the tones of the Masters from the BDSM lifestyle and enjoyed the company of such, it wasn't his kink. Therefore, the domineering commands rolled right off him like raindrops on a London Fog coat.

"I was supposed to accompany Vince to the Winter Cellars Wine Event tonight, but I had something come up. Can you accompany him?"

Darko shrugged, glancing down his body and the aroused dick he was just about to play with— *down boy*— he mentally commanded it, "Sure. I'll take her out."

"Him." Dane corrected Darko from the other end.

Darko laughed. Getting used to the new Vida-Vince was still sinking in for most of his friends and associates. Vince had been a cross-dresser and then a full out drag queen for so many years. The resurfacing of a face that had been hidden under all the false glam was breathtaking and Vince still came out looking more alluring than most women. However, *Vida* was every bit coming to terms that he was in fact a man and not a female impersonator. Perhaps a little of both. But the *he-she* and name were still a matter of transition— for all of them.

"I'll make sure *he* has a good time," Darko assured Dane, with an added emphasis on the masculine pronoun.

"Good. But not too much of a good time. You hear me? I mean it. No one goes to his bed without my approval." The possessiveness not only coming out as words, but Darko felt every tone of it. There was no denying it; Dane Masters was as possessive of his brother as Trenton Leos was of his little Unicorn, Katianna.

"I know. I'll keep him safe," Darko assured him before hanging up then headed for a shower to get ready. He hadn't had any plans for the night save perhaps playing with himself and missing a certain man. Therefore, he didn't see a problem with the spontaneous night on the town. He and Vida— Vince, rather, had been good friends for a number of years now and it wasn't the first time he was asked to play the part of *date* for Vi— *Vince*. Especially now, after Vince had dropped all the drag queen regalia and discovered his inner beauty. The new Vida-Vince drew more heads than any man or woman combined, and Darko liked how it made him feel, claiming sole proprietorship of the androgynous beauty, if only for show and for the one night.

Darko had to admit, once there it wasn't the usual night he was expecting. Because as he had said, the new Vince simply turned heads.

They played around the banquet of sample foods. All while memories of Maxum feeding him at another winery event played in the back of his mind as they acted out a similar game, but more like two high school kids goofing off, than as lovers.

And while Dane would likely ream him for it, Darko gave Vida some room to let a few flirts have a chance to say hello to the man he was charged with escorting.

A little later, they ran into Lars Mickels, attorney and friend of the Dominion Brothers so they stopped to chat awhile with him. "Vida you're looking so extravagant these days. I swear every man and woman in this room is harboring some fantasies of you right now. I confess I have some of my own. Can you imagine at the next Elysian Fields auction? Trenton having you work at his side where everyone could see you? The guests would go absolutely bolloxed."

Darko gave a nervous chuckle, "That might not be such a great idea. The last one, Trenton had problems with the guests daring to touch Katianna and Paris. If anyone tried touching Vida, Dane would go mental."

Lars let out a hearty laugh, "You're probably right. Forget I mentioned it." He turned, spotting someone he knew and waved them over. "Speaking of *Salientis du Deliciarum*, let me introduce to you one of its owners." Lars' hand leading the way, dropped over Darko's shoulder, steering him into a near about face. "Darko, this is Maxum St. Laurents. Maxum, I'd like you to meet a friend of mine, Darko Laszkovi."

Darko's face melted at the sight of the man standing before him. He didn't even dare meet his eyes. Unprepared to see what was there— or worse— what wasn't. He kept his focus distracted elsewhere. That, being which, the body he craved to have pressed against him right now— yesterday— tomorrow. The black silk suit and pewter grey shirt Maxum wore were richly exquisite. As always, tailored to fit him in perfection. Only, Darko's gaze followed the muscular arms that were dropped stiffly at his sides, only for one of them to be gripped by the arm of another in a rather clingy form. An arm that led to the presence of *another man.*

Darko's mouth went dry, not knowing how to respond.

If Maxum was feeling anything like he was, he managed to mask it considerably better as Maxum leaned in offering up a handshake. "How do you do?" He nodded mechanically. "Pleasure to meet you." All business and playing as if they'd never met before.

"And I'm sure you know, Vida Masters, Dane Masters' brother," Lars continued with the introductions, not even picking up on the cold disposition between Darko and Maxum.

"Vince." Maxum acknowledge him by clasping both of Vida's hands, following through with a lean to kiss both cheeks.

"Hon, he just said her name was Vida not Vince," the man at Maxum's side gave a polite scolding that was mild in comparison to the bug-eyed glare the man made. Maxum's arm moved around his backside, tightening around the man's thin body and mumbled something at him that silenced him then turned back to Vince. "Enjoying the wines?"

"Always." Vince forced a smile back to the familiar face.

"And—" Lars stalled a moment, "Forgive me, I forgot your name?" His attention on the man with Maxum.

"Simeon. Simeon Correl."

"Simeon—" Lars nodded, "Darko Laszkovi and Vida-Vince Masters."

"How do you do? I'm Maxum's significant other." A soft hand was offered in greeting— *titles and lines drawn out and circled*— and then came on the plastered charm. "You look so familiar," Simeon spoke toward Darko but not actually *to* him.

While it made Darko uncomfortable, he was acutely aware that had Simeon dared to actually chat *with* him, the act would have been welcomed with even more distain. So here was the man Maxum was supposed to have broken up with.

Darko had waited days to hear back from Maxum only to come face to face with the reason why the call never came. He swallowed the bile churning at his insides. In fact, he wasn't liking having to stand there and pretend at all, but he received no signals from Maxum that there were any alternatives. *Maxum.* He stood there like a frigid statue. His hands back down at his sides. He wasn't even drinking. Odd, since Darko knew Maxum loved these wine events, loved the sampling, loved the aroma on his pallet then testing the resilience of flavor on a kiss. He wondered if Maxum hand fed Simeon from his fingers like he had with him. Darko felt a sudden shame for the playful act.

Simeon, however, kept on without any motivation from Darko's part, his hand floated up to his cheek, delicate bony fingers tapped there as he pondered. "But I can't seem to place the face." He turned to Maxum. "You? Hmmm?"

Maxum's face paled at his partner's quizzing.

"No? Oh, well, I'm sure it will come to me later," Simeon continued despite the lacking contribution lent to the conversation from either of them.

Darko hated the obvious and fake social approach from Simeon. He hated Maxum's ability to be so aloof toward him even more.

Then like the flitting about of a butterfly, Simeon changed the topic, "So you were saying about *Salientis*? You know Maxum is the primary financial supporter for the resort."

But even as Simeon struck up the conversation back to the starting point, Darko could see the man could care less about the island and more about that Maxum had just been introduced as *its owner*. Darko knew by the way Simeon's hand caressed down Maxum's arm like— *here stands my rich boyfriend. Yes, he owns an island, whatever it's called.*

"So have you ever been to it?" Simeon sipped on a glass of white wine, with a fickle twitch to his face after each one.

Though the question was posed, Darko could see the reception for an answer wasn't there. Not particularly paying any attention of whether he said yes, no or—*I prefer jacking my dick to the national anthem.* He nearly snorted. *What a perfect question.* Darko's gaze tightened down on the man across from him, Maxum's own eyes burning with a warning of jealousy. "As a matter of fact, Vince and I had just come from a week's vacation there." Darko thought about pulling Vince in against his body, to rub it in more, but knew better than to use his friend that way. "We had to wait until after the championships, but when we won, our coach gave us all a two week reprieve from practice. So Vince and I headed down then."

"Championship?" Simeon jumped on the chance to steer away from the boring topic of the resort but showing his well-rehearsed ability to make a client feel like they were always in the spotlight with a new one.

"Oh, forgive me. Let me, Darko," Lars spoke up, "Darko is a champion sculling rower. His team won the New England Masters this fall for Eight-man sculling and Darko here took solo-men's champion."

"Sculling? Really?" Simeon actually perked up with some genuine interest.

"Yeah, I row on the Greenwich Queens rowing team," Darko answered mullingly, now hating the attention as much as being a pawn in a meaningless conversation but wasn't going to forfeit in front of everyone.

"Oh my." Simeon face brightened as if star struck. "I'm on the rotary from the East Village. We're big fans. We've even held a few fundraiser rallies to help out. Oh, and you have a new teammate now. That sexy supermodel young man. What's his name? Trojan?"

Darko grimaced, his brother's name wasn't that hard to remember or pronounce correctly. "Trofim. His name is pronounced *trohe-phem.*"

All the while Maxum remained silently dormant. Practiced control and tolerance kept him from rudely walking away but evidently uncomfortable, yet any attempt to lure Simeon away would perhaps lead to questions he didn't chance to initiate between them.

"Trofim. I get it. Oh, he is so handsome. So which boat are you on?" The spotlight focused back for the game.

"Single-man team, hence getting the solo championship." Darko's gaze slowly swept back to Maxum. Ironic, wasn't it? Maxum's boyfriend, the one he was supposed to have called it off with was showing more interest in him right now than Maxum did. Darko couldn't stomach it any longer. He turned to Vince ducking his head only some to whisper in his ear, "I could really use a drink."

Vince gave him a look of pity as if he could see it on his face how much he hated the fake conversation that surrounded him. It wasn't really that, it was, but it wasn't. He'd probably hear about later from Pyotr if word came down the line he'd been rude to a local sponsor club, but Darko just couldn't stand there in front of Maxum any longer. The man he'd been trying to draw into his life over the scarce time together scattered across the last two months, only to come blatantly before the reason he had been unsuccessful. It was more than just a slap in the face as to why it would never happen.

"Oh, look, hon." Simeon was pointing across the banquet hall. "There's Coralline and Almere. Oh, we must go talk to them. Coralline told me at the tea the other day, Almere is looking into buying some European energy something or other." And off they went. A heavy sigh from Maxum as they excused themselves and he allowed his partner to lead the way to the next networking trivial conversation.

As the night rolled on, the stressful game of avoidance continued. Darko finally excused himself for the bathroom, only it wasn't even a minute when Maxum was in there right behind him.

Maxum had Darko backed against the wall, "You're fucking him?" Maxum was seething red in the face as he leered at Darko.

"What business is it to you who I am fucking?"

"Are you or are you not fucking Vince Masters?"

"No! I'm not!" Darko brushed him back to gain some personal space.

"Don't lie to me!" Maxum shoved Darko back against the wall and leaned toward him to keep him pinned there this time.

Darko's chin came up in defiance. "Why would I care to lie? Believe me if I had something to throw in your face right now I would— save my fist."

"Then what are you doing with him?"

"Vida and I have been friends for years. We go out together every once in a while, sometimes at Dane's request because Dane trusts me to date him and *not* sleep with him."

"And the trip to *Salientis*? You're going to tell me you didn't do anything there?"

"Of course not. There were still plenty of sex-slaves on employment while we were there. Though, I spent most of my time with Paris," Darko's confession tightened, hoping that throwing a name out would hurt Maxum enough to make him back off. He watched every line and contour of the man's face grow taut, but Maxum didn't move. So Darko pushed further, turning the tables. "And what about you?" Darko sneered, "You and that pajama wearing queen sashaying on your arm. That's the boyfriend you were hiding? He pushed me away for that?"

"What about the pajama wearing queen?" Simeon's shrill question shot towards them from just inside the hotel restroom before Maxum could defend himself against the foul play.

☙❧

Maxum spun around to see Simeon standing just behind him, hands on hips that were jutted out to the side in perfect hussy pose. And just behind him was Vince, only Vince's expression looked far more wounded than Simeon's did. *Shit this night was a total cave-in and the aftermath from it was certain to last a while.*

Simeon turned on clogged heels and stormed out; Maxum's heavy gaze flickered to Darko for a fraction of a second then went after the ex-significant other who shanghaied him here in the first place. If, for no other reason but to see to it his hands weren't forced into anything else before the night was over. "Dammit, Simeon. Wait!" Maxum was calling out as he left the restroom.

☙❧

Darko let the air out of his lungs with a hard huff through his nostrils, turned and slammed his fist into the stall door.

"Does Dane pay you to go out with me?" the fragile question from Vida-Vince pleaded with him.

Darko shook his head. None of what he said should have sounded that way, but he could see from Vida's point why it did. "No, Vida— Vince, I mean. He does not. I promise," Darko's voice turned deep and low with the pain that ripped at his chest, and he punched the door again throwing everything he had into it.

Hinges snapped, sending the door reeling back with a hard slam into the marble wall, as well as something else sent ricocheting off into flying shrapnel. Only the rebounding door came back so quick it smashed against Darko's knuckles, unprepared for the return and his hand recoiled with a sharp pain far worse than the original punch had created.

Maxum returned inside after chasing Simeon out to the street where he'd hailed a cab and took off without him. He rubbed at the cheek, smoothing out the sting from yet another slap. His emotions stewing over just that one thing. His tolerance of them, overly used up whether he rightfully deserved them or not. He spotted Darko and Vince at the bar he'd fully intended to park his ass at to drown his simmering emotions before heading home, but he held back a moment just watching the two.

Vince was taking a bar towel of ice from the bartender and holding it over Darko's hand and was clearly crying. Darko was wiping the tears from Vince's eyes and gave some attention to his forehead a moment before pulling the fragile man against his chest and kissed his head in the same way he had watched Darko kiss his sisters. Or the girl Darko's older brother now called daughter. In the same fashion, Dane would kiss Vince. *Intimately— but not sexually.*

Something he and Darko had said in that argument upset Vince and got the man emotional. Something Maxum was certain he'd hear about from Dane come tomorrow.

With that, Maxum mentally added the word *putz* under the words *alone* and *failure* on his self-loathing chalkboard list, then turned, and left.

CHAPTER THIRTEEN

It was a Sunday but that didn't matter in Tokyo. *Only Americans think weekend is time for no work*— Mr. Hasamoto had often been heard to say of US businessmen, but so far had never said it to Maxum. He sat in his office after getting off the conference call, realizing he'd yet heard from Dane. It was nearly two. Even as a night person, the man would have been up by now.

His new barely out of the box phone on his desk where the old one used to sit buzzed with the call from the front desk. "What is it, Lee?" Lee being his weekend assistant and intern who over saw most of the quiet operations. If something came up with a client, usually one of the overseas ones, and if was more than the average to-do, Lee knew to call him or one of his employed men if needed. After all, they were Americans and Maxum didn't force his staff to work seven days a week. Lee was a godsend in the sense too. A graduate student working towards his Masters in Global Marketing, who had so many classes crunched into his semesters, he didn't have time for a nine to five office job. And so few financial firms came with weekend schedules that paid well. Maxum needed more than a gopher in the office, so the arrangement worked well for them both, and to show his appreciation Maxum sponsored most of Lee's student fees and his tuition. However, it came with a four-year contract of employment too. As Maxum always said, he invested in the long term, and he knew when he had a good thing in front of him. Except, perhaps, when it came to Darko Laszkovi. Darko spun him about and made him all sensation and emotions until he couldn't think straight at all. Maxum was so predetermined to invest in the long run, it made enjoying the short term bliss he had with Darko complicated and painful.

"You received a call from Vince Masters while you were on conference. He seemed upset. Something about his brother going after him? Do you know what he was referring to?"

"Shit. When?"

"About a half hour ago."

"Dammit." Maxum's mind raced to establish the scenario. It'd take Dane about an hour to reach Darko's shop from his house out at the Hamptons, which gave Maxum only thirty minutes to intercept. "Cancel the rest of my day." Maxum knew the motorcycle shop stayed open over the weekend then was closed on Mondays and Tuesdays, so that's where he headed. He only hoped that's where he would find Darko before Dane could.

Twenty-three minutes and a hand full of seconds later, Maxum pulled into the parking lot of Darko's motorcycle shop. Dane's Audi was already pulled up to the front glass windows of the shop. The driver's side door left wide open. Maxum could hear the heated conflict going on inside when he turned the car off and quickly jumped out to get in there before it got worse.

"I want to know why the hell my brother was seen leaving the Wine Cellars last night while crying, then wound up in the ER, and won't tell me a god damn thing about what took place!" Maxum heard Dane Masters' temper bellowing off the walls like thunder as soon as he stepped in.

"Nobody hurt Vida. I swear it." There was a pause followed by some fast explaining. "I got into an altercation with someone else an—" And that was it. Maxum rounded the front counter of the shop just in time to see Dane's fist come flying at Darko, knocking him back into one of the bikes he'd apparently been working on, and he and the machine went crashing to the floor.

"Dane!" Maxum ran up, but it was too late. Darko was out cold on the floor.

"What the hell are you doing here? Was it you?" Dane lurched towards him. "You, I can fire! Though it won't do much good. I can't afford to buy you out!" Dane spat at Maxum. Flames cooking in the man's eyes like he was sucked-up into some peripheral war zone hallucination.

"Dane! Calm yourself!" Maxum shouted back at him. His own focus flickering to his lover on the floor, still not moving.

"I don't want to be calm! I want to know what happened to Vince last night!"

"Darko and I got into an argument. I accused him of being more involved with Vince than he is. In the defense of Vince's honor, Vince was inadvertently hurt by it."

Dane eased back on his heels, reining himself back in and took a deep breath to Maxum's relief. Obviously, Darko hadn't exaggerated about Dane trusting the two of them would never wind up in bed together. "What the hell were you two arguing about?"

Maxum was next to take a long deep breath. Running his fingers into his hair as he glanced down at the unconscious body that still managed to arouse him somehow.

"Start talking or I start punching again," Dane warned.

Maxum's gaze flicked to the other men in the shop, hovering nearby like they wanted to come to the aid of their co-worker, but smart enough to stay clear from the Titan's involved. "Darko and I have been having an affair. And last night he discovered Simeon and Simeon discovered Darko."

"Fucking great. An affair. That doesn't explain why those two ended up at ER." Dane's hand waved back to the body on the floor.

Maxum glanced back down at Darko's right hand sporting the black arm brace and his fingers taped to a splint. "What happened to Vince?" Maxum asked the only question he figured Dane would care to answer right now.

"Three stitches above the left eye. I had to yank them out and glue the cut shut so he didn't have a permanent scar. Fucking idiot doctors!"

"I'm sorry, Dane. I don't know how that happened, but I'll take a wild guess and say a bathroom stall door had been involved."

Darko felt the piercing pain long before he even thought to open his eyes. Damn, his head hurt, but— *oh yeah*— Dane was punching him. He jumped with a start.

"Whoa, whoa, whoa there. Easy now. The match is over. Just sit tight," a familiar voice spoke while a warm hand settled over his shoulder, easing him back down on the sofa. There was a flash of white light that hit him when Darko opened his eyes, dimmed and there in its place was Maxum, sitting at his side. The man's face drawn up as if he was actually concerned over something.

Darko reached up his hand, searching until he found the weight holding him down and brushed Maxum's hand from his shoulder, feeling the flood of his own pain and anger coming. "What the hell are you doing here?"

Maxum took a deep breath just contemplating him, "I tried to beat Dane to the draw. Guess I had the wrong car with me today," Maxum tried joking, to make light of the circumstances, still pressing the cold compress to Darko's cheek.

Darko wasn't taking the bait or letting go of his emotions so willingly. He shoved Maxum's hands from him, grabbed the wet washcloth, and tossed it across the room.

"You should leave it. You took a quiet a punch," Maxum mildly scolded him for the defiance.

"Yeah, well, there's still plenty more to come when Pyotr finds out I can't practice for two months. It was only fake-luck I got out of the ER before Pavle discovered I was there," Darko grumbled. He brought his arms up, crossing them over his eyes, and just lay there silently fuming— beating back tears as he retreated mentally from the man sitting next to him on the edge of the beat up shop-sofa.

(•ω•)

Maxum wasn't sure how Darko's brother, Pavle, played out in all this, but he figured right now probably wasn't the best time to ask. He could only think to offer whatever request Darko might ask of him, and the remorse he felt rang out in every word. "Is there something— anything I can do?"

(•ω•)

"Yeah— get the fuck out," the words spilled before Darko could second-guess them. But there was no taking them back and it was probably best when the man didn't refute him.

He peeked out from under his arms and watched as Maxum got up and left. Even in the dim light from just the small desk lamp in his office, Darko could make out the man's body inside the tailored slacks, and crisp clean shirt. No jacket hiding his perfect ass this time. *That was odd.* Maxum never stepped out without his jacket. *Must'ah been in a hurry to get somewhere.* And that's when he felt the punch to his chest and the sting of tears threaten his eyes further.

Shit.

☙❦❧

Maxum stepped out, closing the door behind him. He stalled, his hand still holding the door handle. Just hovering there, a moment. He knew he wasn't welcome and he had been ordered to go, but he couldn't bring his feet to obey and take him away.

He heard Darko moving inside the office, followed by his forlorn voice.

"Zdravo. It's me Darko. I was just calling to check— hey, you're up—" Maxum overheard Darko's caring voice from inside. *"No, no. I'm good. Everything's fine. I just wanted to make sure you were okay."*

Darko'd obviously called Vince. Maxum could tell, because Darko spoke to Vince the same way everyone else did. Overly nurturing. Like a big brother.

What'da ya say we go out tonight? Say dinner and a movie, my treat." There was a pause, *"Yeah— talking would be great."*

Maxum finally forced himself to step away. He had no right to feel jealous or lay claim. Darko had made it clear, if he wanted Darko all for himself, he had to keep him, and Maxum hadn't done that because he already let someone else get in the way. Darko had every right to move on.

CHAPTER FOURTEEN

Darko had given up on hearing from Maxum; phone calls he never made that would have gone unanswered even if he had. He'd thought for sure their weekend together at his brother's had gone well. It was necessary from his point of view, the attraction they shared was so searing hot they needed some kind of grounding, just to prove that even an intense attraction like theirs could be a serious and committed one. That they could in fact share a real relationship, not just an affair of excessive fucking for a flighty moment. For all that, not even the sex had happened between them, since their weekend together. Nothing more than the possible chance he might have glimpsed him at the club then the run-in at the Wine Cellars' Christmas Event that didn't go over well at all. The three fingers of his right hand still taped and splinted were a reminder of that night. He'd since tossed the arm brace so he could at least start working out again.

He sat at the bar at the Tavern pub, picking at the label on his ale. It'd been weeks since he'd heard from Maxum, not that he should, after telling him to get the fuck out of his office with a tone that sounded more like *fuck off.*

His attention drifted to his friends as the laughter kicked up a notch over at the pool tables. It'd been just as long since he'd let the guys from the rowing team talk him into going out, but being here didn't make him a part of the evening. Now, just days after another Christmas— *alone*— he just wasn't into it. Even now as he sat in the local pub, filled to the brim, bulging with young hot studs that would willingly jump in his bed with little more than a wink on his part to pique their interest— his wasn't. Darko had already ruled them all out, not one stirred his lust like the powerful man he'd spent numerous afternoons and nights fantasizing of having under him all over again.

He dropped the empty bottle on the bar and right on cue, another was pushed in front of him. He took a long swig, letting the dark chocolaty malt tones of the brew slide down his throat. Thinking how one man's kiss would taste of potent scotch or of a dark nutty sherry against his palate. Potent dark flavors, fancy food, fast machines, and strong men. Just naming a few of their compatibilities.

"*Heyyyyy*— I know how to get your freak swinging again." A drunk slur and a warm arm reached over to wrap around Darko's shoulders from behind.

Darko grabbed the hand that tried to slip into his shirt and unlaced it from around his neck and placed it with a firm hold on the bar. "Not tonight, Josh. I'm not in the mood."

The man he'd called, Josh, sloshed his lean body into the bar stool next to him. Drunk eyes trying to focus in on him. "Since when are you not in the mood? I've heard stories about you."

"Ya, well, you know what they say about stories—"

"Uh-huh, Laszkovi's are great in bed," Josh jeered and leaned in, his arms attempting to make a move on Darko once again.

Darko's hand went up, slapping flat against Josh's chest, stopping any further approach. He flinched from the pinch of pain caused by the splints pressing his fingers back. *One more fucking reminder*— he shook his head and pushed up from the bar, heading for the back pool tables. "Bralick, how 'bout you keep your slut to yourself tonight?" Darko barked at his teammate, as he passed by him.

"You can have him, if it'll put you in better spirits." Bralick groped his crotch in Darko's direction with a pump of his hips. Taunting him as if that would do anything for his attitude. *It didn't.*

"Shit man, you know Darko don't go for that kind," Hemi became defensive, stepping around the pool table and headed for Darko. The New Zealander's dark-skinned arm slipping around Darko's waist with a smooth brush of his fingers and swung around to offer his own body's contact for his pleasure. "Come with me, sugar, I'll make you feel right again."

Darko let the New Zealander lure him back towards the pay phones that no longer served any function other than as a dark corner for necking. He and Hemi had fucked a number of times out of nothing more than familiarity, but there had never been any chemistry between them. For as big a brute as Hemi was, along with his savage tattoo-faced, warrior looks he was too soft, too passive in bed. No fire to get the engines really revving and it wasn't enough to want to be anything more than a quickie with each other. At least not for him. Hemi on the other hand had offered to be a number with him despite what was lacking. Only, Darko didn't see the point in claiming any kind of a commitment with someone he only saw as a friend with benefits. Still, for the moment, here and now, Darko allowed the man's approaching offer, hoping maybe those benefits would do him some good, and break him from his funk.

He leaned back against the wood paneling, offering up his neck for the man, letting the tattooed Māori have free rein with him. His position mechanical, without any personal input, letting Hemi do the work while he drank his ale.

One of them had to help.

Hemi's hand dropped over Darko's crotch, palming against his package, gently trying to bring him to erection with the heavy friction of his palm against the denim of his jeans. "Come on, baby, you know I give good sugar, but you gotta want it." Hemi pressed in, his hand trying to work Darko up, but Darko's body was just as reluctant to step up to the plate to be played with by Hemi as his emotions were.

Darko turned his head and closed his eyes, maybe if he just visualized the man he did want rubbing up against him, then maybe he could trick his dick into becoming hard. He tipped his head back, emptying the last of his ale in one long chain of endless swallows and still— *nothing.*

A shuffle out in the bar and the crash of a falling chair shocked Darko from his thoughts, his eyes popped open to see a man rushing for the front door. Odd how the man kind of looked like Maxum from the back, down to the details of the navy wool peacoat he often wore.

Okay, enough was enough. His body wasn't into Hemi tonight, neither was his head. Now he was fooling himself into thinking he was seeing the man that did stir him but didn't want him in return.

Fuck this.

"Hemi." Darko pushed his friend off, giving him a reluctant shake of his head, "It's just not gonna work tonight."

Hemi's arms tried to sweep around him again, but Darko just brushed him off. That was the thing with Hemi, the one of many things severely lacking for Darko; the man was too much a last resort lover. No fire, no octane. He was vanilla without the bean spice. Yet a good friend. Darko caressed the man's cheek with his palm a moment then slipped past him. "I'll see you guys at practice." He grabbed his coat and slung it on as he headed out.

The New York cold slapped his face as soon as he stepped out. Somehow or another he figured he deserved it, some self-suffering or shit. But damned if he knew why. He had done all he could to do right by Maxum. *Octane.* Never mind too much octane, there was too much NOS. Not that he was complaining. He was loving every drop of it, but how do you convince a man you can still have a real and deeply committed relationship while burning bright like that? He obviously failed that attempt and now he was stuck trying to cope with accepting his life would have to settle for something far more mediocre. Having glimpsed and tasted what he wanted now— *that idea sucked.*

He turned and headed down the sidewalk, grateful to have the long walk ahead of him. The ice on the roads forced him to leave the bike at home, that and he had fully intended to drink Maxum off his brain. Not sure, what happened to that plan since he wasn't near as buzzed as he wanted to be, he obviously failed that one too.

Darko didn't even glance over his shoulder when the car cruised up, rolling just a wheel width behind him, and revved its engine a bit.

"Get in," a man called from the vehicle.

"Get lost! Hookers are around back." Darko turned to shoot the driver a hard stare but froze in his tracks. There weren't too many men driving around in Pagani Zonda Roadsters in this city and certainly only one would dare be caught in front of a gay bar. Now Darko was more than just annoyed, he was livid on a number of levels.

He stepped up to the car, dropped his hands on the door rim, and bent down to peer in through the rolled down passenger window, "*You* can especially fuck off!"

"I didn't ask. Now get in," Maxum growled out with an equal amount of frustration and anger.

"I'm not some cheap fuck you can just snatch up when your other lover fails to get your nuts off. Go blow another ten grand, maybe the fairy will put out this time. You can surely afford it. I'm not for sale." Darko shoved off the car and stomped down the sidewalk at a fast pace.

The high-end rocket car lurched forward with a whiny, high-pitched rev then idled down as it rolled beside him.

"Get in before the police come patrolling by and really think I'm cruising for ass!"

"Aren't you? Go home, Maxum. I'm not the man for you. You said so yourself, remember?"

The car revved again and lurched forward, jumping over the curb in front of Darko, blocking the sidewalk. Darko stopped, his lips rolling in a tight purse while his jaw clenched, biting back the words he wanted to say. The pain he didn't want to admit to.

He sidestepped to go around only to have the car roll backwards, blocking him still.

"Dammit, Maxum!"

"Then get in and say it to my face!" Maxum called out to him.

Darko bent over, eyes flaring at the man inside the car. "Oh, don't even try going there. You're the one who's been playing both sides of the fence here!" he yelled back, making it vividly clear there wasn't a sweet word between them.

"And now I'm telling you to get in!" Maxum revved the car and slammed the stick into gear. "Before I decide to just run your ass over!"

Darko straightened, fury grinding in his bones, but he wanted some answers. Like why Maxum was here and, why the hell he kept running in the first place? The answers, if he got them, would be worth a short ride.

Darko grabbed the car door and jerked it open, dropped into the seat, and slammed it shut. Mentally envisioning breaking something as he did. His gaze straightforward, jaw clenched shut as Maxum drove them deeper into the city.

The silent tension had only built between them as Maxum drove them to the new Beekman Tower— the odd skyscraper of twisting steel and glass that stood higher than anything else for the time being. Darko did his best not to look surprised when Maxum entered a key card and the gates on the third floor of the adjacent parking garage opened up to another level reserved all for Maxum and the collection of cars he'd obtained over the years. *He owns an island, remember?* Darko mentally berated himself with loathing silent sarcasm.

His gaze silently shifting from one parking space to another, noting the variety of exotic sports cars, a few classics and a few he wasn't sure what classification they fell into. Yet, each held a charm for a boyish delight hidden in the grown man Darko had fallen for. He turned, glancing at the stricken face as Maxum parked. Emotions like billows of smoke jetting out around him like a roadster spinning its wheels and ready to take off down the track. *Damn him.*

They went in through a side door reserved for private residents, allowing them to bypass the hotel entry that took up the whole lower main section of the tower. An elevator took them up beyond the hotel and up through the business section that made up the second tier. The elevator ride was a straight shot up towards the top before being accessible to any of the upper floors. Dropping them off on the private access, Terrace-2 level; first floor, third tier.

And all the way up, the tension grew still, only now Darko's anger was smoldering into need. Oh, he fully planned to drill into the man; with his cock, first, *then* he'd have his answers.

"You live here?" he asked as Maxum led him down the corridor passed a few doors until they came to the last flat at the end of the hall.

"Yes," Maxum answered with a flat tone as he pulled his wallet out.

"Batchlor pad for rent boys?'

Maxum glared at him. No. This is my home. One of one."

"You know there's still several more floors up." Darko goaded for the man's vanity if only to mask his own gaping.

"Yes, but I have the terrace." The exalted claim trumping any notion that *he who has the top floor had the better spot*. After all, twenty-five more floors when you were already fifty-one floors up didn't make the ants below look any different. It was the added accessory that made *his* the cut above all the others, and he knew it. Maxum swiped the credit card sized key through the security slot on the wall and showed his abducted guest inside.

Darko glanced around; the place was immaculate and spacious. And the exterior glass walls made it accessibly viewable— to anyone with a helicopter that is. A man this rich could afford a mansion so why here? "I can't even begin to guess how much this place costs or comprehend why you'd want to pay it."

"I'm one of the investors for the developer. I worked out a deal for it. Besides, I like living in the city and I'll be damned if I was going to sit in my office and look at this thing and not live in it."

"Work?" Darko asked and for the answer, Maxum pointed out one of the glass walls that looked out over the city. Darko followed the direction of the finger and glanced across at the Woolworth's Tower just the other side of the park below.

Okay that explained it— potent flavors, fancy foods, fast machines, strong men and king of the hill egos. His eyes swept across the space as he moved further inside. It all seemed so familiar to him. Like it had been designed and laid out to meet his own taste and that's when it struck him. It could have passed for his place, in the way of druthers in furniture and color, except the part where the things in Darko's own flat cost only a few hundred dollars in total. Maxum clearly had paid out for the several-thousand-dollar upgrade.

He turned, still taking it all in until his eyes came on Maxum, and he froze. The air around them going silent. All but the mutely intense smoldering between them like fire and brimstone being stoked up with a fan. *Fight or fuck.* Those were the only choices they had right now and he didn't figure Maxum had brought him to his home to fight. That became evidently certain when Maxum stepped toward him, reaching out and grabbed Darko's coat collar, tugging him in until their mouths met in a crushing embrace.

Fuck or fight.

Darko's mind launched into a decision because if he didn't give into a fierce fucking, he was going to start a fight. Too much emotion, too much nitrous oxide fuel between them to go unchallenged in some form or another. Of course, he wasn't opposed to ruining another set of clothes either. He fought his way into Maxum's coat finding the buttoned down shirt and ripped it open, sending buttons pinging and bouncing across the hard wood floors.

Maxum reciprocated. His own hands finding their way under Darko's shirt and latched on to his nipples with a commanding pinch before palming roughly down toward his belt. Like gladiators in a battle, they fought more for control of who was getting whom naked first, and few things came off without some form of damage. The only thing left were a pair of denim jeans and a pair of slacks between the two of them. Flies open and hungry, angry cocks jutting out to salute the other's arousal.

Darko's cock swelled with full, rutting life. "Fuck, yes." He lunged, grabbing Maxum around the nape and dragged him in for a hard, grinding kiss, complete with the clank of teeth, and bruised lips. Just as their tongues met, demanding a rougher tangle for domination, he pressed his hips forward, his shaft coming in full contact, finding the other man's cock just as eager to meet on certain terms.

"Damn you," Maxum growled, both his hands coming up along Darko's head, gripping at the curls of coffee-black hair. He pulled him tight in his grip and wrenched his lips away. "I shouldn't want this."

The confession rubbed over raw emotions inside Darko and his fiery lust turned bitter in an instant— *fuck or fight*. Looks like they were fighting after all. "Oh, well, here." His hands slamming against Maxum's chest and shoved him away, "Let me arrange that for you." He turned for the door.

❦

Darko hit him so hard it forced Maxum back, nearly stumbling off his feet, he caught himself but seeing the man heading for the door had him filled with a rage he didn't know what to do with. "Don't you dare walk out that door!"

Darko only barely turned, glaring heatedly at him over his shoulder. "You better have a damn good reason for bringing me here. Because I don't usually hang around to play games."

"I tried to stay away!"

"You were getting good at it too."

"No, I wasn't. And when I saw that man pawing at you—"

"Oh, now I see." Darko came about to get in Maxum's face. "You don't want me, but you'll be damned if you'll let anyone else have me either. Is that it?"

"No!"

❦

Darko' protesting insides were in full rage. "Really? First Club Pain— that was you, wasn't it? That I saw running out? Then the Wine Cellars. Now this?" But there was another, far more pressing question nagging at him and Darko let it out with an accusing bellow. "What the hell are you afraid of?!"

"You!" Maxum's answer came back in a flash, "I don't know how the hell I can control you, to make sure you stay!"

"Maybe I don't need control!" Darko stormed towards him. "Maybe I am perfectly capable of knowing exactly where I belong best." The space between then snapped shut by their bodies and Darko's mouth came crashing over Maxum's, forcing its way in for a deep hard probe that ignited carnal lust from the start and there was no refusing the heated exchange this time. Instantly they were both clawing at each other's bodies. Darko's jeans forcibly getting pushed down by his own hand as well as Maxum's, until they pooled at his ankles. Maxum's slacks were next. Mouths locked, hands claiming bodily flesh when their clothes lay at their feet. Darko started walking their bodies towards the large sectional sofa in the middle of the living space. "Forget all you're rationalizing and just let yourself have what you want," Darko growled between brutal kissing.

Maxum took a parting step from him. "It's not that simple. What my body wants and what my head wants are two different things."

"What does your body want?"

"It wants you."

"Then *I* am what you are going to get tonight."

The second those words passed Darko's lips, and his fingers reached out to brush against Maxum's lower belly— *such a fucking erogenous zone for him*— Maxum shuddered and pounced. Any shred of resistance to maintain some kind of distance or control evaporated in a shot. The chance of going slow ceased to exist, not that it ever had much of a chance with them anyways. Maxum clutched onto Darko's head and delved in for a violent kiss of ownership, forcing his way inside the man's mouth and marking territory with every lick and bite.

Hot, firm male flesh burned a brand into Maxum's hands everywhere he touched, and the fact that he felt up the man he wanted with a frightening intensity only spurred the dangerous lover on more.

Darko kissed, licked, and chewed over his lips and jawline, while his hands ran wild all over Maxum's body in return, growling his burning need and rough intention to him under his breath every time their mouths broke for air.

Maxum parroted the same growling conjectures back, and that somehow turned Darko on even more.

Darko dove his tongue into Maxum's mouth with the same aggressive manner he wanted to rip into the man's ass, hoping the kiss would give him a measure of reprieve. Instead, it only ratcheted Darko's base desires up another dozen notches and thickened his cock to a wickedly rigid and painful degree. Everything inside Darko flared up for more— faster, quicker, and hotter— like an engine burning rich. He was full open throttle so his body could achieve release inside Maxum's body. And he didn't care how he achieved it.

Unable to fight the tornado of need tearing through him, Darko severed the kiss and shoved Maxum facedown onto the back of the living room sofa. "I need a condom."

"Back pocket." Maxum growled back over his shoulder; the carnal sound more warning to get on with it, than concern for the requested protection.

Darko shot a look over his shoulder to the black slacks on the floor. "Don't you dare fucking move," he ordered, stepping for the slacks, snatched them up, and searched the crumbled fabric to find the pocket. He recovered the wallet, fished out the foil package, and tore into it with his teeth.

"Damn it, Darko, hurry up and fuck me or so help me, I am going to flip you over, and drill you myself!"

Darko was already right behind him, his hips shot forward slapping Maxum's ass, sending him into the sofa. His cock crushed between his belly and the crevice of Maxum's cheeks. He rocked his hips with a teasing motion and dipped down letting the blunt end drag against Maxum in a long stroke of affirmation of his position and claim. "The hell you will." Darko stepped back, hands spreading Maxum's cheeks apart and bent down to silence the fussing. His hot breath blew against Maxum's hole and then he tongued over the surface, delivering his subject to a trembling mess. From the foil, Darko discarded the condom, using only the lube packet, and spread it over his hard shaft. He stood, keeping Maxum pinned down with a firm hand on his back, stroking over his hard flesh a savoring moment, then lined-up the head against the tight pucker and punched in.

Maxum's entire body tensed up at the abruptness of Darko's entering him, but salacious greed overruled— the muscles relented and he pushed back, forcing the head of Darko's cock past the tight ring of muscle. They both growled out a gasp that only slightly transformed into moans as Darko slid in deeper. Darko's hand came over Maxum's where he held on to the sofa back, his fingers interlocking into his then fisted over, pinning him as the slide of Darko's cock continued it's descent. The grip Darko put on Maxum's fingers might have crushed a man with smaller hands, but Maxum welcomed the bruising force. He felt the invading body folding over him, feeling the husky breath just as Darko's lips came to rest against Maxum's cheek, whispering, "I've never enjoyed a man as much as I enjoy you, *dragi.*" Darko seemed to curse out a foreign word Maxum could only assume was Serbian and yet nothing else existed. That was until— *oh sweet fucking God in Heaven, baby*— Darko's hips bunched against his ass and Maxum felt the last several inches of his cock pushed all the way into his ass until Darko was fully seated inside him.

Maxum moaned low and deep. It felt like his ass opened up in welcome to accept Darko inside. Once Darko had buried every inch to the root, Maxum's passage closed around him in a squeezing vice. It felt different, like there were more nerve endings involved this time, more delicious abrasion and— he spun about shooting a hot glance over his shoulder at Darko. "You didn't put the condom on?" Shock rang through his system.

"That's right." Darko remained folded over him to growl in his ear.

Maxum could even feel the gloating smile.

"I know damn well you don't let anyone else inside you and I've never shared this with anyone but you. So tonight— nothing between us. I intend to brandish my name inside your body, because by god, if this is the last time I ever get to fuck you— you're going to remember me being here for the rest of your life."

Darko drew back through the clamping fist Maxum's inner walls put on his shaft, moaning as every thick inch sparked friction in Maxum's ass on its way out. Leaving Maxum empty and begging for just a heartbeat, before Darko pushed back in with a sharper, less controlled thrust. Fiery discomfort tempered around Maxum's entrance, but his grunt was one of pure base pleasure at feeling Darko invade his very being.

"Oh damn— Maxum— Maxum." Darko pumped his cock into his lover a third and a fourth time. "Fuck yes— it's so fucking incredible inside you." Letting go of one of Maxum's hands, Darko burrowed his fingers into Maxum's hair and pressed his own face into the side of Maxum's head. "You feel so fucking tight and hot. Like you were made for my cock and mine alone," Darko breathed the sultry dirty words heavily against Maxum's cheek, dampening the skin with beads of sweat.

Maxum careened his head around to look despite the fist that gripped into his hair, holding him. He found Darko's heated gaze, eyes wide, holding some feral depth of polished azure. A moment's pause for some silent communication between them as their eyes met. Driving hunger spoke wordless intents from Darko to Maxum that this night was a matter of no-holds-barred fucking and branding. It's what Maxum was wanting and he was about to get it. When the licentious connection was over, the onslaught of a wild fucking cut loose and there would be no stopping either of them until they had crossed the finish line.

As if he couldn't control himself, Darko cursed repeatedly as he used his dick to pierce Maxum's body again and again and again, stretching his hole— *so fucking good.* They both clamped their jaws as Darko roughly asked, "Am I hurting you?"

"Ahh, fuck no— so hot. Keep fucking me, babe," Maxum growled, trying his best to push his ass back into each drilling from Darko's cock, *wanting* with everything in him, to feel overpowered by this man. "Don't stop." He twisted with every intention to lick over Darko's arm, only Maxum bit into him instead as Darko speared into his ass with a pointed shot and took him to the hilt, ending with a rough grind into Maxum's stretched hole.

"Fuck me! Harder, damn you!" Maxum pleaded without censor. He tossed his head back in a violent launch to stand erect against the man drilling him one throttle at a time from behind. Maxum careened his neck around and bit at flesh blindly, nipping Darko's chin who complied to the command, picking up speed, and pounded Maxum's ass with more force. Each strike from Darko into Maxum's shaft clearly fueled them both for more and the harder they went at each other. Darko used full force of his hips, pile-driving Maxum into the back of the sofa with a precision throttling, time and again. Forcing the sofa to bang against the floor, working its way out of arrangement with the other sections.

Building sweat dripped from Darko's body to Maxum's back, and each thrust of Darko's hips sent his balls slapping against the smooth skin of Maxum's inner thighs in the most knee-buckling manner.

"So fucking hot and tight, Maxum," Darko murmured, his voice full of raw awe. He shifted down into a deep micro grinding only long enough to lean down over Maxum, his tongue licking over Maxum's ear, tracing along the shell to lick a line down the slope of his shoulder. "Never felt anything like you in my life." He rotated away; drawing almost completely out then sank into Maxum again, this time stuffing Maxum full with the slowest damn easing-in of his cock. He squeezed Maxum's hand and pressed a soft kiss to his shoulder blade. "And you will never find another one like me who can fuck you like this." Darko shifted suddenly, yanking his hand from its holding sending them both folding over the back, where the thrusting started up again.

Maxum couldn't hold onto his struggle any longer and he folded over the sofa, his face landing in the seat cushions, his cock intrepidly wedged under him, getting jacked by the pounding slide of his body over the soft buttery leather upholstery.

"Darko— oh fuck— please, baby." Emotion began to overwhelm Maxum, while his body was surrendered to pure salacious sensation. Making him moan relentlessly in a way he never had when taking a cock before. With his ass filled to capacity, Maxum's prick stiffened to a painful degree. His nuts grew more sensitive with every slap of skin, and his rectum clenched in a brutal hold around Darko's buried thickness. Maxum groaned again, his cheek planted in the seat cushion, but reveled in the sudden arrival of Darko's chin right there on his shoulder.

Somehow, Maxum found a blur of eye contact through the closeness and shadows and locked onto Darko's desire-filled stare. "Make me feel you inside me forever." God, he didn't know what he was saying, yet bizarre words blundered from his lips regardless of his purpose or not in them.

ᑎᴥᑎ

Darko's breath caught audibly. The motion rolled through his whole body and slid his cock deliciously within Maxum's silky inner walls.

Darko tugged on Maxum's hair, lowering his voice as he went in for a kiss. He teased over Maxum's lips against the edge of his mouth with the tip of his tongue. "There's a reason why we're meant for each other—" his forehead came to rest on Maxum's temple. Darko placed his lips right on Maxum's ear and softly spoke the answer, "High Octane." He pistoned into Maxum, sending his hips deeper into the sofa back. "I like badass motorcycles with lots of power, torque, and flare. You like sports cars, fast, exotic, and rare." He shifted, his body climbing and re-angling. When Darko settled for a new angle and tempo, he burrowed his forehead into the back of Maxum's head with a hard roll, as his hips curled up grinding even deeper inside him, forcing them both to let out a hot growl. "You like strong flavors. Musky, hot, masculine spicy. It doesn't get any better than me. Anything else is lifeless. And just like the precision machines we like to ride, with proper care, they last forever."

Darko lifted one of Maxum's legs setting it up on the sofa back, following in the position with his own leg and throttled up into him harder and deeper than he'd ever been inside the man. His own hunger devoured in the instant, chewing him up, and spitting him back out. He closed his eyes only to find the room spinning out of control underneath them. "Oh fuck, I'm gonna cum," Darko growled into the back of Maxum's head. He didn't want to, not just yet, but he wasn't in control any more. There was no stopping the storm of piqued sensations coalescing in his balls, drawing up, and preparing to fire. He felt the tightening— his scrotum— his thighs— everything spiraling up. His mouth gaped open, trying to say Maxum's name, but nothing came out. Pistoning, throttling up the pressure like a combustible spring that coiled up tighter and tighter, driving him torturously toward release. He felt the pressure kick over in his balls, his entire body twisting into one supercharged quaver, folding over inside Maxum's body. Where one ended, the other began, but damn if Darko knew where the lines were just now. He cried out, then in an instant came down, and latched on to Maxum's shoulder. Biting into him like some savage beast claiming his wild mate.

Darko's hips jerked up into Maxum several times, his arms spiraling around his waist, lifting his hips so Darko could climb in even deeper with an undulating roll of his hips. His thrusts forced Maxum's cock against the back of the sofa and igniting his own release to let go. Maxum's ass sucked a vacuum all around the embedded cock with his prostate orgasm.

"*Ahhhhh*— fuck!" Maxum gasped, "*Ah*, fuck." He bucked beneath Darko with a bone-jarring jolt, and he cried out as pain shot through his hips and thighs. The sharp, lightning lanced over his muscles, calling them to contort, but he pumped his rigid, ultrasensitive cock into the pillow back repeatedly in the throes of a second release that had his cock soaking the leather upholstery with a puddle of cum trapped between it and him.

They both shared in the post struggle, gasping for breath as Darko's load still shot out inside Maxum. The euphoric release sweetened by the tight hug of Maxum's shaft.

"Damn, I can feel you coming all around me." Darko kissed the back of his head, soaked with damp hair now. "Can you feel me soaking your walls," he growled with a ragged breath as another sharp contraction inside Maxum suffocated his cock. Darko slumped over him and surrendered to his panting. "It's incredible."

Maxum pulled Darko's arm around to where he could reach him and kissed it with everything in him, needing the contact, terrified of losing himself completely as the orgasm continued slamming through him with the power of a category five storm. Maxum's ass contracted again, and Darko pushed into him with one final throttle, shuddering as the last of his rattled through his body.

Still heaving and trying to regain his breath in the aftermath, Maxum attempted to push up, but Darko kept him pinned to the sofa back with his solid frame.

With his face buried in the curve of Maxum's neck, Darko muttered, "Don't move a muscle," Just before he nipped at Maxum's nape. "I'm not done with you yet."

Darko began creating a roadmap of kisses across Maxum's shoulders and upper back, and immediately started stirring recently sated body parts. Maxum hadn't even regained his breathing when he started to feel the tremble in his body as Darko brushed his lips over his back and sipped at the perspiration dotting his flesh. He sucked in new air with every contact of nubby-chin hair from the man's proficient tongue. Darko let go of him to add his fingers to the mix, grazing the pads of his fingertips over skin in a way that raised the hairs all over Maxum's body. As Darko licked and kissed his way down his spine, Maxum burrowed his face into the cushion, stifling yet another moan. His whole body was lit up, still sensitized from the fierce fucking. His cock twitched in its fight to get hard again. When Darko reached the cleft of his ass, the man grazed his teeth over the globes of fleshy curves and then he felt the blow of cool air right down his crack. The sofa leather creaked under the movement between Maxum's thighs, and immediately thereafter the pad of a finger brushed down Maxum's crease and across his still-pulsating ring.

"Shit— oh shit." A second passage of Darko's finger over Maxum's tender hole shot every nerve ending in his ass to new life. Maxum couldn't help it. His legs bunched up, leaving his body just dangling over the sofa, but his arms pushed up, arching his back inward he sent his ass out towards the man's taunting playing. "What are you doing?" He growled, Maxum knew what he wanted, but he didn't dare hope. Not right now. Not in this moment.

Maxum felt rather than saw Darko's smile. The imprint fucking branded the top curve of his left butt cheek. "Finishing what you brought me here for." Darko murmured. "You may not think I am long term keeper material," —he spread Maxum's ass cheeks and licked his way down the crack— "but I don't think I should leave my man hungry for something he loves." With that, Darko flicked his tongue back and forth over Maxum's rear entrance, racing heightened awareness to the recently used cluster of nerves.

Oh, shit. Goddamn motherfucking son of a bitch.

Darko continued to tease his tongue all around Maxum's pucker, and with a hoarse noise he couldn't stifle, Maxum shamelessly pushed into the contact. Nobody had ever rimmed him after fucking him, and the sharpened, extra sensitivity to his recently taken hole and passage increased the sensations a hundredfold. Maxum already craved this brand of kiss more than he liked his partners knowing, and Darko somehow figuring it out, making it better, and more intimate by licking him at this moment shredded what little if any reserves Maxum had left.

"Tell me, lover," Darko's tongue traced over the under curves of his ass as he spoke, "Has that boyfriend of yours ever done this to you?" And just then Darko sank his tongue deep against the loosened rim of Maxum's hole.

Unfathomable pleasure racked Maxum's body, jamming up his thoughts so he couldn't speak. He could only moan and toss unrecognized curses to establish he was overwhelmed by the carnal attention Darko lavished his rectum with. Nevertheless, the answer was no. Simeon was not a thrill-running lover. He was a receiver and little else. He had been the dowdy wife every man complained about because he wasn't getting any at home. Despite that, what Sim had been, was consistent. Simeon could win over even the stuffiest of crowds at a business social, which made it easy to take him to the number of boorish dinners and fundraiser events Maxum was so often expected to attend because of his money.

Darko was none of these. The man burned through his system like a herd of stallions, leaving Maxum's mind and his body unhitched and thrown from its axis. He was a total whirlwind in the man's company; just having him in his thoughts was lethal. Come morning, Darko would be gone, back on his twin-engine horse, and riding off for the next lover who begged for his acrid touch. However, right now, it was his own body that was doing the singeing under a touch Maxum had never had. He was no stranger to giving the pleasure of rimming, but he'd never been on the receiving end.

"Fucking do it. Do it." Every guttural moan Maxum released sounded less and less human. He circled his ass into Darko's face, mindless of whether the other man wanted it, or to how the motion enhanced the tightness growing in his leg. "Eat me."

Darko let out a tight growl, his face burying between Maxum's buttocks. He smacked Maxum's ass and then held him wide open again, switching from fluttering his tongue to full-on sucking, to finally probing into Maxum's hole.

Maxum encouraged him with base, coarse language, and Darko accommodated with every swat, lick, and piercing he did to Maxum's fluttering ring, all the while murmuring noises that made it seem as if he enjoyed it as much as Maxum did.

Another intense wave crashed through like a storm, washing away Maxum's turmoiled thoughts, leaving nothing behind, but gibberish and curses trying to hang onto reality.

His body strained with tension as he rocked back on the attack from Darko's mouth. Just when Maxum didn't think he could even breathe anymore, let alone handle the pleasure Darko so freely offered, his adrenalin lover speared into him with his tongue again and slipped it inside Maxum's ass. "Oh fuck, fuck, fuck!" Maxum let loose another shout that scratched his throat. *Yes.* Darko stabbed just into Maxum's body again and again, tongue fucking each of the countless nerve endings there into a wild delirium. The action swirled Maxum down into a vortex of obliterating desire where nothing else mattered. Darko flicked and sucked Maxum's tender hole and then moaned before nudging his tongue into Maxum's sensitized ass once more. Every move was drenched in such intimacy they quickly catapulted Maxum toward his endgame.

"Help me," Maxum was now reduced to begging. His emotions zinging as high as his body was and his shields completely melted away. His very being writhing from top to bottom, shaking out of control, Maxum shoved his hand between his legs to grab his straining cock. Just as Maxum wrapped his hand around his dick and pulled, Darko swiped the flat of his tongue from the back of his balls all the way up his taint, and over his sensitized pucker, then finished it off with a hard nip to his left ass cheek.

Darko vanished from his backside and when Maxum was able to summon up enough brain cells to look, he found Darko coming around in front of him then dropped down on the sofa and wriggled up under him. Darko grabbed his legs and coaxed Maxum to come fully over the sofa and before he knew it, Maxum's knees straddled Darko's head, and he was feeding his cock to the man.

Maxum's head lulled back, drenched in a dizzy wave as Darko sucked in the whole of his half flaccid cock that wasn't going to stay that way for much longer the way Darko moved his mouth to nurse him into a painfully rigid condition. Darko's head bobbed up and down to suck him in and out, stem to tip; his tongue greedily washing every inch along the way.

Maxum felt Darko's hands sliding over his hips, petting him more so than holding him. Caressing over the curves of his ass. Fingers stretching their way into his crease until one finally made its way into his used hole, and steadily began finger-fucking him to match the attention his cock was getting inside Darko's mouth. As a consequence, the painfully sweet contraction in his balls fired off and he was cumming way faster than he thought possible. Maxum yanked his hips back, pulling his cock free from Darko's mouth, and quickly wrapped his fist over his shaft, jerking off with a mad frenzy. He forced his eyes open, watching the alluring man under him, looking down at him, waiting for the prize.

"*Ahhhh!*" Maxum's head kicked back on his shoulders, sending his verbal release to the ceiling as ropes of cum shot over Darko's face and chest.

When the aftershocks subsided enough, he practically crumpled over Darko, landing in arms that welcomed his weight over him. They kissed with simple connections of their lips, too exhausted and spent to do much more. The product of their sex pressed between their sweaty bodies and scented the whole room around them.

Maxum dropped his forehead to Darko's, hovering there for a long moment while they still settled to restore a normal breath between them. He finally let out a harsh moan, unable to form words to label the moment in his memory. Then finally chuckled to himself, slumping over to wriggle in between Darko and the sofa back, where he surrendered completely.

They drifted in and out of slumber, limbs caught up in a chaotic embrace of arms and legs stretched out over the sofa, Maxum's mind never going completely silent. After the brutal, unrelenting fucking Darko had just delivered to his ass, he would not have been surprised if the lover, who kept him so off axis it scared him, had left him to deal with his own skeletons, and the pain of a fuck-em and leave-em aftermath. However, that was not where they were right now. The man who had topped him with full ownership, was now surrendered to his arms for post coital cuddling. An act Maxum had a weakness for and received so little of in his life. And that— that had him leveled. How was it that the very same man who fucked like a beast could also curl up like a pussycat in his lap?

Brimstone and caramel.

It didn't make any sense. He didn't even have to ask for it.

Unable to silence the race of thoughts in his mind, he fished out the remote that had gotten pushed down between the cushions and turned on the big screen tv, careful to mute out the sound first. Instantly, the screen filled with the whizzing blurring colors of formula racecars speeding past a track camera. It's luminous glow spilling out into the room to create eerie shadows.

He watched as one after another sped by with violent down-shifts on the RPMs just as the specifically designed vehicles went into the hair pin turns then throttled down and gunned it before they even cleared the last curl, shooting for the straight-a-way.

Maxum could feel his heart pounding in his chest, felt the adrenalin rush coursing through his veins even now, as he lay sated and spent, next to the man who was ultimately, and intimately his racetrack.

This wasn't fucking helping him at all. Yet he was nearly startled when he saw his own hand of its own validity roaming over Darko's body in the darkness. Mapping out every detail, every hairpin turn. The soft hairs that stopped half way up Darko's thighs. The love knots just over his hips. Darko's cock now flaccid and laying over his thigh, still sticky with their juices.

Shit.

Maxum pulled his hand away and scrubbed over his face. *What the fuck was wrong with him?* Something wasn't right inside. His chest wasn't just pounding, it was hurting, and all he could think about was putting his hand back where it was and finishing what he started. Loving the body next to him.

"While watching formula racing at two in the morning isn't new, it's not what I am in the mood for, but you either turn the volume up or start talking," the groggy voice grumbled just as Darko rolled to look up at him with those deep blue eyes of his.

Maxum took a deep breath, scrunching up his face; he was so deep in his own lost mind it took a moment for the voiced order to even make sense to him. "I'm okay. Just fighting sleep."

"Bullshit." Darko repositioned until he was flat on his back over Maxum's lap and now looked up at him more solidly. "The fucking gears grinding in your head are making so much noise, I can't sleep with them."

Another deep breath and whether Maxum had intended to actually reveal his insecurities they came out anyways and regrettably in a manner that irrefutably sent them both in the wrong direction, and one they weren't going to be able to back down off of. "Tell me who that man was back at the bar."

"Hemi? He's a friend as well as a member on my rowing team."

"And what else? Why did you let him touch you so freely?"

"He comes with benefits and nothing else, if I want it."

"Do you let him fuck you, when you want it?"

Darko sat up, removing himself from the comforts of Maxum's body and turned to glare at him. The way Darko saw it was if he was going to get hit with accusations, he was going to be in a position more suitable for his defense. "I don't let *any* man fuck me."

"I fuck you," Maxum groaned, dropping his forehead into his hand propped on his elbow on the sofa arm.

"Yeah, and you're such a pain in the ass about it, I don't know why I bother."

Maxum saw the track he had laid out now, but he couldn't turn back. He needed to understand or rather, he was pushing for an excuse to stop feeling what he feared he was. His hand came down over his face, scrubbing at it a few times then glanced at Darko watching and waiting for the next stone to be tossed. "So, this friends with benefits and nothing else arrangement— that's what you like in a man?" He shook his head, suddenly furious with himself that he'd gone after this man again only to hurt himself in the end. Darko was everything he desired and all of what he feared in a man. He didn't even give Darko a chance to answer. "I can't do this with you." Maxum bolted off the sofa and began to pace across the room, "I can't have a no-strings-attached relationship. I need something steady. Anything else would wreck my life."

Even though Darko had already pulled from Maxum's arms, the absence of their closeness in the cooling air of the room was immediate against Darko's skin when Maxum moved away. "Funny you should say that because any notion of something beyond fucking your ass and all I see is your *ass* leaving."

"It's all we have. It's all that you want."

"No. What I want is *you*." He caught Maxum by the wrist when he paced back within reach and pulled him down over him, despite Maxum's reluctance to return to his side. "Nothing. But. You. Only I want you all the time. Not just for the intense fucking, when you feel up to some strange away from that clog wearing, light loafer you call a boyfriend." Darko reached up, his fingers tangling into the nape of Maxum's neck and pulled him to drop back on the sofa with him drawing him in for a deep kiss. "Of course, don't expect me to give that part up either." He released his grip, letting his hand slide down the man's chest as he straightened beside the sofa, his eyes following, enjoying what he saw as well as touched. But he saw those gears still cranking away inside Maxum, he could only try one more ploy to get him to let go and trust him. "Remember all the gay-harmony rubbish I pitched to you that one night?"

"Yeah, I remember." Maxum pushed back up to his feet and stepped away.

"It wasn't rubbish." Darko let his head drop back onto the pile leather cushions, staring up at the ceiling letting out a heavy sigh. He wouldn't lie here and tell fairytales of who or what they could be together. Intense passion begat intense everything else. They already showed their equilibrium to pull away as hard as they slammed into each other. But he couldn't deny his feelings to try and have Maxum in his life. He couldn't explain what it was, but the chemistry, the burning attraction was beyond just lust. He just didn't know how to put it into words that Maxum would hear or convince Maxum to stay around long enough for them to share anything but the sex. And they both seemed to be refusing to put that part of their engagements off.

Darko popped his head up to look at the man standing beautifully naked in the middle of the room. Maxum looked like he'd leave any minute now. Run away. Only problem was this was Maxum's place. "Be my date for New Year's."

Maxum drew away once more, going back to his pacing, and his heavily laden thoughts, shaking his head. "No, I can't."

"Sure you can. There's a big bash being held by some of my brother's friends and I've been invited. Who knows, it might be fun." What he didn't tell him was it was a fundraiser being hosted by Diesel Gentry for the cancer center. The last thing he wanted Maxum to think was he would use him the same way his boyfriend did. He wasn't asking Maxum out to make a donation, he just wanted the man to be with him someplace outside the bedroom. Or within range of some other easily fucking accessible area of the homes they occupied.

Maxum sauntered over to the sofa and sat along the edge with an almost apologetic expression. "No, I already have plans and I can't break them. Obligations that are expected of me."

"Fine. We can go to both; we'll start at one and finish off at another." Darko reached out with a lazy hand to pull him down, but Maxum swung his hand out of his reach and pushed off the sofa once more. It was clear Maxum wanted to be near but not close enough that his barriers could be breached.

Maxum stabbed his fingers into his hair, combing it back forcefully. "I told you this can't work."

Darko's last-ditch hope faded. He had been left in the dark for too many days with this one, only to run into him at one of this *fancy-shmancy* socials parading the very man Maxum was supposed to have called it off with. Then out of nowhere he showed up like a prowling roadster, wanting to go for a ride on the hotrod tracks. Darko was starting to realize just how used he had been, despite any emotions that Maxum displayed that he was hoping told him it wasn't intentional. But enough was enough, he couldn't call a man into the pit that didn't want to be on his team. "What can't?"

"This— whatever you want to call it, this relationship. It won't work between us."

"What relationship?" Darko sat upright to interject, "You're so intent on running and rejecting, you haven't even let it have a chance, yet so quick to shun it. Tell me, Maxum, why have you been following me? Why do you keep showing up if we can't be anything with each other?"

Maxum's face tensed, Darko could see the ripple of clenching muscles along the man's jaw while he strode to source out a viable argument, but just then the phone rang. Maxum let out a hard huff, his eyes glancing at the time posted on his wrist.

There was probably only one person who dared call Maxum at three in the fucking morning and unless Maxum had clients in Japan, Darko was certain he could guess it right on the first try.

And, as if to pay off on the silent bet in his head, Simeon's voice came over the answering machine, trailing down the corridor toward them from wherever the machine was stashed away. They both listened as if hearing the ticking of a time bomb set to go off any second when they both heard the voice over the phone, *"Come over, Hon, I missed you tonight."*

The line cut off and the air around them went dead silent. All except for the growing discontent Darko was feeling inside that seemed to roar inside his head. The phone rang again and once more Maxum made no move to answer, letting the machine do it. *"Maxi won't you at least talk to me? I know you didn't mean what you said and I forgive you. Just come over and it will all work itself out."*

When it rang a third time, Maxum still made no move to answer it. He stood there locked in place. His eyes smoldering. Something had jammed up in the gears now and Darko was guessing it was him, he was still the fucking affair.

When the machine picked up, the wailing act of a desperate man came across. *"I'm going to kill myself if you don't talk to me, Maxi, hon. Please. I'm gonna do it, I mean it."*

Maxum dropped to the sofa, elbows landing on knees and his face fell into his hands. "I can't deal with this," he mumbled, then let out a raging growl of pent up aggravation, before throwing his hands down and surrendering to the caller's ploy.

But to whom was Maxum mumbling it to, Darko wasn't sure. To him? Or to himself? Either way, he wasn't planning on sticking around for any more of it. He watched as Maxum grabbed the phone from the table and without even glancing in his direction answered, playing out his best *you just woke me up* tone, "It's late— is anything wrong?" Maxum dragged his hand down over his face then back up to swipe his hair from his face. "No. It's late. I was sleeping, what else would I be doing?"

Darko felt the rage singeing on the cusp of jealousy, making it worse was listening to this man lie to another about what he had just been doing. Maxum wasn't cheating on him to play husband to the *June Clever* of queers, Maxum was cheating on Simeon to have his nuts sated by him.

Darko shoved up to his feet and came around the sofa, to the pile of clothes that lay there and began to dress, torn between wanting to make all the possible noise he could, and just slipping away quietly with his pain clamped around his chest like a vice. It was probably a good thing he didn't have a bottle of ale in his hand or he'd most definitely send it catapulting across the room, because right now nothing would feel better than a sudden surge of physical energy. "I'll be damned if I'm going to sit here quietly while you play the loyal husband to the man you supposedly broke up with."

"I did break up with him." Maxum's head popped up, his attention shifting from the phone to the man who had departure written all over his face. He dropped the phone to his lap, he reached to catch the dodging body of Darko, but was unsuccessful, and his eyes followed the man.

"Then why is he calling?" Darko growled a low response. He was beyond caring what the answer was right now. Pain was threatening him and he wanted to be out before it hit him hard. He'd likely punch the man for it.

"Why do you think? I'm sorry if my break up isn't as friendly of a cut and dry ordeal as perhaps yours turn out."

Darko shook his head in disgust, "You deserve the pajama wearing pansy."

"Your insults of him are not making this any easier for me right now. So why must you?"

Darko knew he was in the wrong and under normal circumstances, he could care less what Simeon wore or how he acted. Nonetheless, Darko's own selfish heart was in the mix and he needed a kicking cat. "Because you insult *me* at every turn treating me like I'm just some free rent boy!"

Darko's emotions were steaming like a kettle when a hand grabbed his arm and spun him around. The phone, still in Maxum's hand, was pressed against his thigh to block any incriminating words. "Where're you going?" Maxum scowled at him.

Oh, narcissistic royalty must have lurked deep in this one's lineage to ask such a vain thing, Darko thought and shoved Maxum back, sending the man stumbling, but regrettably not hard enough to send him to the floor. Darko eyed the other set of clothes and to the wallet that he had retrieved the condom packet from, the greenish white corners peeking out lured him down to snatch it up. He flipped the edges open, took out several bills and dropped the rest back to the floor. His pain steeped into full stinging rage in his eyes as he glared at Maxum trying to read the look he had, watching him take the money.

"The *fuck* was on the house as usual, but you will be covering my cab fare home." And out the door he went, not bothering to have everything buttoned up before he made it out. There was still a long elevator ride down.

Maxum stood there stunned. He waited with bated breath, half trying to convince himself that the man would come raging back in, but he didn't, and Maxum felt the sinking in his chest as clearly as if he was feeling the elevator take him away. Despite all the fuss and argument he made, Darko walking out on him was the worst feeling of all, and he finally realized why.

"*Maxi, hon?*" Simeon's voice bled over from the phone and Maxum slowly lifted the receiver back to his ear.

"Don't call me anymore, Simeon. You and I were over a long time ago. It's high time I got on with my life."

"*But—*"

"No, Sim. You don't love me and I don't love you. The man I love just walked out the door of my apartment on account of this phone call and now I need to find a way to convince him I'm worth him coming back to. Goodbye, Simeon." And his thumb hit the button, disconnecting the call.

CHAPTER FIFTEEN

New Year's Eve, Darko showed up at Diesel Gentry's *New Year-New Hope Event*, toting a last minute date. He hated things like this, absent his preferred choice of some self-indulged company and factoring Dane wasn't fairing him to be Vince's date again anytime soon, one of the guys from the team hooked him up with a friend, and already Darko was wishing he hadn't. However, things with Maxum had him feeling a little insecure and he'd spent the last two nights obsessing over what he might have done differently to be seen as more than a good romp in the sack. He really should have gone to talk with Pyotr but had opted to keep away. His brother already had his mind and heart breaking with Kimmi's steadily failing health. Instead, Darko gave himself the answers he figured his brother would have given him.

Some fires burn too hot. While they like it, it's not easy to partake and not fear getting burned— Darko let out a heavy sigh as the drummed up answer rolled through his mind. He could hear Pyotr saying something along those words— or something remotely like that. He interceded the groan he'd likely have dispelled as more thoughts and discouragements leaked into his head, realizing he just didn't have his brother's insight enough to answer his own questions, but he didn't want Sognac listening in on his thoughts either. He wished he could have spoken to his brother; especially when Maxum's name kept coming up on his caller ID. Still, Darko couldn't bring himself to bother Pyotr with this. He'd find a way to manage on his own. He just wished he hadn't chosen Sognac to do it with. The man was trying too hard to be the top and it agitated him further.

Even when they pulled up in front of the hotel, Sognac gave instructions so he could lead. "Stay where you are so I can get the door for you, baby." Then he hopped out to dash around. Darko rolled his eyes, shaking his head, and he opened the door to step out just as Sognac was reaching for it. His date gave him a flustered look and Darko only patted his face like a *better-luck-next-time-ol-chum,* smack to the face.

He should have done this solo. He'd have enough friends and family here to enjoy himself, but the truth was he brought a date to distract his thoughts from the man he wanted to be with.

To his relief, Maxum spotted Trenton Leos and Diesel Gentry right away, and as usual they had already retreated into a partitioned off corner for a spell. Maxum wasn't quite ready to take on the crowd of social butterflies. So, he made a fast B-line to join them, stepping up to the small private bar tucked out of the way from the blustering of guests mingling at the event. He pointed to the two bottles on the shelf knowing they were reserved specifically for him. The bartender held them up, one in each hand for a closer look, "Which would you like to start off with?"

Maxum eyed the *Bodegas Dios Baco, an Imperial Amontillado Jerez* then the bottle of *Remi Martin*. He rubbed his fingers together considering his objectives for the night, "Let's start with the Jerez first."

The bartender nodded, filled a tall stemmed tulip, wine glass halfway, and set it in front of him. As Maxum took a moment to savor the aromatic plume of the sherry, he glanced over at Trenton to acknowledge him.

"Played it smart and left Simeon at home for a change, huh?" Trenton came up, reaching out to greet Maxum, shaking his hand. He waved him to the end of the bar to join him and Diesel where they sat. Also with them was the always present, Katianna Dumas, who was both his slave in their lifestyle, but also his beloved lover, presently sitting *on* the bar, while Trenton resumed his position between her legs and leaned on the bar's edge.

Maxum was rather surprised at the jest; aside that Trenton had been rather socially concave since the attempted abduction of her, Trenton was never a big jokester either. However, he knew Trenton's brothers were pushing him to resume his iconic position in the community so Maxum dismissed it as just a foolhardy, albeit poor attempt to start up light conversation, and he dropped into one of the bar seats next to him but sparing them the details, thinly admitted his change of life, "No. Simeon and I have gone separate ways now."

"Good," was all Trenton said as he tipped a shot of his preferred platinum tequila back then followed it with a dab of hot sauce that had been mischievously distributed on Katianna's fingers, then took the lime she held up for him.

Maxum felt rather contrite by the comment for all of a split second. Unsure how to take it as he watched Trenton feed a glass of wine to his little female. Such a strange and unique relationship they had. Yet, it showed that between them as well as in their faces, they were happy. Then realized himself, *it was good*. Simeon had not been the right partner for him for some time yet it seemed everyone but *him* had known it. There was no need for remorse, or offense for that matter.

"So, now what?" Trenton asked, waving the bartender for another round of drinks, then pulled Katianna over for a kiss before releasing her, his eyes floating down her body to the thighs outlined by the soft fabric of her evening gown that clung to them. He brought a hand up and stroked over one of her legs, devilish thoughts reflected in his eyes, clearly entertaining himself silently. Since Maxum couldn't come up with an answer, the man's misbehaving thoughts went on until the bartender returned with their drinks and Trenton passed them around, holding his up for a toast. "To new beginnings."

Maxum hesitated, he hadn't meant to but the words just fell short of a meaning for him. Was this a new beginning? Or was there a grey area one had to suffer through before a new start came? He had a great business that made a lot of people wealthy, he had a home that recited his taste perfectly, he had a garage of cars— all his favorites.

~~ But does it have a white picket fence? ~~

TALON PS

No. It did not. Maxum dropped his eyes, staring at the drink in his hands, he could feel them looking at him, even if they weren't judging him. He looked at the reflecting images on the surface of what was most likely tequila that had been handed to him. White picket fences were things you added to the home after working everything out, so how would he ever have that now?

"You know, just because you gave up on someone doesn't mean you didn't care. It just means you realized that they didn't."

Maxum's head snapped up to the woman and was met with a teary smile. Her face so warm it touched and held him and quite suddenly what she said sank in. Weight— so much weight lifted off of him just then like vapors and a small huff of a chuckle came out. She was right— so very right. This wasn't his fault. "To new beginnings." He held up his shot glass then turned it up to catch up with them in the toast.

He downed the shot glass and set it on the bar taking up his glass of Jerez once more. *A new beginning,* but his thoughts fell upon the new beginning he had already had a shot at and blundered. Perhaps that one was his fault.

"Maybe a vacation to the resort. Paris already has a single's mingle on the books for May. Get out, Maxum. Meet some new guys," Diesel commented, setting his empty shot glass down on the bar and stroked over Kat's thigh teasingly as he pulled back.

"I already did." He saw the surprised look on Trenton's face, "Meet someone, I mean." Maxum nodded, drinking down his glass until it was gone, thinking about how quickly he could possibly finish off the bottle of Jerez.

"He was everything a man could fantasize about. Heady, full-on, open-throttle octane." He set his glass out on the bar for it to be filled. "He was kinda my wake up call. But I hit the kill switch too many times and pretty much blew it." He fell silent, taking the refreshed glass and swallowing down a long draw of his drink. Behind his eyes, he saw his and Darko's lovemaking in his mind; burning impressions that would forever have him searching for *Darko* in every man he met for the rest of his life. "I tried calling him so we could talk, but he wasn't taking my calls. I must have called at least ten times."

"Only ten times?" Diesel smirked.

Maxum grimaced. "I seem to have picked up an unfavorable habit of throwing my phones in a manner that is terminal for them."

Diesel let out a chuckle and shook his head.

"It's not funny."

"Actually, it is," Trenton answered to the response, the fascinated smile hovering just under the surface of his face.

"Glad to have been some amusement then," Maxum stewed.

"Don't get me wrong, my friend." Trenton set his tequila shot down to focus on him. "We've known each other for a long time. We're here because you helped us maximize our spending funds. But you— you're one of the most potently self-sufficient business men I have ever worked with. A member of the fortune 500 and you have more money than myself and my brothers combined. I have never known you to waver about any decision."

"That's business, this is about emotions. Something I have no batting practice with. For all the worth Simeon had, our relationship had the emotional oomph of a dried out brick of clay. This man sends me on my ear with a simple brush of his hand and the burning desire in his eyes. He was an affair I had. How could I see anything but compulsive hazards there?"

❦

"Maybe instead you failed to see the growth potential in a new concept. One you haven't tried before. The highest gains are made in a playing field of high-risk margins. You taught us that," Diesel chimed in hoping to make an analogy his friend would grasp. He understood that when a man had already had set definitions, how hard it was to break out of them. So perhaps this way, he could give the man a push. It was worth the try. Someone had the man's heartstrings, and was dragging him out to sea, because neither was making the final connection. That was something Diesel knew himself. Though he knew exactly where Paris was and what he was doing, the distance between them was painful. A separation he planned to fix soon.

❦

"I've grown very reserved over the years," Maxum refuted with his poor excuse for his position.

Trenton sucked in a deep breath, taking in a more direct look at him, but gave a softer expression than one would ever expect out of a man who held the title of Dominus within the high-end BDSM community. "No, just gun shy at a new starting line."

Maxum mimicked the hard breath and let it out with a huff. He turned back to the bar and waved the bartender to bring another refill and watched as his glass was topped off from the bottle of Jerez. His thoughts wandered about as he held the glass up, just letting the dark nutty tones of the sherry, touched with seawater and white plum, seep into him a moment before drinking it down; far faster than one usually did with a Jerez that cost $75.00 a bottle. Then again, Trenton was right, he could afford it, and seventy-five bucks was nothing to him. Trenton knew him well enough to understand his tastes, not only for the high dollar brands, but knew he had a taste for the dark and uncommon flavors like the bottle of *Daniel Bouju Cognac* his gaze just spotted behind the bar and he was half considering the idea to bottom it out as well before the night was over.

He dropped the glass down to the bar and turned glancing at the man. Outside of knowing his tastes, Maxum couldn't say they'd ever grown close, but he knew he could always trust in Trenton to speak a truth or nothing at all. Trenton didn't beat around the bush or mince words, and he certainly seemed to have a global perspective on people. Though, that seemed rather irrelevant at this point. "I suppose it doesn't really matter any, now. I've fucked this one up and threw the qualifications before I gave the race a trial run."

If Trenton's expression were any hint, Maxum would have said the man didn't share his ideas of defeat. Further, damned if the Dominus didn't look like he already knew to whom Maxum was all bent out of shape over. He had this oddly amused *cat that caught the canary* look. Maxum shook off the notion. They might be in a small circle of social affairs, but Maxum dismissed it as an unlikely possibility. Trenton couldn't possibly know his affair had been with Darko Laszkovi. *Could he?*

"Come on." Diesel brushed away from the bar with a nod towards the crowd, "Time to mingle and work up the contributions."

Maxum gave a reluctant nod, but not so much as Trenton's was that it had him chuckling to himself, well that and the look Diesel was giving him like he would wrangle him out there if he had to. Likewise, well, you had to know Diesel Gentry to understand he was the kind of man who would do exactly that.

Trenton downed another shot, then lifted his little slave from the bar, placing her on her feet to walk in front of him. His hand slipped under the long wavy trusses of light brown hair, claiming the back of her neck where it stayed for nearly the remainder of the night; a posture that told everyone— *mine*. Not that anyone had to be told. Anyone who knew who Trenton Leos was, also knew his lifestyle and who the petite woman, with the sapphire studded platinum collar around her neck, was in his life.

Maxum had to admire them. They lived out a relationship the world didn't understand and scrutiny came before witnessed understanding, yet it marred nothing between them. Trenton never held back how he lived or what he felt for Katianna. Something Maxum too had relished in his life. Being gay in the business world wasn't always a welcomed candidate to do business with, but he stood by on both aspects of his life. Made men rich and was never secretive that a man slept in his bed.

—Or rather, he had wanted one there. Just one. Sadly, his understanding of *who* that one could be may have come too late.

Socializing at parties was always the sentient nightmare of Maxum's job. He hated walking through them alone. It was the touching— that was the part he disliked the most. The singles-hunters always reaching out to touch him as if doing so would make him want to be with them. Aside from that, he could wander a crowd as if it were never there. However, going it alone he felt more vulnerable as if he wore a neon sign that screamed— *I'm single come touch and take a chance.* He loathed word getting out that he was now an available bachelor, just on that one thing alone. Luckily, Trenton and Diesel weren't the type to announce it, not here and so far, the touchy-feely encounters had been sporadically few. Save the red head that always grabbed his arm and pulled him to her, to mark his cheek with her richly, red lipstick. That particular *cougar* did so whether Simeon was on his arm or not. *She just didn't care. She* was also one of his long time clients, apparently very good at her game of gold digging. So, he endured the lipstick offense, but had never allowed her to cross the line beyond that.

The four of them waltzed through, stopping for small talk with a number of elitists, friends, and celebs that lived in the area. Social club members, and even a few reps from the governors' team came to support the event in place of the governor himself. On top of the presence of many of New York's finest were a few globetrotters along with prized possessions, no doubt purchased by means of Trenton's Elysian Fields Slave auction. *It was always the adoration in the submissive's eyes that gave them away.*

"Excuse me, I see someone I need to say hello to." Diesel patted Maxum on the back and disappeared into the crowd. Maxum not interested in fairing the crowd alone stuck with Trenton and fell into a more relaxed and friendly conversation with Dane Masters and his beautiful brother, Vince Masters, tucked guardedly under his arm.

However, if Maxum's emotions weren't already out to sea in *that* conversation, the stormy waters had just become worse when he heard the familiar voice of none other than Simeon Correl, just on the other side of one of the buffet tables.

"If you'll excuse me." He nodded his apologies then quickly ducked away before Sim could spot him.

Darko had just sequestered Sognac off to get drinks, while he could use another to settle the turmoil roiling in his gut all night; it was more just to have a moment's reprieve from the man.

"So what is he?" Diesel asked with some inclination of teasing him. "Flavor of the night?"

Darko scrubbed over his chin a moment. It was almost laughable, if only he had been in the mood to laugh. He and Diesel talked often enough, Deez knew the man he brought wasn't his type. "More like a spontaneous emotionally, driven defiance and last minute bad planning filler." Darko managed a light chuckle while his eyes drifted out across the crowd. He'd been doing it all night, looking— searching for a face that wasn't there. It only made his nerves curl a few more times. At this rate, he would be able to launch a small jet across the salt flats test field for all the energy pinging in him. *Where the fuck is Sognac with his beer?* he wondered, now looking for the least likely man he wanted at his side.

"Oh, by the way, I don't know if you two have ever met—" Diesel called Darko's attention back to center point.

Darko anatomically returned his gaze to Diesel along with the person he was about to be introduced to only to come face to face with—

"This is Maxum St. Laurents." Diesel dropped a soft grip to Darko's shoulder, "Maxum, this is my friend, Darko Laszkovi."

If the earth had come to a screeching halt at that moment, Darko would surely have been thrown right off and into outer space for all the lack of anchoring he felt just then. And that coil of energy was suddenly exploding inside— small bombs detonating in his gut, his head and his heart. *Fuck!* His head screamed.

What seemed like a frozen, silent eternity finally dropped and reality kicked in, he glanced around and— Maxum was flying solo. *Where was June Cleaver?*

"We— we've met," Maxum stammered as did his hands. First frozen at his side then seemingly considering offering to shake hands, but that failed too, and they dropped back down to remain at his side. There was a ripple of emotions over Maxum's face that seemed to match what Darko felt but gone too soon to know just which ones were winning out. Save the last lingering one of puzzlement, "What are you doing here?"

The question of suspicion hit Darko wrong, he was almost inclined to either ignore him and not answer, or say something rude, like pointing out that Diesel used the word *friend*, but he bit the retort back. He wouldn't do that in front of his friends— or to Maxum for that matter. It wasn't the place to stage a personal drama. "You remember—" he paused not sure of just how privately Maxum and Diesel knew each other and perhaps— *well fuck, this was just getting harder.* He wasn't the type to hide behind smoke screens, but then he had been Maxum's affair and realized what he was about to say would be incriminating and quickly rephrased himself. "My brother Pyotr recently adopted his lover's sister as a daughter—"

"The one I met at your brother's house. She was sick," Maxum's comment dismissed any secrecy and his concern showed. It was a small comfort for Darko. Maxum was snapping his fingers, "Kimmi—" the snapping stopped and he pointed a finger as if pointing out the answer to his silent question, "Wasn't her name Kimmi? She has leukemia? I'm sorry," Maxum surrendered some grief that may have also been to him as well as for Kimmi, some portion saying *I'm sorry, I should have known.*

Darko was almost surprised that Maxum would risk outing himself, but it fazed him little. It was hard standing here before to him pretending to be little or say nothing at all of how they knew each other. He hated even more that he was still strongly attracted to the man.

"Yes. She is still sick." Darko's head motioned towards Diesel. "He's her guardian angel. This gala is for others like her."

Maxum suddenly stiffened up, right in front of him. He looked almost nervous like he was ready to bolt and Darko had to wonder why he would react so strongly to unless—

Diesel grew antsy as well. "Say, Maxum," his hand taking the man by the shoulder and pulling him along, almost pushing him towards Darko— his eyes watching something else in the crowd of guests, "why don't you take Darko out on the dance floor for a tune."

"But I don't know how—" Maxum choked up an attempted excuse to refuse.

Diesel cut in right away, "Yeah, but Darko does and he loves to dance."

Next thing Darko knew, Diesel had practically strung he and Maxum up together, and sent them rushing in another direction, while Diesel took off in the other direction. Even Maxum seemed to glance over his shoulder a moment. Darko bunched his brows up in a near glare at Maxum who now had him by the arm, intent on doing just what Diesel had instructed him to do and steered him more toward the center of the crowd before finally pulling Darko around to face him.

The *Schiller* tune wasn't fast and grinding like the music that called to Darko at Club Pain, but not so slow it was like cowboy-slow dancing. Nevertheless, Maxum was suddenly two left feet, save for his arms that quickly took their place around Darko's body as if it was the one thing in life Maxum needed in order to live.

Darko, for a moment, melted right into it, for the same misconception— *he needed it.*

He did what he could to lead the man into a moving tempo of simple footsteps, but he wasn't doing so well himself as emotions bum-rushed him, and he finally just surrendered his forehead to Maxum's, closing his eyes while the two of them just rocked in place.

Darko felt himself leaning into the strong arms that held him, almost as if he needed them there to hold him up. He heard the low rumble of Maxum's own surrender to the moment and relaxed into him, feeling a warm brush of fingers up his spine. But Maxum's mind was someplace else. The grinding of gears evident. "What has you so deep in thought?"

He felt Maxum shake his head stutteringly, then looked up at him, pained and troubled by something. Maxum's hand came up to caress his temple, eyes wandering over his face and hair as if to— well Darko wasn't sure really. "You're not a rent boy. I'm sorry I made you feel that way. I—" he shook his head again and his face clearly said he wasn't happy about the words that fell from his mouth, "I wish I had treated you better, because you deserved better." Their dancing came to a grinding halt and the room fell away until it was just the two of them and nothing else. "I wish I could have another chance to be better for you."

Maxum's deep tenured voice rolled across his skin, speeding up Darko's heart rate. His breath drew in deep and felt heavy in his chest.

Schiller's mood swimming lyrics filled the ballroom with words that seemed to talk just to them.

~~I've been here all the time— I've been here all the time — As far as I know doing right— I've always waited for

the moment that you would come walking through my door. ~~

Darko's eyes filled with his presence. Maxum had always looked good, but tonight he was different. He still had on the suit jacket that hid his masculine frame. Yet, the hand-died silk shirt underneath was thin enough, Darko was certain if he tried, he could taste the man through it, and that alone had his mouth watering for a taste he knew he enjoyed. *Fuck, the things this man made him feel.* He felt the pull to lean in, kiss Maxum, and let him know he could have it—

"Mind if I cut in?" A rather agitated voice broke through the spell and they both snapped around to see Sognac standing there next to them and none too pleased.

Maxum's expression collapsed and he took a step back, "Of course," he surrendered Darko respectfully to the date he brought with him.

Once more, the planet was slammed to a halt and Darko even felt the tilt from the centrifugal force in his chest as he watched Maxum in silent, emotional horror disappear back out to the mingling social crowd.

FUCK!

Maxum found his way back to Diesel, spotting him talking with mutual friends, Bob and Sandra Prats. Both known for their outstanding involvement in community improvement and if there was a fundraiser gala being held, they were likely to be there. He caught words about the earmarked funds for the new wing at the cancer center when he stepped up, only to freeze in his footsteps to see Simeon chatting among them, as always, the usual social butterfly as if waiting for Maxum to arrive. Bob was quickly drawing Maxum into the conversation while Sandra went on about the Guardian Angel's Program getting a large boost of funds from tonight to help cover personal care expenses not covered by standard insurance and to help low income families. Maxum was about to make an escape for the bar when he turned and there was Darko with the intruder who had stolen the moment he was hoping to rediscover with the man.

Well, fuck me— wasn't this a thrill ride through Dante's hell? He might as well drive his car into an oncoming train for all the wreckage he was feeling inside right now.

Someone behind him commented to Maxum directly about something, his brain clicking into autopilot, staying his feet, and he answered without really paying attention to what he said or what the conversation was anymore. He just stared at Darko. *Fuck, he wished he could erase all this, start all over again. Do it differently. Something— Anything.* He just wanted to say he was sorry and beg Darko to let him have a chance to make things between them right.

The conversation about the treatment center shifted to names of people or children there, and something sank in. Something Darko had said— before the dance floor. And quite suddenly Maxum was interrupting them all, directing his question to Darko, "Back there, you said this event was for others *like* her. *Like Kimmi*— but you didn't say it would help her. Why?"

Darko kept silent even as everyone turned to look at them both. Sensing there was far more being said then what they heard. Diesel shook his head and took Maxum's shoulder with a firm hand, "Kimmi signed her terminal declamation papers."

"What does that mean?" Simeon asked, having held on to every word said between them. It annoyed Darko— no— it pissed him off actually. He didn't care if Simeon cared or not.

"It means, Kimmi will die of Leukemia." Darko fell laconic and stepped away. His New Year's evening going from glum to dismantled wreckage in two-point-five-seconds. Had to be a world record for cursed luck. He didn't even bother to see if Sognac was following him and he hoped he wasn't. He just didn't need to be consoled by someone whose compatibility felt like sand in his carburetors. He stopped at the bar and ordered a double shot of the strongest stuff they had, then turned leaning back on it, looking out to the man, he left standing with Diesel. His heart wondering if he troubled Maxum's mind as much as Maxum St. Laurents troubled his. Darko almost didn't notice when Trenton Leos stepped up.

"Do you want to be with him or not?"

Darko's head nearly spun off at the question, and it took a long moment to form coherent words. "I— I'm not sure anymore. I mean, I wanted to, just not sure it's worth being tossed away over and over."

Trenton nodded to him in understanding.

"I mean, what's the point if he is still with his partner."

"Maxum and Simeon are no longer together. Maxum came alone, only Simeon came alone as well, knowing he would be here, and is trying hard to hang onto his bragging rights."

Darko leaned forward a bit at the revelation of news. "So why don't you throw him out?"

"Wanting something you took for granted and now can't have, isn't a crime." Trenton's gaze moved from him out into the crowd of people, "Besides, it seems there will be more discovered and learned tonight by letting him stay." Trenton let out a heavy sigh. One that was practically mirrored by Darko. *Why the fuck did life have to be so complicated?*

"Maxum is an extremely powerful and clever man. He doesn't make his living off of directing businesses, he does it by being in charge of people's private personal funds and knows how to direct people to his will. It's also a very volatile and high stress job. So when he comes home he wants something comfortable and secure." Trenton turned back to him and smiled, the Dominus' Bailey's-n-crème eyes glinting with the understanding of the pleasures that came with power. "Hard to believe he is so mellow inside. Only, it's hard to find comfort foods when you have bold tastes like he does. However, there is one thing you can count on. He will sacrifice so much; he will flex, bend, and even give up things to make you happy." Trenton's attention moved to Katianna who sat quietly in his lap, listening and watching the crowd herself. His eyes floating over her features, taking in every detail of her body before looking back at Darko, "Can you say you would have ever done as much for someone you wanted?"

Darko had listened but more so, he saw —*taking in every detail*— just as Maxum was looking at him only a moment ago. "But I haven't asked Maxum to give anything up. I just wanted him to let us have a chance by trying, to not get dismissed just because we started off fucking like a fire storm."

"Perhaps you should have." Trenton's smile almost chuckling at him, the way Pyotr always did. "Asked something of him," the man added to be sure Darko caught on.

Maxum watched Darko walk away. He knew not to chase him down, but his eyes tracked him to his very location. Nor was he going to leave him there for long. He looked at the man who had interrupted his moment with Darko out on the floor. "I'm sorry, I don't believe I caught your name." Maxum extended his hand out.

"Sognac. Like cognac but with an *S*."

Maxum nodded, not sure why the man felt he had to give a reference for his name. Saying it was good enough without the example of enunciation. "Sognac. Okay, I'm Maxum and this here's Simeon." Maxum pulled Simeon up, his hand gently pressing on his back, bringing him up to play the social butterfly.

Sognac easily traded hands for Simeon's. Like clockwork, Sim fell into a well-rehearsed dance step of approach.

"So how long have you known, Darko?" Maxum struck up conversation.

"Just met tonight. A friend of ours hooked us up, kind of last minute thing."

Maxum nodded. For some reason that bit of information made him feel better and he was noticing that Sognac hadn't actually let go of Simeon's hand yet. "Say, ah, Sognac, why don't you and Simeon go to the bar and get some champagne. I'd like a chance to talk to Mr. Gentry alone a minute."

Simeon swayed up to the man without even a glance in Maxum's direction. Something that, in the past, would have only added to Maxum's misery in their relationship, but not this time. This time, he planned and banked on it. He was watching this ship sail for the last time. He almost wanted to wave them farewell, but it would have been a bittersweet gesture of mockery. Not so much that Simeon did just as he figured he would and was so easily detoured by other men, but that this was what Maxum had kept shoving Darko away for.

Maxum glanced at Diesel who looked as if he already knew what Maxum was going to say. Though Maxum wasn't really sure himself. "I-uh— I know we're business associates and never really been close, but I don't know who else to turn to."

The man just looked at him, quietly. That was something he'd always noticed about Diesel Gentry; he wasn't a talkative man. Quiet came easily for him. "It may not be my place to ask or your place to answer, but I really do need some insight on the man."

"You mean, Darko, don't you?"

"It seems I've turned rather transparent over the last month or so."

"Not necessarily transparent, but the energy between the two of you is strong enough to either qualify as its own power source or bomb a small city off the map."

"That's pretty much how our encounters are, too."

"It's not usually my place to advise. Trenton is the one you should really go to or Darko's brother, Pyotr. But since you're asking me, the answer is, *be with him*." And like that, according to Diesel, the solution of life was revealed.

"I just—"

"No buts," Diesel interrupted the muck and mud Maxum was about to pile up on his simplistic solution, "Darko is a good man, he's got his life in order, knows what he wants, and he's never afraid to go after it. *And*, he has strong family ties. He might make you high as a kite when you are together, but he's well grounded, too." Diesel chuckled slightly, perhaps some inner thought, then looked back at him once again, nodding agreeably. "Invest in him and the return will make you a very rich man."

Maxum looked away, his eyes catching Darko sitting at the bar looking his way. Just sitting there like one of those exotic sports cars, he had a weakness for. It also wasn't going unnoticed that Trenton Leos was talking to *him*.

"Look. No one said you had to get married the same day, just take it for a test drive. But do it on the right kind of track," Diesel added.

Maxum could see Diesel out of the corner of his eye watching him watch the man of his desires. He turned, facing Diesel over his shoulder, who was smiling at him, as if pleased to know he would make match-maker of the year for this. Diesel didn't, for a second, look concerned over any future involvement with Darko. Rather, he seemed like it was the best choice Maxum had before him. And right then for the first time, Maxum felt it too. There was just one last thing to do. He glanced around but didn't spot Simeon at either of the bars close by, but he pretty much knew where to look, so he headed for the restroom.

He heard the moans the second he stepped in. He strolled past the stalls, stopping at the sink and decided to wash his hands. Some symbolic thing, he guessed. He used one of the towels on the marble counter, dried his hands then dropped it in the hamper, then turned and leaned back for a moment of reflection. He wasn't angry, in fact, he felt free for the first time in a long time. Even knowing the second he walked out he was going to snatch Darko up in his arms and beg him to give him a chance to do it the right way with him, he still felt free. Free to have what he wanted, what he ached for. He heard the groan behind the stall door followed with a murmured complement. He almost laughed. *Ain't that rich? Simeon wanted him back yet the other man still got the blowjob.*

"Hey, Sognac! You don't mind giving Simeon a ride home do you?" He started off for the exit, "Thanks, I appreciate it." And stepped out, walking right into Diesel who was grinning at him.

"Remember, use the right track."

"Which one is the right track?"

"The qualification track. Not the race track."

Maxum stilled at the answer— *he got it!* He actually got what Diesel meant. Because, he had every intention of just snaring Darko up and dragging him to his studio so they could burn the sheets between them. Consequently, that wasn't the right step to take right now.

"And don't forget to drop a check in the donation box on your way out!" Diesel called out after him.

Maxum threw a nodding smile over his shoulder to him and headed for the bar.

He was grateful to find Darko still sitting there and no Trenton Leos. Even more so, that his target didn't try to storm off when he approached. Signaling the bartender, Maxum pulled up next to Darko, his gaze dropping to the bar where he folded his hands, and carefully told him what he knew he needed to say first. "I never cheated on you."

Okay, so it was an awkward start, but it was a start and when Darko said nothing, Maxum continued. *Something— Anything—* he reminded himself. "That day I left to pick Simeon up from the airport, I tried to cuddle with him. I actually had to guilt trip him to do it, because I was already missing you. I might as well have been hugging a mannequin. I think I got one kiss out of it. That was it. I never even tried again after that. I didn't try, because you were right. I was with the wrong person. I just didn't know it yet and I am so sorry for screwing that up with you. But I did not cheat on you, if that helps me get another chance with you." Maxum chanced a look. Darko just sat there looking at him. *What the fuck was he thinking though?—* "The other night when you left, I realized something, and it took losing it to actually know it even existed."

ʕ•ﻌ•ʔ

"And what would that be?" Darko dropped his eyes to the dark ale he now drank, picking at the label with a finger. The two overturned shot glasses on the bar blurred in his vision as a reminder of the pain he was trying to drown out.

"My heart," Maxum answered, "The sinking feeling I felt after you left was a pain I don't want to keep feeling—but I don't want my heart back if it doesn't come with a full package. Meaning you."

"Me too." It was all Darko said, but it was enough to have Maxum's head snapping around. Only Darko kept his posture unwelcomingly closed, warning Maxum to maintain space.

Don't rush him yet. *Fuck or fight.* They were both good at that, but *this*— this was new frontier for them.

ʕ•ﻌ•ʔ

Maxum returned his gaze to his hands still on the bar, his weight leaning on his elbows. He cleared his throat, summoning up more things to say. "I like overpriced, overly fancy, rich foods. I like holding hands and driving a fast car on a slow Sunday. I hate going to flouncy socials, but I like reaping the benefits from the networking, so I go to them anyways. I like watching porn on Saturday afternoons—" he paused recalling one of Darko's comments about not giving up certain curricular activities and he grinned mischievously, "And— I would really like to fuck you on my desk overlooking the city, as well as, on the black glass top of the boardroom table."

The silence from Darko was nearly killing him and his insides collapsing, dreading that he was still failing to gain Darko's pardon for another chance.

"So where is Simeon?"

Maxum's head may have been slumped forward, but the smile that came over him was impossible to miss. In the wreckage that threatened to strip away his last chance to ask Darko to be with him, he had executed a plan. Plan to do away with bad investments and competition. It had gone together rather successfully. That alone had Maxum smiling.

"What the fuck is so funny?"

"He's in the bathroom giving your date a blowjob."

Darko's face melted into an incredulous expression. Then without a word, bolted off for the hotel restroom.

Maxum didn't budge, arms still on the bar, holding his weight while he sipped on a glass of cognac— *with a C—* and just waited for Darko's return.

It wasn't a moment longer when he heard the request behind him.

"Seems I could use a ride home."

Maxum pushed off the bar and turned to look at Darko, grateful to see he didn't look as pissed as maybe he should. "I'd love to give you one."

Darko made a double take as Maxum pulled the Bugatti into the garage at the Beekman Tower Gehry, "What are we doing here?"

"I— I need to take a piss and I won't make it to your place in time. You mind?"

Darko gave it some thought, it was a poor excuse, but he was willing to play along to see what was really going on. "Nah, I don't mind. I could use a pit stop myself."

Darko followed Maxum's lead as they went up to his flat in the tower, only this time they weren't clawing each other's clothes off. In fact, they were rather calm and reserved— it was almost floundering in a way, but Darko wasn't about to dismiss the new behavior for them. A new discovered pace, to show they could putter around and perhaps after that they could finagle a cruise control for them. When they walked in, Maxum seemed to fall into an automated routine, keys and wallet went into a dish that sat on a buffet table against the wall in the foyer, his coat in the closest, followed by his suit coat that went over the back of the chair sitting next to the table. Then he offered to take Darko's coat and hung it up.

Maxum's tie was next, pulling it loose as he turned, and stopped to look at Darko. He was quiet; even the gears normally grinding and trying to shift were quiet. Darko wondered what it all meant. Had all this defeated the man, now he was just a lost pup who was willing to follow whoever was willing to feed him a few morsels? Darko nearly shook his head to refute the thoughts but stopped himself. He didn't want to give Maxum any more doubts than what were already there, but he was at a loss to give anything else either.

"You want a drink? I have several dark ales and even a couple of black ales if you prefer." Maxum fished out a comment as he broke from their gaze and crossed the living room to the stocked bar along the wall.

At the mention of the selection, Darko quickly fell in step and followed him over, "No one keeps black ale on hand unless you drink it yourself," he protested, "Which, you don't." But just as Maxum opened the small fridge under the bar, certain labels grabbed Darko's attention. He took the door from Maxum's hand and opened it wider. Sure enough, aside from the four or five dark ales, three of which Maxum had seen him drink before, there were just as many black flavors— Butchertown, Imperial Iba, Föroya Bjor Black Sheep, and Point 2012. Darko opted for a bottle of Brains Dark Ale instead, while Maxum poured a glass of high priced scotch over ice.

As Darko swigged down the ale, he scanned over the bar. It wasn't really the kind of selection for— *say*— a party with cheap-thorough-fairs for a multitude of guests, but rather customized for Maxum's own palate. Perhaps a select few dinner guests and little more. Maxum had obviously purchased the black ale just in case he ever got the chance to bring him home with him again. Trenton had said Maxum was the kind of man who would bend and fluctuate to fit with the person in his life. However, not a bottle of champagne or floral wine to show that a certain someone else had ever had the pleasure of having a drink with him here.

And that thought struck a note deep inside Darko.

He glanced around the immense apartment— *nothing*— not one thing hinted of Simeon's presence. Even outside of Darko's biased dislike for the flaunting male, he wasn't so unfair he refuted that Simeon was just different stock. *Because he was.* Simeon personified the feminine male. His home was probably a muse of pastels, houseplants and the latest works of a local artist. Not one thing here in Maxum's flat said, *Simeon was here.*

Had Maxum just been thorough of wiping him out? Or was the gap between those two so great, Simeon never fit in, in the first place? It was all just Maxum, hung up on his morals about making a relationship work. *There was only one-way to be sure.* "Mind if I use the bathroom?"

"Sure. Down the hall, first door on the right." Maxum pointed with his glass then went over to the sofa to find the remote pad.

Darko made his way down the hall, finding the bathroom easily enough, but the one he really wanted to see was the one in Maxum's bedroom. He wandered farther down, finding an office and a guest room that looked as though it had never been touched, a third room that had not a single solitary item in it, and then finally finding a master bedroom that was about as big as his own pad in total. "*Dayyum,*" he gasped, taking in the décor. Darko took a quick glance over his shoulder; he could hear the Times Square crowd's cheer spilling down the hallway, but no Maxum. Coast clear, he walked in. The bedroom, unlike most everything else Darko had seen in the luxury residence, was a straight out black-n-white color scheme with a Grecian trim for added flare. Black walls with white trimmed frames set the stage with a king-size canopy bed with its tall posts curtained in with black drapes that had the typical Grecian block border design. Though it took him by surprise, he actually liked it. A canopy bed wasn't usually a man's first choice, but it made sense, since like everywhere else in the apartment, the exterior walls of the flat were all glass. So, bed drapes were a necessity if one wanted to sleep in on Sundays.

Not wanting to stray for too long that he would invite Maxum to come looking for him; Darko found the bathroom and went in. It was nearly as big as his bedroom at home. A double sink vanity, a jumbo-sized shower with an overhead rain showerhead, even a waterfall chrome plate, and jet-massagers on all three stone tile walls. Everything a rich man could invent for a bathroom was present. Only, Darko didn't find what he was looking for. Instead, he found what he needed to know. No second toothbrush, or personals one would find if another person lived or stayed here frequently. In plain truth, Simeon wasn't here. He never had been. Simeon, for all the effort Maxum had put into building a relationship, had never filled the spot. Maxum wasn't grieving over losing his long term partner, he was grieving over never having found him.

Glancing at the high tech Jacuzzi with the large screen tv mounted on the wall in front of it he nearly laughed. All the toys and gadgets, and no one to play with. Perhaps now he had.

When Darko returned to the living room, he found Maxum standing there. The large screen with the New York party crowd from Times Square filling it frame by frame behind him, but for the man, it might as well have been blank for all the concern he wore on his face. Darko saw it right away; Maxum was waiting for the rejection.

"Why'd you bring me here, Maxum?"

Maxum's shoulders slumped, "To beg." He turned away and wiped over his face, perhaps to hide his disappointment or something stronger, "I'm sorry. I'll take you home."

Darko stepped into Maxum's path, blocking him when he headed for the closet. Their eyes met in silence.

Maxum, for all the smarts he had didn't have a clue where he was in his life or what Darko possibly wanted from him. Darko, for all the years with his brother, couldn't find the words to tell Maxum or ask him to try again. So he kissed him.

It was soft and tender; he could even feel some small bit of pain in it. "I wish I had some grapes right now." Darko murmured against Maxum's lips as they paused in the embrace.

Maxum pulled back a step, his face screwing up in a question.

Darko smirked and offered a lighthearted shrug. "That sweet kiss stayed your ass that day in front of my brother's house when you wanted to leave then; I was thinking maybe they could come in handy right about now."

Something melted, some shadow sliding right off of Maxum's face, "You want me to stay?"

"I want you to try to be with me." Darko reached out taking Maxum's hands in his. A boyish smile on his face, because he had to admit it felt strange. For him, as well for the both of them, but he wasn't about to let go either. "I want you to give *us* a try."

"You'll give me another chance to make things right?"

"Things were already right from the start; I am giving you a chance to stop running."

Maxum let out a heavy sigh of relief. "No running. I want this." He fell silent a moment, gathering some resolve for himself. Maxum had never considered himself as a real risk taker. Life to him came with two options. For him there were challenging hurdles, numbers he knew how to calculate far in advance of what direction they would take that meant reaping the rewards, and then there was foolishly throwing money away. He liked spending his money on enjoyable things, not tossing it out without purpose or usefulness. Darko had, until now, seemed like a huge risk that came with instant rewards, but no certainty of the long run. "I'll be honest, no one has ever scared me like you do, but damned if I can make myself let go of you. I want you. Hell, you're already brandished into my veins. I'm not letting go so you might as well come to terms with it."

"Only, I have something to ask of you."

"Anything."

"No, not anything, just this one thing."

"What is it?"

"That you let me show you how much I want to be with you. That I can be the man you will be with for years to come."

"So how do we start?"

Darko's gaze flickered to the large television screen and the crowd it showed in the city below. Cheering and party favors abound as the moment approached. "Well, it's almost midnight. Maybe stepping into the New Year with an old tradition is a good start."

"You want me to make a New Year's resolution?"

"Kinda. How much money did you donate tonight?"

Maxum sucked in a deep breath and let it out in a solemn sigh that ended in a warm smile. "A hundred and fifty grand."

Darko cocked a brow up at the six-digit sum. "Well, that might get you a kiss." Despite the dim lighting of the room, the copper brilliance Darko had seen in Maxum's eyes the first time they met sparked back to life and he realized he had missed the flickering color.

"A kiss? That's all I get?" Maxum suddenly put on a pouty bewildered look, "Not even a door prize?"

Darko shrugged, trying not to laugh at the playful look at his knight. "What were you expecting for just a hundred and fifty grand?" Darko mirrored the surprised expression along with a wicked grin.

"Well, I don't know. I was kinda hoping I got to keep the man giving the kiss." He took a step in, bringing them almost nose to nose.

Darko took on a rather cocky arrogant air. "I think you're over calculating the value of your money here." He leaned in nudging his nose against Maxum's in a taunting glance. His smoldering blue eyes dropping down to consider Maxum's lips in a visual caress he could feel. "Perhaps we could consider it a down payment and work out some kind of arrangement." He drew one of Maxum's hands toward him, depositing it on his hip, then took Maxum's hip in his own. "With your budget, I'm sure we could work it out in installments. Maybe even a parking space." He brought an arm over Maxum's shoulder, delivering more of that smoldering aura he was well aware were among his seduction skills. The countdown on the television at Times Square began just as the starting-lights for Darko's approach had.

Ten— nine—

"I might have to put in a little overtime, but I think I can manage that." Maxum grinned at him.

Seven— Six— Five—

Maxum's smile paused and he let out a deeply contented sigh. "I want to make a New Year's resolution here. I want to promise that I can be a forever man and I am willing to devote the rest of my life to prove it to you."

Three— two—

And just as the countdown reached its climax with the ball dropping at Times Square being shown on the television screen, Darko pulled Maxum in— kissing this man he'd spotted on the side of the road one early winter morning and knew then, they were meant for each other— a rough attraction— like rocket fuel and fast cars.

EPILOGUE

EHRA-LESSIEN TEST TRACK, GERMANY

It was early summer, and just the right temperature for the track, which by track rules, they still had to wait to well after the noonday sun before being allowed to take even the first run. Maxum had gone first, reaching a heart stopping thrill ride of four hundred and nine kilometers per hour. Then while his car made a pit stop for new tires, refueling and an over-all-check while it cooled down, one of the certified drivers from Bugatti took their newest super-sport models for a test spin to really show what the car's design could do. Breaking a previous Bugatti record of 431kph.

Now it was time to let the man, Maxum St. Laurents brought into his life on the eve of this year, have a go at the adrenalin rush. He leaned down on the door of his La Blanc Bugatti, peering in at his heart stopping handsome lover, Darko Laszkovi, sitting in the driver's seat adjusting the harness straps of his seatbelt, and made a double check on his helmet gear, "Do me a favor while you're out there—"

"Sure, what is it?" Darko was more automatic response as his focus remained on the car and perhaps some of the willies he was likely having. Maxum sure had them when he was psyching himself up for his first run this morning for the first track run of the day and he was having a small amount of them again now.

"Don't wreck and die out there. I plan to propose to you tonight at dinner."

Darko gripped the wheel with both hands, let out a long nervous breath and nodded, "You bet." Darko then gave the car a rev, his eyes scanning over the gauges for the hundredth time. His expression paused a moment as he received communication in his earpiece, "Ah, roger that, I'm as ready as I'll ever be."

Maxum grinned and pushed off from the car. He had really wanted to land a kiss on Darko before letting him go, but that would have just been damned impossible with the small window space, the helmet, and well hell— Darko was already in that adrenalin rush. Which wasn't too much different than the sub-spacing some of his friends talked about. So, he let it go.

Maxum removed himself from the track and settled behind the control team, watching both the car on the track and the multitude of monitor screens. One showing the road from inside the car, one aimed at the driver, and the other two would follow the car down the track through a series of high tech security cameras throughout.

A few additional screens would monitor speed and performance on the vehicle itself.

Using the same countdown stack of lights used in racing, Darko was given the signal to go and the car revved, and jumped forward, but only to come to a screeching halt about a hundred yards down.

"WAIT! Where's Maxum?!?!" Darko's excited voice was shouting over the head set. "What the fuck did he just tell me a minute ago?" And within minutes, Darko was climbing out of the Bugatti, and running down the track, back to where he'd started.

Maxum stepped out from behind the crew, but for all the flip-flop and adrenaline that was crashing through his gut just then, it might as well have been him sitting right back in the driver's seat of the damn car.

"What that hell was that about dinner tonight?" Darko pulled the helmet off as he came up to Maxum.

Maxum chuckled, if for no other reason, but to get his nerves to settle down a tad, but it was also kind of funny how Darko presumed to be mad at him. "I'm gonna ask you to marry me." He wiped at his chin with the back of his hand, trying his best not to start sweating.

Darko let out a hard, husky breath as if it just got pushed from his lungs, "Fuck that! Ask me now. Right here, on the tracks."

The biggest grin a man could wear split across Maxum's face, but his face went a sudden red as he realized both the Bugatti and track crew were all standing around, watching and waiting. Maxum scratched at his nose then placed his hands inside the pockets of the jumpsuit he was still wearing, for a moment. Another itch that was just nervous stalling and he pulled his hands from his pockets, took one of Darko's hands in his, then slowly lowered down to one knee before him.

"Oh fuck. You were serious," Darko gasped and his knees went a little weak under him before gaining his composure. It just wasn't going to look right if he passed out in front of all the other guys watching. But it might be a good idea if just one of them would think to call an ambulance because his heart was thumping at a speed that could possibly make track records.

"Darko Laszkovi, I have never met a man like you. You meet me in the middle head-on and yet I landed in soft strong arms. Every time I turn to look at you, it takes my breath away because you're already staring back at me." Maxum paused, taking a nervous breath. He wanted this to come out perfect without stuttering— or forgetting his words— or for god's sake without passing out. He'd been practicing too long to blow it now when it counted. "I don't want you to ever let go or stop looking at me. I want you in my arms and in my life forever. So won't you please marry me and be my husband?"

A century must have passed in that millisecond that he waited with bated breath for Darko's response, a breath that was equally shared with the crew for all the silence going on over there, he reckoned. But not Darko. Suddenly, Maxum found himself being yanked up and those arms he mentioned coiled around him with a less than soft embrace this go around, as they crushed him into his love's body.

"Fuck yes, you'll marry me," Darko growled, just as his mouth came over Maxum's to seal the deal between them.

Life couldn't get any better than that moment for Maxum. He was on top of the world, standing in the middle of the most private and prestigious speed track in all the world, within the arms of his newly engaged man, who one morning pulled over on the side of the highway to rescue him with a crushing kiss much like the one he was receiving now. A kiss that left more than a grimy mark on his suit. And after all that, Darko called him his *Knight-in-Shiny-Armor*, when in truth, Darko was his.

TO BE CONTINUED—

ABOUT THE AUTHOR

We Came— We Saw— and then we made it sexy.

And that's pretty much how the Twins came to write Erotic Romances and Dark Fantasies. Both Talon and Tarian have been writing together since they were kids, challenging and competing with each other, and always each other's biggest supporters.

Writing has always been an affair creating fictions of Dark Apocalyptic Fantasy and Film Scripts in Action/Drama and Sci-Fi. It wasn't until they began an Ancient History Fantasy together that the works turned to the Erotic Genre and they've been hooked ever since. However, the final product comes out as richly detailed as we believe all stories should be created: holographic worlds of love, pain, frustration, and challenges beyond the every day. We believe a good story should take you on an emotional ride, pluck your heart strings, and zing you about until you're dizzy. All for readers to submerse themselves into and escape from their day when they need or desire, and to whet your appetite for more.

So, make sure to reserve plenty of private time, pour a glass of wine, and find a cozy spot, because as Talon always says—

" I'm about to make you wet

Talon ps.

TEASER FOR WHAT'S NEXT

TAKING OVER TROFIM

THE DOMINION OF BROTHERS SERIES: BOOK 5

MM-Romance / Forced Seperation to Second Chance / Conspiracies / Abusive Family / Erotic Romance / Exploratory BDSM

Trenton Leos has always been known to many as the Dominus, the man to go to for the perfect D/s match. However, Trenton and his brothers are about to find out that he and their lifestyle has become the target of a political cleansing. A shady operation with very deep pockets comes to the surface when Trenton is asked to investigate a dark secret that threatens the future of Pyotr's younger brother, Trofim Laszkovi and his lover, Shay Wilks.

Trofim Laszkovi would never forget how right it felt to be in Shay's Wilks' arms five years ago. But Shay's father made it abundantly clear with threats hard to ignore, that Trofim's family would pay the price if he didn't stay away from Shay. So with the help of a friend,

Trofim made a career move that put him an ocean away from his family— and his heart.

Even now, having finally returned home, only a year ago, to the family he missed, Trofim hadn't dared allow himself to look in Shay's direction.

☙❦❧

Shay Wilks has done everything he could to keep his father's plans for him at arm's length and protect his internship as a doctor from ruin by the same man. All in hopes that the only man Shay has ever loved will one day return to him.

Now, five years later, Shay finally has another chance to be with Trofim. If only he can convince Trofim they are better together than apart as well as get out from under his father's brutal hold in time before Shay loses Trofim again— for good.

☙❦❧

4-Stars! ~ "Loved, loved, loved the mystery and suspense that accompanied the relationship in this tale, and hopefully opened the doors for future intrigue. I'm a sucker for a good romantic whodunit, especially one that is self-sustaining." ~Books n Cozy Spots Book Reviews

5-Stars! ~ "Oh. My. God! The twins have done it again! I want to tell so much more but that would give away too much. What I will tell you is that this story is true to the Dominion of Brothers series. It will have you laughing, crying and cussing throughout the whole book." ~ Author Ava Snow

EXCERPT FROM CHAPTER ONE

Trofim finished his shower and went to his locker with nothing more than the towel tied at his hips. He needed to get out of there. Instead, he found himself dropping down to the bench, overwhelmed with old feelings. That face up on the bridge, looking down, just as his team rowed underneath— he knew that face, remembered it all too well. It still hurt to see him after all this time. Why Shay would suddenly show his face at their first outdoor practice seemed more than coincidence. It would be just like Shay Wilks to come sneaking around, but Trofim's heart couldn't take it.

"Are you joining us for dinner?"

Trofim heard the gentle question reach him through everything else that bombarded his mind. He looked over, finding his brother's concerned face. He never could hide anything from Pyotr, and it was no mystery that what he felt now had started back in the fall at the championship race.

Shay had been there too. Shay was pulling stroke seat on the New Rochelle Masters' Rowing Team. Trofim was only grateful he hadn't seen him on the river during the race or he would have likely created a similar wreckage of oars for his teammates as Shay had for his. *So, he was told.* No doubt Shay's father, former Senator Benjamin Wilks had been there as well and saw what caused his son's failure. The New Rochelle Team would have taken third place in the Masters if it hadn't been for that calamity. A wrecking ball Trofim was grateful to have been oblivious of.

Except when Shay came running up to congratulate him after receiving the championship trophy, Trofim nearly crash-landed off the back edge of the platform trying to get away. Seeing Shay again brought on a storm of old emotions, both good and painful. The worst of them was knowing Shay's father would see them together, and Trofim couldn't allow that.

"Trofim?" Pyotr's fatherly tone broke through the clouds in his head again.

"Sorry." Trofim averted his eyes. Pyotr had just gone through the death of his lover's sister, Kimmi, and both Cliff and he were still nursing the pain and grief of the loss. The last thing Trofim wanted to do was dump his five-year-old broken-heart melodrama on him. "Nah, I'm good. I think, I'm just gonna grab something and head to Club Pain. Fashon will be expecting me there."

"When you're ready then." Pyotr gave him a long assuring look, like a pillar only a brother could provide before he vanished behind the wall to head out. It was his brother's way of saying he would be there for him whenever he was ready to talk. Even with a new love of his own, Pyotr would never stop being Pyotr. Nothing was too important to keep him from family. Always the big brother that looked after his siblings as if they had always been his own children, and in a sense, they were. After all, Trofim himself, had only been eleven years old when their parents sent them out of Yugoslavia to flee the coming civil war. Pyotr became the only mother and father they had after that.

Trofim stared at his locker, hating the sinking feeling he had. Even less, he lacked the motivation he needed to get dressed and forget what could not be changed.

"I got tired of waiting outside for you," someone spoke from behind him.

Trofim spun about, jumping to his feet and backed against the lockers at the familiar voice. His heart dropped the millisecond his eyes came upon the handsomely refined face of Shay Wilks. "What are you doing here?" He swallowed hard, trying to regain his bearings and hopefully some resistance.

Shay took a step towards him, closing the space between them that wasn't nearly enough, and placed one hand flat against the lockers next to Trofim's shoulder.

Trofim's eyes followed the possessive move of Shay's arm still molded with the muscles of an athlete and took that as a sign to move away. One step and Shay slapped his other hand up, blocking Trofim's escape.

"Still running, I see." It was more of an accusation than something arrogant. So much of the *rich boy* attitude was at work in Shay. *When he had Trofim in his targets, Shay fully intended to have him.*

"I didn't run. I left. I got that break into modeling. It required a lot of travel," Trofim blabbed out in his defense. Even if it wasn't entirely the truth.

"Yes, I know. But were you so busy you couldn't pick up the phone and call you the love of your just once? I didn't even get a *sayonara* from you." Shay let his eyes drift down Trofim's body, lapping up the very sight of him. Then back to Trofim's eyes. Blue like the night was long. Not a light blue or a sky color, but deep like cobalt stone. The kind of blue most had to accomplish with contacts, but Shay knew first hand Trofim's eyes were all natural. The color of his soul— so deep, it was staggering.

"Senator Wilks saw to that," Trofim snapped, stifling the rest of the words whereas the shakiness of his voice conveyed there was more he wanted to say.

Shay stilled, just inches from Trofim's face. He had always known his father had some doing in Trofim's sudden departure, but no one, not even Trofim's brothers would speak of it. "I was angry for months after you left and then I saw the first modeling release of you." Shay laid a soft feathery kiss against Trofim's jaw. "I saw how beautiful you are, but those first few pictures also showed your pain. I saw in your eyes you were hurting too." He kissed him again with light, lingering contact. "I tried to reach out to you, but you never came back— 'til now." Shay leaned back, his gaze washing over Trofim's body as if he had done so with his hands. "So handsome," he whispered, as if remembering something far more intimate. "I think I've managed to collect every photo ad ever printed of you." His hands dropped from the lockers to Trofim's arms, delighting in the feel of the exerted muscles of his biceps. Shay's eyes locked on the muscular curves, "Damn, rowing has been good to your body." Shay moved his hands up over his shoulders, gliding down over his chest. Using both hands to firmly squeeze the firm gentle rise of pec muscles, then caught one of Trofim's sensitive nipples between his fingers and pinched him.

Before the gasp could barely break past Trofim's lips, Shay came over them, his tongue plunging past his own lips to lapping at his tongue. Claiming Trofim all over again with a deep hunger that had never been quenched by anyone but Shay.

Trofim was spontaneously drowning in the kiss, feeling the man's arms tighten around him like a snake coiling around its prey, refusing to allow even the slightest chance for escape. Yet it was the kiss which made Trofim stay.

Shay had a mouth that could get him drunk on the euphoria of its caress, as if his kiss were made of honey wine. And Shay was force feeding an entire barrel of it into Trofim's mouth that very moment. Delivering and eating all at the same time. Moreover, to ensure there was nothing left of his resistance, Shay pressed in, delivering a firm grinding of his hardened arousal against Trofim's own cock. Shay's hands wandering farther down and grasped Trofim's hips, pulling them to ride against him.

Despite every brain cell sending up immediate alarms to get away, Trofim's body knew he was in the arms meant to hold him and everything lit up. Awake and wanting. Convincing him to stay where he belonged.

DISCOVER THESE OTHER TITLES BY TALON PS & TARIAN PS

DOMINION OF BROTHERS SERIES
Becoming His Slave
Domming the Heiress
A Place for Cliff
Rough Attraction
Taking Over Trofim
Right One 4 Diesel
Touching Vida~Vince

LA SERIE DES FRERES DU DOMINION - {French Edition}
Devenir Son Esclave - Partie 1 & 2
Dominer l'Heritiere
Un Havre pour Cliff
Attirance Brutale

QUANTUM MATES:
Pt 1~ What Torin Wants

DEAR SOLDIER SERIES:
Dear Soldier, With Love
Dear Soldier, With Love II: A Lost Soldier Named Grey

LYCOTHARIAN COLLECTION:
Bond of the Lycaon Concubine

TALON's KEEP COLLECTION:
Feral Dream by Talon ps
Danny's Dom by Nick Hasse

That's My Ethan

Muse Me Only
Inspire Moi Seulement {French Edition}

THE TEDDY BEAR COLLECTION:
Their Plane from Nowhere
Big Spoon & Teddy Bear
Ivan vs Ivan
TIME: Wounds All Heal
Shaggin' the Dead

THE SADOU ORDER – A Dark Taboo Series
Perfect Boy / Perfect Son

TARIAN ALSO WRITES UNDER THE FOLLOWING
PEN NAMES FOR SEPARATE GENRES:

STEPHAN KNOX ~ *Historical Fantasy And Post Apocalyptic Sci Fi*

Anáil Dhragain (Dragon's Breath)

Keeping With Destiny

ROCK HARDING ~ *Adult Coloring Books*

The Adventures of Hugh Jorgan

CONNECT AND FOLLOW THE TWINS:

WWW.TALON-PS.COM